THE
Dis- ORIENT
EXPRESS

Greg Lawson

This book is a work of fiction. Places, events, and situations in this story are purely fictional. Any resemblance to actual persons, living or dead, is coincidental.

ISBN: 1-4140-2155-0 (e-book)
ISBN: 1-4140-2154-2 (Paperback)
ISBN: 1-4140-2153-4 (Dust Jacket)

This book is printed on acid free paper.

1stBooks - rev. 01/30/04

I Would Like To Thank

Randy Hanshaw, PhD, BS
For the support of humble beginnings

Jane Goetz at Dog-eared Books
For reference and enthusiasm

Betty Craig, M.Ed.
For kindness and insight

For My Wife Lynn

who provided the patience, time, encouragement and
dedication to see this work completed

NOTICE OF VACANCY

Position to be filled: Mental Health Officer
Range: Police Officer Pay Scale (CS5 thru CS20)
To be posted: Open to Certified Law Enforcement Officers
Projected fill date: Immediately

POSITION DUTIES INCLUDE:

Responsible for evaluating individuals suspected of emotional problems for the purpose of assessment and possible involuntary commitment. Must be able to deal (in person and by phone) with people suspected of mental illness, and professionals in the mental health community. Must be able to maintain a professional and courteous demeanor when dealing with staff, the general public, and outside agencies. Must become knowledgeable concerning the legal aspects of the Texas Mental Health Code. Applicant must possess good verbal and written communication skills. Must be willing to work a flexible schedule, which includes weekends and holidays. Must meet all minimum physical standards regarding weapons qualification, vehicle operations, and possess the abilities to take physical control of another person as needed. Must possess the ability to work with minimal direct supervision and be capable of making independent decisions.

PREFERRED QUALIFICATIONS:

Applicants who have prior experience and knowledge in dealing with aspects of the Texas Mental Health Code. Any specialized skills (such as bilingual in Spanish or Asian, sign language or patrol experience) or training (such as Mental Health Certification) as it relates to the position.

*Considerations may be given for diversity, special skills, or other factors
contributing to the overall mission of the department.

One can not learn from doing things correct.

Murphy's Law - Revised

CHAPTER ONE

Good Intentions
"Friday, December 13th, 9:20 pm"

Adam paused quietly outside the door and listened. He could hear the traffic on Park Lane and some music coming from an apartment just above, but nothing from inside. He leaned back and looked at the curtains in the living room window to see if any lights were being turned on. The curtains were just as before, faintly illuminated by the dim stove light in the kitchen. Adam had been here enough times to know where the light was coming from.

He turned his flashlight around and banged the butt of it four more times against Patricia's front door. "Patricia, it's Adam Thompson with the Sheriff's Mental Health Unit. Come to the door," he said complacently, as he had so many times before. She was always a test in patience.

He stepped off the tiny porch and walked around the corner to her bedroom window. He banged the flashlight again. "Patricia, come to the door," he shouted at the window.

Still nothing.

He returned to the front door, stowed his flashlight under his belt in the small of his back and pulled out his key ring. He flipped through a dozen keys looking for a master that might work on Patricia's lock. Adam heard a thump in the living room and froze. He strained his ears for any sounds. There was another thump and a clang from what he thought was the kitchen area. It sounded like an empty coffee can being dropped on a tile floor.

1

He knocked again. "Patricia, Sheriff's Department. Come to the door. You're not in any trouble. I'm just here to help."

Adam noticed an orange glow flickering from the living room window and stepped off the porch to get a better look. There were long flickers of orange light coming from the window and suddenly the curtains brightened. A hideous shrieking came from within the apartment.

"Shit—shit—shit," Adam repeated as he turned and grabbed the front door knob. He twisted it both ways, but it wouldn't budge. He stepped back and with all of his strength, he kicked the door open. Shards of wood and dust scattered and the opening revealed a beautiful, however deeply troubled woman being consumed in flames. Patricia Hammond stood in her kitchen with her arms outstretched as if she were being crucified, still clutching a rolled up news paper in her left hand. The woman's waist and chest were bathed in flames as she stared at the ceiling. A small gasoline can lay spilled a few inches from her feet, and Adam could see a flame trail flashing toward the container's spout. He recoiled and covered his face as it exploded. The metal of the can split open and luckily for Adam, Patricia had poured most of the gas on herself. Very little splashed around the apartment. With the explosion and the outside air fed by the swinging of the door, the flames engulfed her. She took in a breath of scalding air and shrieked again.

"Get on the ground!" Adam yelled. "Get on the ground!"

She stood fully covered in flame. Black smoke with the stench of gasoline and burnt hair boiled off the ceiling. Another scream came, and she began to flap her arms.

Quickly, Adam looked around the living room for something, anything that could help extinguish the fire. The only thing he could find was a crocheted blanket draped across the back of the couch. Adam grabbed it, and just as she began the fire victim's dance, he threw it over her. Because of the holes in the crochet pattern, the flames began licking through and devouring the blanket as well. As carefully as he could, Adam followed her around the living room padding and fluffing the blanket, slowly extinguishing the blaze.

Patricia could stand it no more and slowly fell to her knees, then to her side into a fetal position. Adam crouched down with her in the heat and the smoke still slapping at the flames. He noticed how parts of the blanket had melted onto her skin and were sticking to his hands. The blanket was made out of some sort of synthetic fibers and now was causing more harm than it was doing good. As soon as Adam extinguished the last flame, he removed the parts of the blanket he could before they buried themselves deeper into her skin.

Patricia reached over and grabbed Adam by the arm with a greasy claw. He stopped what he was doing and looked down at her. Most of her facial skin lay on the carpet near his knee.

"Why?" she croaked.

"Your going to be okay," was all he could think to say in his panic. He stood up and saw the apartment was no longer in danger of fire; the flames had disappeared. He reached for his hand held radio but decided it would be faster simply calling 911. If he went through county dispatch they would have to transfer to the fire department and relay the information. He grabbed her phone and made the call.

Afterwards, he knelt back down. "Help is on the way," he assured her.

She opened her eyes. Surprisingly, they were as blue as before, untouched by the flame. "Why?" she asked again.

"You're going to be okay," Adam repeated. "Help is on the way."

Painfully, she raised herself up onto her hands and knees. Adam could see pieces of her skin sloughing off as she moved. "You need to stay still. I'm trying to help you. It's going to be okay," he said again. He could hear the sirens coming.

"Look at me," she hissed. "Look at me. I'm not going to be... okay."

"The ambulance is on the way," Adam tried to comfort her. He saw at least half of her was severely burned; her body, face and one entire arm were all loosing skin.

She inhaled air into her scorched lungs. "You did this to me. Look at me!"

"We're here to help you," Adam said, and checked the empty front door. He heard the chirp of the air brakes and could see the flashing red lights of the fire truck reflecting off the apartment's walls.

"If you would have...left me alone...it would be over now," she grunted. "It would be over!"

3

Adam knew he hadn't done this to her. She had tried to burn herself to death, and he had saved her life. He was sworn to do that, to protect.

But to what ends?

"I just wanted to make sure you were okay. I want to help you, Patricia," he said.

From her hands and knees, it took great effort for her to turn her head and look directly at him. "I didn't want...your help." A string of slobber dripped from her mouth.

The fire paramedics rushed in and pushed Adam aside.

"I...didn't...want it!" She growled.

CHAPTER TWO

That Morning
"Tuesday, December 17th. 6:00 am"

The day Robert was murdered, Adam Thompson started off his morning like most others. He received no premonitions of the impending doom of his partner. No overwhelming desire to tell Robert he had to stay home today, that something was going to happen and it wasn't safe. In reflection, Adam would be able to recognize the signs, just as any armchair quarterback can do. But this day seemed to be, just another day.

Adam intended to get up around six in the morning, but at six, his expectations were thwarted by a greater and what he felt was a more honorable ambition, sleep. He rolled over, twisting himself even tighter into his favorite Mexican, wool blanket. It was very rare that he had the fortune of sleeping in late, except on the three to eleven, evening shift. When working midnights, Adam could rarely decide when he was supposed to sleep. Right after work, or wait a few hours, then sleep, or what? Usually, he would wait, and then getting the same as most others would, a couple of hours before they had to be back again. With day shift, he just stayed too busy. Getting up too early and staying up too late. The day shift was just too normal and too easy to take advantage of.

He finally rolled out around ten o'clock and cursed himself for his laziness. It seemed every time Adam rewarded himself, he would feel guilty. The recovering Catholic in him, he supposed. Trying to suppress his laziness, he got on his sweats and wandered around the

5

apartment looking for his running shoes. His apartment was a two bedroom one bath located half a mile from Sixth Street and the partying district. Not only was it a great location, it was also free. For only one walk-through a day, and to be on call for any problems at night, Adam paid nothing for his little place in the world. He decorated it in cheap, black lacquer and brass, livened the walls with framed prints that were on sale at the mall, and kept a two hundred gallon aquarium with fresh water fish from all over the world. His aquarium was his real pride. It not only brought him enjoyment, it brought him peace.

He found his shoes under the glass coffee table, and after slipping them on, he left the apartment. Walking out into the parking lot, he noticed a moving van parked in front of one of the adjoining apartments. He walked closer to get a look at the new tenants. A man in his fifties, neatly dressed, stood beside a younger man carrying an overstuffed chair. A woman with a young girl came walking out of the apartment and joined the two men. Apparently, they were in some sort of disagreement on where to put the chair. The young girl, or woman, Adam noticed, was at that precarious stage in her life between high school and college. An adult, but not quite. She looked over at him and smiled. Adam returned the smile and started walking toward the road.

"Excuse me," the girl called to him.

Adam turned and looked. She said something to her father, and then they both started walking his way. Her mother and mover went back to the apartment.

As the man got closer, he reached out to shake Adam's hand. "Bruce Blackmon, this is my daughter Michele."

Adam shook his hand. "Adam Thompson," he replied.

"I told my Dad you're the security officer here," she smiled. "The manager pointed you out when we were looking at the apartment, last week."

Adam didn't remember seeing her and that surprised him. Now that he got a better look at her, she was stunning. Still very young, eighteen, nineteen at the most, flawless tanned skin, obviously from a tanning booth this time of year, and almost white hair, thickly braided behind each ear and down to the middle of her back.

"Do you work for the police department?" her father asked.

"No sir, the sheriff's office."

He nodded. "It's pretty quiet around here?"

"Yes, sir, I hardly ever get a call; she'll be fine," he said, as he looked over to her. She was giving him eyes and a smile that if her father had noticed, would have caused a family disturbance right on the spot. It took Adam by surprise; he quickly looked back at her father and smiled.

"Well, I'm sure you'll take good care of her if something should happen."

Adam almost choked with what was going through *his* mind. "Yes, sir, I'm sure she will be just fine. Ya'll have a good morning."

They said their goodbyes and Adam purposefully did not look back at Michele again. He thought for sure she was playing one of those games. Flirtation just under Daddy's nose and taunting a little danger. A little excitement. Adam knew exactly what she was doing.

He trotted across the road through bustling vehicle traffic and headed for a quiet neighborhood street. As he settled into his jogging pace, he worked his way through the shaded streets and pushed himself forward toward City Park. Adam wasn't a great runner, but at six foot two inches and 220 pounds, he could hold his own within his weight class. He took this run at least three times a week. It wasn't nearly as demanding as the ones in the Army at Fort Bragg, but that was because he could now set his own pace. Back there, it seemed like every first sergeant and company commander was five foot eight inches and 160 pounds. They would fly like the wind, and they kicked his ass every week. He even thought he was going to die a couple of times, but he hung in there. He prided himself on the fact that he never fell out of a run. Never. But now, he didn't have to push it; he set his own pace.

He was having a problem with getting Michele off his mind. Five foot two inches and maybe a 110 pounds of energetic fun. He saw nothing but sheer physical perfection, and that was dangerous. He shook off the thoughts.

He always intended it to be a five-mile track, but in the past year, he had finished it only twice. Usually, about a mile and a half into the run, he found himself under one of the pecan trees in the park admiring birds. He knew the way he felt this day, it would be the same thing. But as long as his feet were moving, he convinced himself otherwise and pushed ahead. *Five miles, nothing less.*

He followed the road bending around the groomed soccer fields. The cool air started to sting his lungs and he slowed his pace a little. A soccer goal net fluttered slightly with the breeze and reminded him of shrimp nets he saw when taking vacations with his parents along the Texas coast. That was a happy time for his family. Everything held together until his Dad died. Adam missed those times and tried not to think of them very often.

He glanced up at the sky; it was clear and the sun shimmered off the waters of Town Lake. Taking in the beauty, he changed course and found himself slowing near the benches that lined the mouth of the Springs. There, where the Springs spills its frigid waters into the lake, he sat down, letting his breath catch up. He drank in the beauty, the nature. Two squirrels dug around the base of a pecan tree. Three gray cranes flew in from over the trees and landed gracefully in the cold water. Even some ducks, which, for whatever reason, decided not to head south for the winter and swam toward him. They waited at the bank for some seeds, a bread crumb, or a Cheeto. Watching them, Adam felt somehow responsible for their feeding.

"I'll come back on my days off and bring you guys something to eat," he promised.

Two more gray cranes circled high above the huge Spicewood trees lining the bank of the lake. They soared in formation like the protectorate eyes and ears for their three brothers who were now enjoying the water. Adam longed to fly again and have the wind in his face. Airborne school at Fort Benning was a good start, but that is exactly what it was, a start. Military parachuting had its moments, but it just seemed too much like work. Civilian skydiving was where he believed real freedom and excitement was. Adam wasn't going to be able to go again this weekend. His last outing had practically drained his checking account and the sport had long ago devoured his savings. It was an addiction, pure and simple adrenaline. Each sixty-second adventure turned into a fifteen-minute story at the end of the day. Standing around a campfire on the drop zone with beer in their hands, everyone would have their turn at telling stories of the day. Grown men and women with their arms outstretched demonstrating swoops, dives and flips, mimicking what they had done and making fun of each other's mistakes. Adam's adopted family.

He smiled sadly.

As he sat, he knew deep down he was just wasting time. Anticipating the passing of each hour until he could go back to work. He was ready to go back to work. He loved his job and to deprive him of it two days a week seemed unfair. Mental Health Unit 1273, Adam Thompson. His name was actually in the county phone directory under Mental Health Investigator.

Adam had more miles than most his age, but he was still a very young man.

After a quick shower and a McDonald's sausage biscuit, he found himself behind the wheel of his mental-health car. The mental health sedans were much like regular patrol cars; they just weren't equipped with quite the same features. Painted a light tan, they displayed no official markings, but had extremely dark tinted windows to protect the identity of the poor soul in the back seat, along with windshield-mounted spotlights. The inside was a little different, also. No shotgun rack in the front floorboard; however, it did have a very interesting safety feature, a spring-loaded, plexiglas window. This window could be placed in the down position to ease conversation between the front and back of the vehicle, but with the first sign of danger from the back seat, the deputy could release the spring and the window would slam shut, trapping anything sticking through it.

It was about 2:45 pm when Adam pulled into traffic.

He picked up his radio microphone. "Unit 1273, to county."

"Unit 1273, go ahead," the dispatcher answered.

"Unit 1273, I'm in service, en route to mental health office."

"Unit 1273, 10-4. I have one call pending, 707 Cawfield, on an escapee from the state hospital. Do you want me to hold you en route?"

"Unit 1273, 10-4. I'll need a case number, title it Unauthorized Departure."

"Unit 1273, 10-4, 14:46 hours."

CHAPTER THREE

The Visit
"Tuesday, December 17ᵗʰ, 2:31pm"

Harold thought he heard a noise from the garage. He wasn't sure. His hearing wasn't what it used to be.

There it was again. It sounded like Scooter's old doggie door, but it couldn't be that. Scooter was dead, going on four years, maybe five.

Harold slowly forced himself onto his feet. After adjusting his robe and slippers, he walked from his Lazyboy in the den, through the kitchen and to the garage door. His reading light was the only lamp on in the house, but beams of the day's sunshine found their way through seams in the closed curtains and were diced evenly by the blinds in the kitchen window. They cast a smoky appearance in the dust-filled house.

He reached for the knob to the garage door, and then strained to listen for the sound again.

It was there all right; the sound of the dog door swinging back and forth. The hinges squeaked and the plastic made a muffled thump as it passed in and out of the frame. Turning the knob he freed the lock and tried to slowly open the door, as not to surprise whatever little animal might have gotten into the garage.

BLAM! Without any warning, the door exploded toward him. The bottom of the door raked across the toenails of his left foot, tearing them from their roots. Stumbling back, he caught himself on the edge of the kitchen counter, screaming in pain.

11

She appeared in the darkened doorway wearing a black, knee-length skirt and a dirty, Aqua Festival T-shirt. Her hair swung like a crown of lifeless snakes, and glittering dust swirled around her in the slices of sunlight.

"Hi, Daddy. Did you miss me? I've been gone for such a long time," she hissed, slowly walking toward him.

"Sandra, please," he gasped. "You don't suppose to be here. Please don't, Sandra. You've cut my foot."

Almost the same size, but with an age gap of about forty years, she reached out and took the old man by the back of the neck. Digging her long, dirty nails into his flesh, she forced him toward the back of the house.

Toward her old bedroom.

With a bath and some make-up, she wouldn't have been unattractive. Actually, she would have been quite pretty. Her complexion was a bit ruddy from teenage acne, but her face was pleasant, if it were absent the scowl it now manifested. Her braless chest was full and round and with the help of the cold weather clearly shown through her T-shirt. Her legs were smoothly shaven and absent of all color. Milky white. Yet somehow, even though she possessed the pleasant proportion of a desirable woman, her personality seemed to ruin all of that.

Somehow.

"Your little girl is home, Daddy. Aren't you glad to see me!" she screamed and threw him up against the closet's thin, sliding doors. He crashed though them like paper and stumbled over the clothes and pieces of door under his feet and then fell to the floor.

Even though he was out of breath, he managed to pant, "Please, Sandra. You're sick. You need help."

She froze, staring at him. He was older, much older now. His hair had turned totally gray, and he was dressed in a bathrobe and slippers. He looked so weak sprawled there on the floor with his hands shaking. His gray hair entranced her; she had never seen him like this.

"You're old, aren't you, Daddy? You look old and sick. Like the fucking little old bastards at the hospital! They can't ever remember a thing. Have you ever tried to talk to someone that can't remember what you said two fucking minutes ago?" she shouted.

Suddenly, calmness overtook her. She stared down at his bleeding foot. Her eyes not leaving it. "Oh, Daddy, you hurt your foot. How did you do that?"

His foot was deeply lacerated. The toenails were peeled all the way back, revealing the tender meat they normally shielded. They pulsated and he also knew his neck was bleeding. He felt the wet trickles running down his back.

He remembered how years ago the doctors explained, "She thrives on pain, Mr. Graham. That's what she likes to see. I can't explain it any further. The only way I can put it is that it is a sexual experience for her. She needs to go in the hospital before she hurts any more people." "Or herself," another doctor had added. "I've never seen anything like her case in twenty two years of practice."

He tried not to show it, but the pain was excruciating. He knew it would only encourage her.

Slowly, she walked over to him and then raised one foot high off the ground above him. He could see she was not wearing panties.

"Why did you leave me there, Daddy?" she asked, and then slammed her foot down on his chest.

He exhaled, and wrenched with pain.

Ah—she thought, *there it was. He gave in. They all give in.*

She smiled.

Standing above him with her straight teeth gleaming in a wicked smile, he noticed brownish tobacco stains starting to show. He had been so proud of her teeth and had put a lot of money into them. Before she started to get sick. Before it all started. He stared at her in silence and knew there was nothing he could say. He simply fought the pain.

Pulling her skirt up around her waist, she walked over and turned on the light switch. "Daddy, do you want this?" she asked in a deep, sultry voice. Her butt was exposed to him.

He watched.

She waited a moment for an answer, but none came. Turning around and pushing out her pelvis exposing herself to him, she asked again, "Daddy, look at it. The wards at the hospital like it. I've learned all kinds of things there. Things you couldn't teach me." Turning around, she bent over exposing all of her backside. She looked back at him through her parted legs. "The black boys like this

13

best, Daddy." She swayed back and forth running one hand over her butt. "You gave all this to them. And they give me all the smokes and Cokes I want."

Reaching with both hands, she pulled her cheeks apart and shouted, "And up this way I don't get pregnant!"

Quickly she turned, grabbed his arm and pulled him from the closet. She dragged him on his back across the broken pieces of the door into the middle of the bedroom. "See, if you weren't such a goddamn goodie-goodie and did Mom up the ass like you really wanted to, you wouldn't be having this problem now! Would you, Daddy?"

She straddled him, then sat down on the middle of his chest. Reaching down she ripped open his bathrobe. Now he could feel her privates pressing into his sternum. "We're going to give you a cardboard test, Daddy. Remember your playful little test?"

She put her knees on top of his arms, pinning him to the floor. Leaning over him she whispered, "Shhhhh—"

Slowly, curling one finger at a time, she made a fist. Using her middle knuckle, she started lightly tapping it on his breastbone. "It sounds pretty good, doesn't it, Daddy?"

He closed his eyes, wishing the pain away. The pain in his toes was the worst. They throbbed and burned terribly.

"Answer me! Doesn't it?" she screamed and slapped him across the forehead.

"Please don't, Sandra, please. It was a long time ago."

The tapping steadily got harder.

And harder, until it sounded like she was pounding on a thick corrugated box. He started screaming in agony, wiggling, trying to force her off his chest. Sandra leaned back like a bull rider, bellowing laughter and kept it up. She started grinding herself into his chest, as the old man closed his eyes, trying to escape, and praying she would stop.

After what seemed an eternity, she slowed. Then only Harold's gasps for air and whining were heard in the room. She had finished.

Slowly, she stood, running her hands through her hair. It relieved the pressure from his chest and he could breathe again. He looked down. Swollen red whelps marked her strikes on his chest, and a stripe of white fluid remained, marking where she had sat. He could smell her odor, and his stomach twisted.

Was that the way the next-door neighbor's seven-year-old boy felt after she had her way with him? She had been a trusted babysitter until her seventeenth year. No one ever imagined Sandra doing the unspeakable things she did to him. And the things she made him do. That's when it started to happen, when it *all* started to happen.

The change.

The police. The courts. The embarrassment. Two more assaults on boys down the street, but those charges were dropped. Those boys apparently didn't resist enough to the court's approval, even though they were both only twelve. Then the hospital. She destroyed so many people's lives and happiness. The strain had killed her mother, but they kept saying she is sick; it's not her fault. Harold often wondered whose fault it really was.

Now, she came back for him.

So many people's lives.

"So what if she is sick?" he remembered the prosecuting attorney saying. "She did it and there is no doubt of that. The damage was done, and now justice must be."

She stood over him staring. Then, with a look of embarrassed accomplishment, she pulled her skirt back down.

"You wanted it, Daddy. I remember things. How you looked at me. You wanted it." She turned and went into the bathroom.

Raising himself to a sitting position, he reached down and tried to push his toenails back into place. The pain was too much and he jerked back in agony. He held the scream in, somehow.

The shower came on and she walked back into the hallway. Her shirt was already gone and she kicked off the skirt. "I'm going to take a shower now, Daddy. You be good and stay right there." She stood naked before him with her huge mat of hair exposed and fat tits. He said nothing as she disappeared into the bathroom, not closing the door. Looking around the room, he took the sleeve of his robe and tried to wipe the stuff from his chest. He saw the telephone on the nightstand and slowly picked up the handset. Checking for a dial tone, he called the number he referred to many times before, then waited for an answer.

Because of her previous escapes he fortunately had memorized the number.

"Sheriff's Department, Mental Health Unit. Can I help you?"

CHAPTER FOUR

The Return Ticket
"Tuesday, December 17th, 3:05pm"

After about a twenty-minute drive, Adam pulled in front of a nicely landscaped, upper-middle-class home. A shiny new Oldsmobile sat out front. The sun beat down through the clear sky, but the temperature was beginning to drop again.

"Unit 1273, 10-23. I'll be out checking with the complainant," he said on his radio.

"Unit 1273, 10-4, 15:05 hours," dispatch acknowledged.

He parked his car in the road at the end of the driveway. Walking to the front door, he checked for his notepad and pen, then reached around to adjust the gun in his waistband and covered it underneath his coat. He always tried to do this; it just seemed to work better if they didn't think the mental health officers were real cops. Badges and uniforms always seemed to exacerbate the situation. Authority figures, bright colors, especially red, quick movements and an assortment of other little things could set them off.

Strangely, the house reminded Adam of one of the homes he lived in as a boy. Maybe it wasn't the house itself, just the general neighborhood. Late 1960's style architecture, all brick, and lots of green grass and old, tall trees. The whole area definitely had the same feeling as his father's house on Green Lawn. That was a pretty good time for his family. It seemed to be just a stopover for his Dad, though. It was one of the longest stopovers, a whole three years. *The life of a salesman*, his Dad would say. They had moved about once

17

every two years until that time. But, when you grew up moving around like that, somehow, it didn't seem strange. He didn't think about it much. The strange part, that is. Adam apparently inherited his mother's ability to disassociate herself from unpleasantness; she simply just chose not to deal with it. Adam decided that was one of the reasons he made such a good cop; he learned it from his Mom. He could handle any number of disgusting things, then go straight to breakfast for a Mexican, chili omelet.

He stopped at the front door and looked through the gap in the front window's curtain. He noticed the inside of the home looked dark and deserted, but a small light was on in the living room. He couldn't see anything else indicating someone was home.

The wind was starting to pick up a bit as he stood there listening for any sounds from within. There was a light thumping in what he guessed was a bedroom, just to the right of the door.

Adam rang the doorbell and waited.

The thumping sound stopped. He could hear the sound of footsteps shuffling to the door. A chain slid off the inside clasp and it quickly swung open.

"Get that bitch out of my house!" an old man said, feebly. "What took you so long? Get her out of my house!" He shook his finger toward the back of the residence and then shuffled past Adam, heading for the car in the driveway. Adam reached out and took the man by the shoulder. He saw he was bleeding from a large cut across his forehead.

"Wait. What's going on? Are you okay?"

"My daughter escaped from the state hospital. The bitch is in the back bedroom. Get her the hell out of my house!" he said again, then ripped free of Adam's grasp.

"Okay, what's her name?"

"Sandra Graham," he barked, continuing toward his car.

Adam stood there for a moment, confused as to whether he should stop the old man again or to go see the bitch.

He chose the bitch.

Adam thought he heard the name before. It sounded familiar. He imagined, briefly, thoughts of Sandra standing in this very place knocking on her father's door and the old man asking, "Who is it?"

18

Then in a slow, mocking tone, she would say, "Sandra gram." He could see the terror on the old man's face. It would be like Saturday Night Live's land shark episodes all over again.

Adam heard the sound of running water in the back bathroom. Slowly stepping through the door, he studied the interior of the home. Instantly, he could tell Mr. Graham was divorced or a widower; a light layer of dust covered the entire inner surface of the room.

Suddenly, the shower stopped. He froze, listening in the entranceway. Someone was opening and closing cabinets in the bathroom. He didn't want to go in too quickly and have it result in a struggle. But he didn't want to give her any time to get some sort of weapon either. That wouldn't be good. This was her backyard. You don't mess with a dog in her own backyard, or in this case a bitch. Quietly, but swiftly, he slipped through the den and down the hall. Stopping just outside the open bathroom door, Adam listened.

He took a deep breath.

Maybe she'll be calm, he thought. Maybe everything will go smoothly. But then again, she didn't escape from the state hospital because she wanted to go back, especially not back to the extended-care unit. As soon as she sees him, she'll know why he's there. She won't want to go back, and she's already assaulted her father, a helpless old man.

Water dripped on the floor, and then there was the sound of a towel sliding off a metal towel rack.

Shit! he thought. It was the first time it had occurred to him. *That's all I need, a goddamn crazy, nude woman. That's going to look great, just great. I'm never gonna hear the end of this one,* he thought and contemplated about backing out or calling for a female patrol officer, but realistically it was too late. Plus, last time he did that, the patrol officer was a bigger bitch than the patient. He would just have to take his chances. There would be an almost guaranteed sexual assault complaint filed after this one. Father already left. No backup. No witnesses. *Great. Just great.*

"Mrs. Graham? Deputy Thompson with the sheriff's department. Can I talk with you a minute?" he said in his best "I'm with the government and I'm here to help" voice.

Greg Lawson

Well, here it goes. A loud grunt came out of the bathroom door along with an old Stylex hair dryer that smashed against the wall. Adam jerked back as pieces of the machine scattered in the hall.

"Get out of my house!" she yelled. Her arm came out of the bathroom holding a can of hair spray. Without taking aim, she discharged the mist towards him then the can quickly disappeared back into the bathroom.

He knew it had to be now. He had to take her now, clothes or not. In the bathroom, it had to be now. Adam put his hands up in front of his face and stepped forward turning into the bathroom, but it was too late. By law, he made his presence known and it turned the whole affair into turmoil. If he could have just sneaked up on her and snatched her. That would have been so easy. But the law is the law, and rights are rights. You can't lie to them; that would have made the job too easy. *"Hey, Sandra, I got a bunch of rope and little boys out in the back seat of my car. Ya want to go for a drive?"* He would have had her in the car in seconds without a complaint.

Adam tried to block it. He swung down to slap it away, but she was strong, a lot stronger than he anticipated. He took into account her mental condition, adrenaline and her physical strength, but he didn't count on this. She ripped the shower curtain rod from the wall and like a lance, drove it into his midsection. Luckily for Adam, the blunt end didn't break the skin. With both hands on the rod, she pushed him out of the bathroom and into the wall where the hair dryer shattered, only moments before. Dropping the rod, she ran down the hallway and into her room, slamming the door. Adam was surprised her tits bouncing everywhere didn't kill her on the way.

With one hand over his chest and the other one groping for his kuboton, he ran down the hall after her. Pulling the small, black metal rod from his belt, he grabbed the doorknob.

Locked.

Stepping back, he heard her throwing things around in the room. "Fuck you, you cocksucker. Little boy doing a man's job! Fuck you!"

With a hard kick he knocked the door open, only to reveal the naked, deranged woman. With mascara running down her checks from the shower and her milky-white chest bouncing wildly, she ran back at him. Her left hand was holding a can of Lysol, and there was

20

a lighter in her right. Adam raised one leg and planted his foot in Sandra's stomach. Just then, she clicked the lighter and the Lysol ignited. Flames licked at his face, but did not burn him. With a slight thrust, he managed to stop her and send her falling back onto her meaty ass. She held a tight grip on the can and kept the flames shooting everywhere singeing the lace comforter on her bedspread and a crocheted table cloth on the nightstand. Adam planted himself in a defensive stance, blocking the doorway and waiting for the flames to go out.

"SHIT!" she yelled, floundering flat on her back with her legs kicking. She tried to push herself away from him.

It was hard for him not to look at parts of her; his eyes were having a battle between his professional side and his entertainment side. He had never seen one that hairy before. He couldn't seem to keep his eyes off it. It was one of those strange things no matter how hard you try, you can't tear your eyes away from. He almost laughed at the thought of it coming alive, hopping off of her and running back down the hall.

She pushed herself all the way across the floor away from the boy who was getting pissed. The boy who had just about enough and was preparing to whip her ass.

As the flame went out, Adam hopped forward and kicked the spray can from her hand. "You need to just calm down now. I don't want either of us to get hurt!"

"Fuck you!" she shrieked. Rising up, she grabbed both of his legs, trying to dig her nails through his tan jeans. Adam took his kuboton and raked it across one of her wrists, then clamped down. This produced good results, and she screamed in pain, pulling back both her arms and trying once again to retreat instead of attack. He maintained a tight grip on her left arm, and feeling the metal of the kuboton grinding on the bone, he kept the pressure on.

"Stop resisting!" he shouted.

Her right arm came up and violently grabbed his family jewels. Now it was just a matter of who could take the most pain. Being the gentleman, Adam decided he would release her arm first. However, not necessarily for that reason. With his other hand he grabbed her fingers that had latched onto his balls and tried to force them free, and with the other, he frantically jabbed the tiny black rod into Sandra's neck, just under the back of her jaw. After a couple of stabs, the kuboton found its mark and she screamed with pain. Grabbing hold of her hair and keeping a generous amount of pressure on her neck, he pulled her forward onto her stomach. Firmly, he placed his knee onto the back of her head, pinning it to the floor. Quickly pivoting around, Adam put the kuboton back into his belt and removed the handcuffs, which soon secured her wrists behind her back. He had an incredible urge to slap her big ass just below where he cuffed her hands, but somehow he refrained. He also thought a big, red handprint on her backside would look suspicious when he returned her to the hospital.

"Fuck you, you bastard. I'll send you to hell! I'll send you to hell!" she screamed, spit flying from her mouth.

"Yeah, and you're going back to the hospital," he managed to say, trying to catch his breath and swallow his gonads back into place. "Where are your clothes? Your clothes!"

"I'll kill you, I swear!"

"You're going to have to get in line and pack a lunch, sweetheart. There's at least twenty people ahead of you. Now where are your clothes?" he repeated, not letting his knee off her head.

"Fuck you!" she spat again.

"Well, okay, we'll play Burger King, and you'll get to have it your way."

Standing up, he hooked his arm through hers and placed a thumb under her jaw, where the kuboton had influenced her earlier. She flinched to retaliate, but remembered the pain and submitted. Reaching out with his other hand, Adam pulled an old, full-length, teenager's bathrobe out of the trashed closet. Swinging it around, he draped it over her shoulders. Her breathing had become a little labored and he thought he might be choking her somewhat with the pressure on her neck. But at this point, he really didn't care. He didn't relax the technique a bit. It was difficult to keep her under control with one hand and at the same time get an adult-size pair of tits in a girl-size robe, but he managed.

As they walked to the front door, he could tell the pain was really starting to get to her. By the front door, she was walking on her tiptoes, not saying a word. Adam reached back and closed the front door, then walked Sandra to the waiting car. Her body was half exposed as the cold December wind pulled at her robe. He placed her in the back and found himself once again behind the wheel of the disorient express with a one-way ticket to the other side. Like traveling on a track with no detours, switches, or side-rails, he headed straight for the depot of society's outcasts. A warehouse without real therapy or cures, pity or empathy, sympathy or comfort. They simply didn't pay the employees enough for all that. And really, there was nothing anyone could do for these chronically ill people. Many were terminally ill with conditions that just may take forty or so years to run their course. The only real cure, death. That's all. There is really nothing anyone can do to improve their situation. No cures, just potions of mixed drugs to help mask the symptoms. Just a warehouse for the uncontrollable, and the unpredictable.

The unacceptable.

A warehouse of lost souls.

Sandra seemed to liven up a bit as he got in the car, started it, and situated himself. The "fuck you," and "go to hells," could be faintly heard through the plexiglas window, but he paid her little attention. He thought of how bad he felt having to take people to the state hospital. The look on their faces as they headed back down the snot green tiled hallways. Very much like the morgue, but they lived in this building, or existed in, Adam didn't know which was worse. If they were lucky, maybe they would be sent back into society long enough to say, "Hey, I'm cured," and get off their medication; right back to square one.

Adam notified dispatch and headed to the state hospital.

CHAPTER FIVE

The Investigation
"Tuesday, December 17th, 4:35 pm"

After dropping off Sandra, Adam responded to back up Robert Lassiter on a possibly suicidal subject. Their two, tan Ford sedans rounded the corner as Jackie stood in front of the windows of the leasing office. She was gazing down the driveway still shaken from her encounter with Edward.

Dabbing her eyes once more with the napkin, she paced back and forth on the porch, once more, going over her story. Stopping along the railing, she waited for the cars to park. She squinted a bit but because of the dark window tint, she still couldn't see the drivers' faces.

Pulling directly in front of the office door, Robert Lassiter picked up his microphone and radioed dispatch, "Unit 1273 and 1274, 10-23—We'll be checking out with the complainant."

The radio cracked back, "Unit 1273 and 1274, 10-4, 16:35 hours."

Adam pulled to the left of Robert's car and parked.

Halfway out of his car, Robert said, "Hello. Are you Barbara Woodward?"

The question startled Jackie; she had forgotten what she told the dispatcher on the phone. She almost panicked, but forced herself to nod. She remained on the porch in the brisk wind and brushed the long, black hair out of her eyes. She thought if she stayed near the office, it would seem more believable.

The two men joined her on the porch.

25

"I'm Robert Lassiter," he said, in an enhanced, deep voice. "This is Adam Thompson of the Mental Health Unit. What can we help you with?"

Adam learned long ago that Robert loved taking charge at the scene. Assuming Alpha leader, Adam called it. Chest inflated, back straight, voice full and low, he savored the recognition of being in charge, but did not relish the results, which would almost always be a lengthy report. To assert himself as a pillar of strength must have been quite impressive to most who were in need of assistance. His on camera, off camera performances were just what the public needed. Stand erect, carry a clipboard, badge and gun, and point this way and that. Six-foot-five, two hundred and sixty pounds of commanding lawman. Spew mental heath code and psychological jargon of which, he himself only half understood. It made for an impressive production. And after all, isn't that what citizens pay taxes for?

"That was fast," she said flatly. "I'm having a problem with one of my tenants. The police department said they couldn't do anything about it."

"What happened?" Robert asked as he put his hands into the warm pockets of his $490, big-and-tall man's custom leather jacket. The one everybody at the sheriff's department had heard about at least ten times.

Looking down at the ground, her eyes began to water. "Ya see, he left a work requisition in the box over the weekend, and—"

"Wait. Who did?" asked Robert.

"Edward Langtree. We've never had any trouble with him before. You hardly ever see the guy. He keeps to himself. I think I've only seen him about twice since I've been here, going on two years—"

"Anyway, what did he do?" Robert coaxed.

"Oh. Uh, yeah, he left a requisition for us to fix the heater in his apartment. Whenever we get one, I always go to see what's wrong before I call maintenance. Ya see, their office is at another apartment complex and I don't want to waste their time by calling them up, and—"

"And so what did he do, Mrs. Woodward?" Robert cut in, a second time.

She brushed the hair out of her face and remembered the scars on her wrists. Quickly, she concealed them from the officers by pulling her sleeves all the way down and then continued. "Anyway, I got over to his apartment; it's just around back." She pointed behind the office. "And I knocked on the door. I waited for a long time, but he never came, so I used the master key and let myself in. The place was trashed. There are pizza boxes all over the floor, soda cans, and candy bar wrappers. It is disgusting. I can't believe people can live like that. It's unsanitary. You know?" She stood there, staring at them.

"Mrs. Woodward," Adam cut in. "What did Edward do to make you think that he needs to be evaluated by the mental health unit?"

Looking down at the leaves blowing on the ground, her voice started to waver, "Oh, well, I'm standing in the middle of this filth and he walked out of the bathroom yelling at me."

"What did he say?"

Looking back up, she revealed the tears in her eyes. "He called me every name in the book, that's what he said. I was just there to help. He told me to get the fuck out of his apartment. He just kept yelling and walking towards me. I mean, he didn't have any clothes on. He was just holding a towel in his hand. He scared the shit out of me. I mean, he's like some kind of pervert or something."

"And what did you do, Mrs. Woodward?" Robert asked, emotionlessly.

"I got the hell out of there!" she said with a strange look on her face, both hands planted on her hips. "What do you think I did?" Then she thought, *What would the real manager have done?* "But, I mean, I didn't just run off. I'm the manager here and I don't have to take that. I told him he needed to clean his apartment up. We needed clear access to the thermostat and he would have to pick up the boxes. Then he really went nuts, screaming about doing any goddamn thing he wanted to, and that this was his home, and if he wanted to blow his blankety-blank brains out, he could. I want him out of this complex, Officer Lassiter. He's weird. The man is weird!" Tears welled in her eyes, and she tilted her head back to catch her breath.

"What do you mean Edward said, blow his blank-blank head off?" Adam asked.

She smirked and lifted one eyebrow. "He said that he could blow his fucking brains out, okay?" she snorted. "Do I have to spell it for you?"

"Mrs. Woodward, how long have you been the manager of this complex?" Adam asked.

She thought quickly. "Oh, about four years. I'm getting out of school at the end of this semester. I think I'm going on to law school and get—"

"Mrs. Woodward," Adam chose his words carefully. "I think you know we can't just kick the guy out. I'm sure you know the procedures for eviction. If you want him out, you need to go ahead and start that."

"Well then, I want you to interview him or do whatever it is you do. I want him out of here. He was standing there with his dick hanging out!" she insisted.

"I'm sorry, but a man can say or wear anything he wants to in his own house. If it offends you, you need to leave."

"But he said he was going to kill himself," she whined.

Robert was kicking some leaves away from his size fifteen, $695 ostrich-skin boots. "She's got a point, Adam," he added.

"No, when we asked what happened just now, you told us that *he* said, *if* he wanted to blow his blankety-blank brains out, he could. That is not a suicidal threat," Adam assured.

"I don't know; it could go both ways," Robert said.

Robert had been Adam's training officer, and Adam couldn't believe what was coming from his mouth. When he was under his wing, Robert would have pointed this flaw in her statement immediately. He would have used it as a basis for the entire investigation. But, Adam did notice how Robert's subtle glances found two tiny knots the cold wind helped form under the young woman's thin top. That was it. The lone-eyed ranger to the rescue. Adam was somehow sure that Barbara had noticed Robert's interest, and was going to use her assets to their fullest.

She stood there with her arms crossed, propping her chest up on them. "I can't believe you guys aren't going to do anything?"

Robert pulled his hands out of his jacket and reached for his wallet. "Yes ma'am, we'll go talk to him, but we can't promise that were going to do anything." Forcing a smile, he added, "He might have just been upset that you caught him with his pants down. Here is my card."

She stared at it, blankly.

28

Robert motioned to the door. "Do you mind if I borrow your phone? I would like to call ahead and see if we already have him in the system."

She fidgeted for a moment and almost seemed to blush. She had anticipated this and had her answer ready.

"Barbara?" Robert asked.

"I'm sorry. How embarrassing. I don't have the office keys with me."

"That's okay. Don't worry about it. Now, I want you to know that if he does have some sort of problem needing medical attention, we won't be able to tell you where he is or when he will be back."

"I don't understand," she said.

"Under the Texas Mental Health Code, all information on patients suspected of mental illness is strictly confidential. So if we do leave with him, just know that he will be taken care of."

"What apartment was it?" Adam asked.

"114. It's around the back. Did you want me to show you?"

"No, no, that's okay. We'll find it," Adam assured her.

The two deputies tightened their jackets and headed around the office toward Edward's domain.

"Well, that was one person that didn't ask how tall you are," Adam said.

"She wants to be a lawyer," Robert said.

Now he knew for sure. It was the little buttons that had gotten to him. Or it might have been her calves. He had seemed to watch those blowing leaves for a long time. *No*, Adam thought, *he got a look at those young, bouncy breasts*, and that was it. The cold had transformed them from soft little sponges to hard eraser heads. The investigation was shot to shit and now Robert was on a mission.

Edward was doomed.

Adam didn't reveal his suspicions; there was no need. Even as a joke, Robert would be deeply insulted, or at the very least, act that way. He would defend himself stoically against any thought that would violate the sanctity of the admiration he held for his wife and the institution of marriage.

"Kinda strange the apartment manager wouldn't have her keys with her, don't ya think?" Adam asked.

"You've forgotten your keys before."

"Yeah, but she said she used her master key to let herself into the dude's apartment, right?"

"So, what's your point?" Robert said, impatiently.

Adam could tell he was getting nowhere with all this. "Okay, forget the keys. She said she's been the manager for four years, right?"

"Yep," Robert answered curtly, not really paying attention to the conversation.

"This complex hasn't been here that long, three at the most."

Robert just shrugged, "It's the next one up. Are you writing the report or me?"

Adam was waiting for that question. Robert knew damn good-and-well who was supposed to write the report. Robert was dispatched to the call. Robert got there first. Robert checked out with radio dispatch. Robert made first contact with the complainant. *Gee, I don't know!* Adam thought. *Could it be me?*

"You took the call," Adam said, calmly.

"All right, I got it," he mumbled. He stopped at the apartment door and carefully listened for any sounds.

Nothing.

Stepping aside, away from the door and leaning up against the wall, Robert reached out and checked the doorknob. It was unlocked. He waited a few seconds and then knocked. The force of the knock jarred the door slightly open.

"I guess he didn't close it all the way," Robert whispered.

Robert's ability to state the obvious was uncanny.

"Mr. Langtree. Sheriff's Department. Can we talk to you a minute?" he shouted.

Silence.

Adam leaned forward, "We're with the Sheriff Department's Mental Health Unit. We just need to talk to you a minute."

Silence.

Pushing the door open, Robert started to step inside.

"What are you doing? We don't have a warrant on this guy," Adam said sternly.

"Emergency entry doctrine. We're goin' to see if he's all right."

"That's bullshit! This guy didn't say he was going to kill himself."

30

Ignoring Adam, Robert continued walking into the apartment. "Sheriff's Department. Mr. Langtree, we need to talk."

Stepping over the pizza boxes, the big man brushed back his curly black hair with one hand and adjusted the gun in his waistband with the other.

"Mr. Langtree?" Robert repeated.

Adam cursed him under his breath, but followed anyway. At this point, he had no other choice.

As they both stood in the living room of the small one-bedroom apartment, Edward quickly stepped out of the bathroom and into the hall.

"What the hell do you want?" he yelled as he walked toward them. "I don't work for them anymore! Get the hell out of here. Get out!"

Robert held his hands up in front of his chest and tried to calm him down. "Hold on just a minute, Mr. Langtree. We just want to talk to you."

Edward stopped a half step into the living room, wearing only sweat pants that were bulging in the business area. They apparently just woke Edward or walked in while he was taking care of his business.

"I don't want to talk to you. I want you out of my apartment now," he demanded.

"All right, Mr. Langtree, all right. You win. We'll leave," Robert said, as he removed a business card from his $75.00, hand-tooled wallet. "It was nice talking with you. I hope we can meet under better circumstances next time," he added and handed the card to Edward, then extended his hand in apparent friendship.

Adam just stood there in disbelief, shocked at what was about to happen. Robert had been his mental health field-training officer. He knew every one of his moves. Adam saw the big man break the arm of a burglar with one twist. He once put a 280 pound, college football lineman's face through the windshield of a TransAm. Adam knew Robert, his strengths and his weaknesses. And he knew that at this point Robert was taking charge.

Assuming Alpha leader.

Looking somewhere between satisfied and bewildered, Edward reached for his hand. Then suddenly, as if he had a premonition from

God, Edward jerked back in horror. Immediately, Robert struck him in the chest with both open palms, throwing the small man into the wall. Stunned, he slid to the floor, with Robert right on top him, turning him over. In a flash, his hands were cuffed and he found himself lying face down on top of his own trash.

After getting a little air back and raising his head off of some pizza boxes, Edward croaked, "What did I do? What did I do? I'm sorry!"

"Now, I'm doing this for your own good. I don't want to hurt you and I don't want you to hurt yourself."

Edward pleaded for forgiveness as Robert pulled a set of leg cuffs out of his back pocket. Quickly, he cuffed Edward's legs to his hands, hog-tied style. Throwing his hands up in the air like a rodeo cowboy who just finished bulldogging a calf, Robert shouted, "Time!" then smiled at Adam.

Adam stood speechless. What was he supposed to do? Step in and stop Robert from pouncing on the guy? Second-guess another officer? The one the department in its wisdom, assigned to train him. Step up and declare, "Excuse me, but I believe you are using excessive force in apprehending this subject. Please cease and desist your brutality!" Had Adam missed something Robert had seen? A hidden gun? A furtive gesture that would make this big man feel that tiny little Eddy was putting him or Adam at risk?

Standing up, Robert adjusted his belt and started walking toward the bathroom. "So are you on any type of medication, Ed?"

"What the fuck is it to you?" he screamed. Spit shot from his mouth.

You could tell it in his eyes. There was something going on with Edward, but what? Would he meet criteria for commitment? An actual danger to himself or others. Experiencing a psychotic episode? Severe deterioration?

"I'm not playing!" Edward shouted. He turned his head and raised his chin over a Coke can, looking up at Adam. "And who the hell are you, Obi-Wan Doggie? Ya got Darth Vader doing all your dirty work?"

Adam squatted down beside him. "Just hold on a minute, we're not here to hurt you, Ed. Are we, Robert?"

Robert continued his questioning from the bathroom, "Have you been seeing a doctor for anything lately, Ed?"

"What the hell is going on?" he asked Adam.

"I'm not sure. Just wait a minute, Ed. Just hold on a sec," Adam tried to console Edward, but he was in a state of confusion himself.

Walking back out of the bathroom, Robert had several bottles in his hands.

"I don't work for you anymore!" Edward screamed.

With an amused look on his face, Robert stopped, just as he returned to the living room. In a voice as if he were addressing a child, he asked, "And who are we, Ed?"

"You can burn in hell, fluid mover!"

Robert smirked at Adam, then stepped over Ed into the kitchen. Again he searched through every inch of Edward's private life. The life he kept so long sheltered from the others. The one he always knew he had to keep secret. It was his life; there was nothing wrong with that.

"I haven't told anyone," he sobbed, letting his head rest once again on the pizza box. "Just leave me alone, please."

"Ed, how long have you been an outpatient over at the West 12th office?" Robert asked from the kitchen.

Ed lay silent on his stomach, hands and feet behind his back in the air. He whispered to himself, "Water is the perfect pressure."

Adam stood and left Ed's side to join Robert in the kitchen. "What are you doing, man? If this guy isn't crazy now, you're going to make him that way."

"Oh, he's crazy all right. Look at this. He's got part of his last outpatient slip here in the garbage disposal. Schizo-affective disorder. They've got him on just about every psychotropic medication you can think of. By the supply he's got here, it doesn't look like he's been taking any in a couple of months," Robert said, with a sense of accomplishment.

Edward's eyes widened; he was sure he had destroyed everything. All records. There was no way he could have missed anything. Everything had been chewed up and flushed.

Chewed up and flushed.

"As I say again, what are we doing here? What has he done? You need to go in there and evaluate him, Lassiter. You need a reason to put him in the hospital, not just because he won't let you in his house or won't talk to you. He probably thinks you're a complete dickhead."

"He wouldn't be too far from the truth, would he?" Robert smiled.

"You come walking into my house like this and see what I'd do. I guarantee you'll think I'm crazy."

Robert crossed his arms, "Is that a threat?"

"Just go in there and talk to him."

He followed Robert back into the living room. Ed lay on the floor, surrounded by the things of his world, his things. Things he liked and paid for.

"Well, Ed, now that I gave you a little time to think, maybe you'll be able to answer a few questions, huh?" Robert said, tossing the medication on the dinner table. He looked for a place to sit and tried to clear some of the trash off of one of the chairs.

It was quiet in the room where Ed lay, still staring into the pizza box. Only his breathing made a creaking noise as his chest rocked back and forth on an empty Coke can.

He said nothing.

"Now, Ed, I want you to know, you need to talk to me. I'm getting the feeling that you're off your medication and might be having a psychotic episode. I need you to convince me that's not true."

Ed lay in silence.

Adam squatted down again. "Come on, Ed. You were talking to me not just a minute ago. What's the deal?"

Giving up trying to clear a seat for himself, Robert stood over both of them. "Well, what's it going to be? I don't have all day to sit here and play games."

Games…Edward knew the games.

"Last chance, man. I'm on your side," Adam said, softly.

Nothing.

"Come on, let's go. I'm going to give you a ride to the Psychiatric Services Unit at the county hospital. I'll let you talk to a doctor there, if ya want to talk," Robert said. He reached down and unlocked the leg cuffs. "You're not gonna try and run anywhere, are ya?"

Putting the leg cuffs into his back pocket, Robert carefully helped him to stand. They started walking to the door. "Do you got some keys or something ya want to take with you, or is the water running or something?" Robert asked.

"I don't think he's got any more to say to us, Robert. I'll make sure everything is locked up and turned off," Adam said. He turned to go back into the bedroom and check the rest of the apartment.

"Last chance," Robert repeated as Adam fumbled with the lock.

After closing the door, Adam took hold of Ed's other arm and they escorted him around to the mental health cars.

Arriving, Robert unlocked and opened the rear passenger-side door to his car. "Here ya' go, partner. Watch your head," he said, and carefully stuffed him into the cruiser.

The back seat was dark; he could hardly see through the tint. Edward tried to straighten his legs, but the metal frame for the prisoner window took up half of the space between the front and back seats. Leaning to the side, he tried to relieve some pressure off the handcuffs. The bare skin on his back squeaked on the cold vinyl seat.

Adam saw the woman still standing on the office porch. Now two men in business suits accompanied her. Prospective clients, Adam assumed and walked up to the edge of the stairs, to wait for her. He knew she wouldn't want to discuss any problems with prospective tenants near.

She excused herself and walked down to him. "So, what happened?"

"Well, we're going to take him down to the hospital and let him talk to a doctor. I think he's going to be just fine. Just needs a little time to cool off."

"I knew there was something wrong with him. I'm pretty good at reading people. I've got to get him out of here."

Adam took out his note pad and pen. "I need to get some information from you, for the report. May I see your driver's license?"

"Uhm," she looked embarrassed or nervous. Adam wasn't sure which. "My purse is in the office."

"In the office?" he repeated.

"I don't have my keys. Remember?" she said.

Very convenient, he thought, then said, "Full name and date of birth will be fine."

"Barbara Woodward, January 12, 1967."

"Do you have a middle name?" he asked.

"Ellen," she answered.

There was a pause in her answer. Adam was sure he detected it. "Okay, Barbara Ellen Woodward, January 11, 1967."

He looked at her and waited. She stared at him, then stammered, "No, uhm, twelfth. January twelfth."

Adam smiled. "Just remember, Mrs. Woodward, you can't kick a man out of his home for wanting his privacy, or for being sick. If you're going to evict him, make sure he's done something against his lease agreement or else you'll be wasting your time."

"Thank you very much for your help, Officer…"

"Thompson. If you need anything else, please call."

"Oh, how long will he be there?" she asked.

"I don't have the foggiest. He could be there for a couple of hours, or a few days."

"Will you call me when he gets out?"

"Ma'am, we explained that earlier. We can't relay any of that information to anyone."

The woman sighed, "I don't understand. What if he gets out and is mad at me for calling on him. How am I supposed to protect myself if I don't even know where he is?"

"You just need to call 911 if he gives you a problem again. I'm sorry, but that's the way the Mental Health Code is written. I'm sure everything will be fine." Or Adam thought to himself, *Would have been fine*.

She turned and without another word went back to join the men on the porch.

Robert had already gotten into his car and started backing out when Adam finished with her. Making eye contact with him and nodding, Robert dropped his gearshift knob into drive and headed to the hospital.

Robert checked in with dispatch. "Unit 1274, I'll be 10-8 in service, transporting one white male to Psychiatric Services Unit at the county hospital. Could you telephone and tell them I'm en route?"

The radio answered, "10-4, Unit 1274."

Adam felt terrible that he didn't take Robert up on his offer to let him have the call. If he had taken the call he most likely could have saved Edward, or at the very least, made it a little easier on him, maybe arranging an emergency out-patient appointment instead of all this. He got back into his car and radioed dispatch, "Unit 1273, in service, I have one to run by name and date of birth."

"10-4,1273, it might take a while, the state computer is down. Go ahead," dispatch said.

"Woodward, Barbara Ellen, white female, one, twelve, sixty-seven."

"10-4, Unit 1273. Are you available for a call?"

"10-4," Adam responded.

"Unit 1273, assist city department at 8th and Senate. Possible EDP in the roadway. Suspect, white female with no clothes on."

Adam smiled and thought to himself, *God I love this job. Two in one day.*

"Unit 1273, 10-4," he acknowledged. "Do you have a description of the subject?"

"I think she will be the only one there with no clothes on," dispatch answered, sarcastically.

"10-4, en route," he laughed.

CHAPTER SIX

The Trek
"Tuesday, December 17th, 5:20 pm"

Edward Langtree tried to adjust the cuffs to keep them from pinching his wrist bones, but no position seemed any better than the other.

"You okay back there?" Robert asked.

Edward's bare skin squeaked on the car's vinyl seat, but he said nothing.

Robert released the locking lever and pushed the plexiglas window down. "I said, are you okay back there?"

Edward stopped moving and stared straight ahead. He reflected how earlier this morning he had emerged from his sterile-white, artificially illuminated environment. He was used to it. All of his adult life, he had worked in places just like this one. He remembered marching out the double-glass doors and into a new, crisp morning. He remembered how he took in his surroundings. The other employees seemed to be walking in every direction. There was movement everywhere and it was hard for him to pick up anything out of the ordinary. Most of the midnight shift paused shortly when they walked into the daylight. Their eyes squinting, and most mentioning something about how beautiful the day was. Not Edward. The weather was of no consequence to him. He subconsciously acknowledged the brown, dead grass, and how the barren trees clawed their way sparsely across the environmentally friendly, industrial park. He remembered how the clear blue sky opened up allowing a chilly, southerly breeze to volley fallen leaves, discarded candy wrappers, and cigarette butts across the sidewalks and parking lot. The sun had just cleared the horizon when the day shift arrived to relieve him and the midnight crew.

Typical day crew, Edward thought. *Mumbling and complaining. Stumbling around like zombies.* Most of them had cups of hot coffee and managed to spill it on everything but a costar or napkin.

"No discipline," he hissed to himself, as he sat in Robert's back seat.

"What was that?" Robert asked.

"Pathetic," Edward said.

"What's pathetic?"

Edward did not answer.

Edward was not a big man. He stood five foot ten inches, with a slender, but well-developed body. That of a runner most people would think, if they took notice of him. Most didn't. It wasn't that he was unattractive. Just unremarkable. The way he carried himself, his mannerisms, speech, and expression. Everything was, for the lack of a better word, blah. Plain. If described by an inexperienced witness for a police lineup, you would have gotten, "Oh, he was average, ya know, average height. I wouldn't say he was heavy, but he wasn't really thin either. Kinda sandy blond, no, brown hair…" and so on. Edward seemed to be shrouded in the ordinary.

Edward could not understand how Robert and that other guy had found him at his apartment. He had been covering his tracks so perfectly. He had known the government was watching him and couldn't imagine what he had done to give himself away.

He had never parked his car in the same place twice. He varied every movement. Took a different route to and from work. He had parked his car around the back of the manufacturing complex today. It always seemed like a long walk. Maybe he had walked too fast, and they noticed him.

Edward clinched his eyes together, trying to think.

"Edward, are your wrists hurting?" Robert asked.

Nothing.

"It's only about another five minutes, and I'll get those things off," Robert assured.

Edward did not hear him. He remembered starting his car's engine and smoothly moving into the morning traffic. He could see the lot and the string of cars in his mind, but nothing out of the ordinary. No one watching. He remembered adjusting the rear view mirror to see if anyone was following, but there was no one.

He had chosen Micro Invocoustics as his place of employment because of their advanced security program. Cameras, uniformed and plain clothed security officers, none of whom knew him. Most of them wore sunglasses, he later noticed. He started wearing them too. Security watched every move on the property. They couldn't afford to do otherwise. Being one of the leaders in computer technology, they were constantly at risk of compromising classified research and trade secrets. It was a perfect setup for Edward. He thought there would be no better place for him to hide but right under their noses. Micro Invocustics was one of the largest and leading semiconductor plants in the United States, commanding one of the biggest government contracts in the computer industry.

Edward knew he was more valuable than being just a wafer-manufacturing technician, but he couldn't afford to give himself away. It was only a year since the last incident.

Edward felt the car turn and opened his eyes. He didn't recognize the street. He didn't care.

He realized he was reckless last time. They easily discovered he was conducting his own research, and forced him to get rid of his dog. Little Billy was still buried in his porch flowerbed. Edward decided when the government infested Billy with the tiny, flea like robots, he had no other choice but to put Billy down. That was when Edward made up his mind there would be no more attachments; he would not be responsible for anyone else close to him getting hurt. It was from that very moment that he never talked to Jackie again. He decided he would become a listener. No more notes or journals. Nothing they could find or use against him.

Everything chewed up and flushed. He would rely solely on his mind. His own, perfect mind. Not theirs. Not the clouded, drug induced one they forced on him. Not anymore.

Working as an intelligence analyst in the Navy taught him that. He had never operated in the field, at least he couldn't remember if he

did.   He was just an enlisted analyst.   Photographs, radio
transmissions, frequency emissions, things like that were his world.

He met Jackie at the hospital; she liked to hurt herself. Never
anything major, just carve up and down her wrists with an assortment
of sometime dull, sometimes sharp objects. Usually she did it late at
night, when she was alone.   When Edward stopped returning her
phone calls, she made some frantic attempts to talk to him at his
apartment. He would hear her voice calling and the banging, but he
would just wrap his head tighter in the pillow.

"Shit!" Robert exclaimed and jerked the wheel. The car lurched
to the left and they barely missed a bicyclist darting out between two
parked cars. "Dumb ass," Robert added.

Edward looked back at the cyclist. He had stopped his bike and
was staring at them through dark sunglasses. The rider reached into
the jacket pocket of his gray pinstriped business suit and brought out a
two-way radio. Even though the windows were closed and even
though they were now a block away from each other, Edward could
hear the cyclist say, "Tan Ford Crown Victoria, east bound on Pecan."

Edward faced the front of the car, again.

He knew for sure now; they were tracking him.

Robert turned left and now Edward could see the hospital. To his
right, he could also see a lady throw a small, white plastic bag into a
green dumpster. Ed smiled to himself. It reminded him of his last
few days in the Navy, on the ship. He remembered the white plastic
bag he had. *And,* the dead thing in the bag. He laughed and shook his
head.

"We're almost there," Robert said again.

They had constantly harassed him on the ship, Edward
remembered. Made jokes about him, to his face and behind his back.
Mostly behind his back, he guessed. He could never understand how
people like that could be in charge over him. That was the hardest.
He finally came to the revelation they were just jealous of his
abilities. That is why he never received the recognition he deserved.
His work normally went unnoticed. Accepted by his chain-of-
command and nothing else said. He knew what they had been doing.
They had reported his information and kept the credit for themselves.
That was why, sometimes in his reports, he would purposefully falsify

the findings to discredit the greedy bastards. If they wanted to take sole credit for the work he was doing, they could have it.

He was very thorough and deliberate.

It wasn't until the end of his Navy service that he realized things were happening to him. What things, he could never really be sure. On one day his papers would be moved, on other days, maybe the cap to his toothpaste would not be on all the way. Things, words, pictures, like images with white borders, and thoughts would flood his memories as strobes of light, vanishing as quickly as they came. Sometimes it was dreadful, like severe growing pains. Sometimes the sharpest of the pains, searing pains, would stab at his rectum. It usually happened when he was in public, on the bus, in a quiet bookstore, or at the grocery. Those were the worst. The stabs would come and he would have to accept the pain silently, with bulging eyes and quivering hands. His whole body frozen until they passed. They never came to him when he was alone. They would never allow him to compensate for the pain and let him scream. And given the chance, he would have screamed.

Robert parked his car in the empty police designated area of the county hospital's Emergency Room parking lot. "Here we are."

Edward glanced around. He had been here before. He would soon have to talk to the doctors and he would have to be ready for them.

For their interrogations, he thought. *Medications. Instillations. Fabrications. Cauterizations.* His mind clanged over and over. *Medications. Instillations. Fabrications. Cauterizations…*

"Edward?" Robert asked.

He hadn't realized that Robert had come around and already opened the door for him.

As Edward got out, Robert pointed at the sliding glass doors. "Straight through there."

A person sat on the bench, just outside the emergency room doors. He held a newspaper high in front of him, concealing his face. Edward knew this technique. He knew only novice agents tried to hide behind newspapers. Amateur spies.

As they walked through the doors, Edward said, "I see you," to the person on the bench.

Robert shook his head. "Right over there."

Robert walked Edward over to the holding cell, just inside the waiting area. He looked through the small window in the door and seeing that it was empty, pulled the door open.

"Turn around for me," Robert said.

Edward turned and Robert unlocked the cuff on his right wrist and moved the cuffs around to his front. "Here ya go," he said, then locked his hands together again. "Have a seat in here. It might be a while before they come to talk with you."

Robert shut the door and turned to fill out his admission slip. In his mind, he was done with Edward. Done trying to talk with him. Done trying to explain things to him. Done babying him. He was just going to complete his commitment and move on.

Edward stared at the white tiles, then walked over and sat on the stainless steel bench mounted to the wall.

He could remember everything. And he could remember nothing. "What are anomalies?" he remembered Dr. Jarrett asking. *Mister, Doctor James G. Jarrett, Ph.D. Psychology, Bethesda Naval Hospital.* "What are anomalies? Are they people, Edward?"

Edward had tried to explain them to him, but there were things he couldn't tell the doctors. His military security clearance would not allow it. He told him what he could, but definitely not everything.

"An anomaly is an anomaly," Edward remembered saying. "Look it up. You do own a dictionary, don't you?"

Edward had completed his data manager's internship at the Air Force's Space Command in Colorado. That is where he learned of these anomalies, of these abnormalities. Radar blips that aren't military or civilian aircraft, aren't weather related, and change course and speed. An impossibility.

Edward knew the anomalies are what started it. Started all his problems. Simple anomalies.

That was a long time ago.

"Anomaly," Edward said to the empty room. The ceiling tiles devoured his words and left nothing to linger. He knew they were something inconsistent or improper. Space debris that changed course and speed. It didn't seem right. Ed knew bullshit when he smelled it, and this was definitely a pile.

He would need to remedy this problem, once and for all.
Like the dead thing in the bag.
Chewed up and flushed.

CHAPTER SEVEN

The End
"Tuesday, December 17ᵗʰ, 8:01 pm"

Robert's eyes opened again. Things were blurry. He coughed and foamy, salty spittle bubbled at his lips. His teary vision cleared a little, and he saw the dark liquid pooling in the floorboard. A long, gooey string hung from his bottom lip; it swung, jiggled a little, and then attached itself to his collar.

He heard the door slam, but he was confused about what happened? His radio microphone cord was torn from its housing. That wasn't right. His big hands reached for the car's ignition, but found only the switch. Smearing his blood onto the column and gearshift, he fumbled in a frantic search, but found no keys. He was starting to come around a little, and that too, would soon fade again.

"Marla," he choked, again grasping at the puncture wounds in the side of his throat.

He felt air escape from one of the tears.

Stop the blood, he thought, as he applied more pressure to his throat, groping, trying to decide which rip needed the most attention. His head ached and a knot was forming near his right temple.

He pushed down with his legs and tried to force his butt further back into the seat, but he couldn't get traction; the floorboard was too slippery from the life that oozed from him.

Straining, he attempted to focus on the world beyond his windshield. Diffused blackness. A cone of light reached down from a street lamp and cast an obscured glow on the cold, empty pavement. Everything else was void; his windows were too foggy.

His vision blurred again. He had no idea where he was. He felt the warm fluid escaping from his neck. The liquid crept down his forearm and onto his jeans, slowly inching over the gold star, clipped to his belt.

No pain, he pondered. His throat throbbed along with the side of his head. He could feel the gashes, but no real pain.

He blinked slowly and braved another breath, not that he could afford to put one off any longer. The air and blood came in. His throat lurched. The involuntary reflex brought another series of choking spasms. More blood leapt from his mouth. Some of the crimson spray sprinkled across the windshield, while larger globs splattered and attached themselves onto the dash and instrument panel.

He closed his eyes for a moment and could see Marla. She sat smiling at him in full view of the lake behind her. "Don't eat so fast. You'll choke to death!" she laughed. "There's plenty of time. We just got here." Then she whispered, "We have all weekend."

Her broad smile warmed him. Her eyes seemed to take on the color of the waters, and her coal-black hair swung around to one side, exposing her long neckline. Marla was his wife. He made it well known.

Then he saw her on the boat. She stood on the bow wearing a bikini covered by one of his T-shirts. She was grinning her special grin, trying to steady herself against the constant assault of waves.

"It's so beautiful," she said, arms outstretched, displaying their cabin on the shore behind her.

Robert took her picture.

"Why don't we stay the summer?" she pleaded. "Karen doesn't have to be back at school for another two months."

Robert stared. She *was* beautiful. He knew she was talking about the beauty of the lake and cabin, but he was thinking only of her. How could he be so lucky?

She was gone with a blur of black and white images flowing through his mind. Boats, restaurants, Marla and their daughter hopping around in the water.

"Come on in, Daddy," Karen called, pulling her hair out of her face, a miniature image of her mother.

Marla waved. "Yeah, come on scaredy-cat. Come on."

He saw the back of his hand in front of him, waving to decline. He just wanted to watch them for a while as their smiles widened and their eyes clenched during vicious splashing attacks on one another.

Once again, Robert's eyes slowly opened. A car drove past. He sat motionless, not even trying to get the attention of the driver. Not a flash of his lights. No tap of his horn.

Nothing.

Not more than fifty feet off the road to the right of him, a young couple sat in their dimly lit den. They had already assembled most of the parts and quietly debated whether to attach the two training wheels on their boy's first bike. Behind Robert's car, at the end of the block, an overweight, impatient woman dragged a small, leashed dog through the chilly darkness. Leading him from tree to tree, she tried to force the nervous little animal to do his business so they could both get back into the warmth of her apartment.

Five minutes ago Robert had been fully aware of his surroundings. Fully alert, his second sense guarding him, ready to warn him at the least sign of danger. He relied on it. Trusted it. His gut-instinct had never failed.

Now, he was only aware of his slowing heartbeat. He actually felt it. Felt his heart flutter, and the muscle actually spasm. In a desperate gasp, he forced down another gulp of air and blood into his straining lungs. Leaning over toward the passenger floorboard, he coughed. The contraction blew the blood and air back out again, splattering everything. Blood sprayed from the open wounds at his neck, and hung in long tentacles from his mouth, reaching out and attaching themselves to the floor.

He rested across the seat. He was sleepy. Tired. His mouth bubbled, "Marla—I'm sorry."

He closed his eyes and she was there once more. This time she was different. Still at the lake house, but something was wrong. The house had been their only retirement goal, a simple one. Twenty-five years with the department, then a pension. If they played their cards right with everything paid off, they would be able to live well. Not rich by any means, but comfortable. *Their* kind of comfortable.

Now, Marla seemed burdened. She sat on the porch overlooking the water, silently in her chair. His chair was folded and propped up against the rail at the end of the stairs, unused. And she was old. Her hair white, and brow deeply furrowed. Her eyes thinned behind bifocals, and he could see they had lost their luster. No smile. She just stared with a pallor of regret. The breeze blew and the wind chimes swung. A fish-shaped windsock from long ago, flapped lightly against one of the porch rafters. The colors had faded with the years, and the cloth had been rotted by the sun. Its tattered string broke and it swam to the ground.

Marla paid it no mind.

A female's voice broke the radio's static, "Mental Health Unit 1274, checking status."

Robert half opened his eyes and struggled to focus, but saw only the passenger seat adjustment lever and the floorboard. The blood. The torn microphone cord, submerging in dark, thick liquid.

His pupils dilated.

December 17, 8:05pm, Robert Lassiter died.

He was Adam's friend.

It was Tuesday.

CHAPTER EIGHT

The Discovery
"Tuesday, December 17th, 8:40pm"

A patrol car meandered through the quiet rectangular blocks of this aging city neighborhood. The vehicle's shiny paint and colorful rack of lights added to the magical twinkle this time of year brings. Streetlights and the flash of other passing cars sparkled in the red, blue, and yellow bubbles on the cruiser's roof.

Christmas lights hung from some of the weathered eaves and twirled around balding bushes, but they were few. Half of the community were renters who never took the time or imagination to join in the holiday spirit. Mostly, a neighborhood filled with young, struggling couples and spartan college frat houses. The dwellings sat at varying distances from the roadway and seemed to stagger down the block as the patrol car headed south.

There were some lifelong residents still in the area. Mostly bitter, reflecting on the good ole days before so many transients encroached in their tiny part of the world. Before the laws were passed making them powerless against allowing undesirables into their sanctuary. Usually, in this part of the city the only reports to the police came drearily as a deceased, elderly hospice patient or a loud-music disturbance from one of the students' parties. But this night was quiet. With the holiday season, most of the college students were back in their parents' houses. Most escaping from their parental grasps momentarily, trying to prove their independence, but still needing to gather more fruits from the family trees. Mainly, the family Christmas trees. Too old to stay under the wing, yet too young to stray too far from the nest.

Still most of the other inhabitants gathered quietly around their glowing boxes, electronic screens casting a faint blue light, illuminating their faces. Their eyes transfixed. The shows promised to take them far from their homes, on a journey away from this mediocre place. Away from their troubles, if only for a few hours.

Officer Dean Martinez, proud and professional, scanned the dark driveways and front yards as he passed. A twenty-seven-year veteran of the force, who at the age of forty-eight still preferred working the street rather than a desk assignment. As a minority he had seen some of the toughest times in law enforcement. When he was a younger man, he would be ready to go toe to toe with anyone who disrespected his family name or made jokes of Mexican stereotypes. It took him a good ten years to realize that cops will attack your soft spot anytime you reveal it. They poked and prodded him at every turn until he simply gave up the fight. He gave in to their ignorance and pitied them for their stupidity. Many years ago a white officer slapped him on the shoulder and told Dean the other guys wouldn't be harassing him if they didn't like him. Dean didn't care, he didn't want to hear it whether they liked him or not.

He was cresting the hump of his evening shift, ready to hang his hat and go home. It was Christmas time and he had no business being anywhere other than with his family.

Dean knew his job and this neighborhood well; it was his first as a rookie patrolman. He had first served in the theft detail, then reassigned back to the street. Burglary, then back to the street. Warrants, to the street. Auto theft, street. Back to burglary, street. And so on. Each time he finished his investigative assignments, he was sent back to the same district or to one adjacent. At first he objected and felt someone was trying to hold him back. He was suspicious of a predominately white chain of command, forever wanting him to translate Spanish for them and performing this duty, this *skill*, for no extra compensation. But after a couple of reassignments, he was always ready to return to Baker Sector. He liked the residents, and for the most part, they liked him.

The relationship became comfortable.

Comfortable can be dangerous.

After making sure his driver's side window was all the way up, Dean tried once more to turn on the heater, hoping after his last try, it had repaired itself. It hadn't. He zipped up his jacket and felt a little shiver.

Looking up at the road, he turned onto Sager. Slowing, he noticed what he thought to be an unmarked, county vehicle parked on the side of the road, pulled against the curb at an odd angle. The car seemed to be almost camouflaged, sitting in a colorless landscape of shadows, where no streetlight fell. As he neared, he became certain it was a county car. A mental health car. A tan Ford LTD with tinted windows and windshield-mounted spotlights. He turned on his own spotlight and then the high beams to illuminate the surreal scene. It didn't feel right. Slowing, he pulled directly behind it and stopped a car's length away. He stared.

Dean picked up and cued his radio microphone, "Baker 604."

"Baker 604, go ahead," the dispatcher responded.

"Baker 604, I'll be checking out at 4110 Segar, on Texas license plate, AWS386. Contact the sheriff's department; see if they have anything going on at this location. I believe this is one of their mental health units."

"Baker 604, 10-4."

He strained his eyes trying to make out something, anything in the car. The window tint was too dark. *Definitely not Department of Public Safety approved tint*, he thought. But it did do the trick; the tint would protect the identity of anyone who might have to be transported in the vehicle, even in the brightest sunlight.

Dean sat in his car waiting for a response from dispatch. He didn't want to disturb anything the mental health deputy might be doing. Usually mental health notified the police department if they were taking any calls within the city limits, but maybe this one wasn't any big deal. Maybe he was just stopping to see a friend, a *lady* friend on duty. He smiled and understood how easy it was to get a rumor started. Even one created in his own mind.

The radio cracked, "Baker 604."

Dean answered, "Baker 604, go ahead."

"Baker 604, county advises that the unit left the emergency room 35 minutes ago on an Emotionally Disturbed Person (EDP) transport to the State Hospital. They're attempting to raise him at this time."

"Baker 604, 10-4." Dean felt a flutter in his chest.

The radio cracked again, "Channel 2 dispatch to all Units, clear channel two for Baker 604 responding to officer needs assistance at 4110 Segar Lane."

Dean's heart pumped and a rush of blood surged into his brain.

"Dispatch to Baker 604, County is unable to make contact with their Mental Health Deputy. Their Watch Commander advises he should have been at the State Hospital twenty minutes ago. The prisoner is ten-zero (10-0), use extreme caution. Baker 602 and 605, hold you en route to back up 604."

"Baker 602, 10-4." "Baker 605, 10-4," the back-up officers responded over the radio.

"Baker 604, 10-4," Dean said, mechanically.

In a matter of seconds, the peaceful night had been shattered. The radio came alive with officers' locations and estimated times for their arrival on the scene.

Now it had become a scene, Dean thought. These kinds of things happened all the time. On a regular busy night, he probably wouldn't have even checked the car. He would have just stopped and got out for a close visual. Or maybe just a slow, drive-by visual. Hell, probably not even that. On a busy night, he wouldn't have thought twice about a poorly parked county vehicle. *The county probably doesn't even have a driving program anyway*, he thought.

After grabbing his flashlight, he slowly got out of his car. He pulled the waistband of his jacket down and unsnapped the holster to his pistol. Raising the flashlight to chest level and holding it out to his side, he walked cautiously toward the car. Over the sound of his footsteps, he heard the sirens from the backup units responding to his location. He reached to his belt and turned down the volume of his hand-held radio.

Quietly, he worked his way to the car. As he got to the driver's door, he tried to make out something in the front seat. A coat, or blanket, or something. The tinting was so dark it started to make him feel even more vulnerable; his light just reflected back into his face. He couldn't see anything. *Like walking up to a car at night wasn't bad enough*, he thought. If anyone were in there, they would definitely be able to see him.

He pressed the lens of his flashlight against the glass to dispel some of the glare it reflected. Suddenly, a grisly image came into view. His heart wrenched in his chest and he thought it would explode; the searing pain of panic stabbed into his veins. He looked down to draw his pistol from his belt, but saw he didn't need to; it was already in his hand.

Dean now realized his instinct was right. He froze for a moment then suddenly remembered he hadn't checked the back seat, then jerked the driver's door open. A body lay crumpled in the front seat. Glancing through the open prisoner window between the front and back, Dean could see the back seat was empty. The prisoner was gone.

He pressed the emergency button on his hand-held radio and then scanned the area briefly with his flashlight. He took several deep breaths while he looked, bringing his emotions back into check.

Holding the mike to his face, he tried to speak clearly. Unwavering, "Unit 604, I have an officer down at my location. Roll an ambulance and Criminal Investigations Detail, (CID)."

Over faint static, the dispatcher responded, "10-4. All available units respond to 4110 Segar. Officer down."

The crisp night air tumbled tiny leaves from the looming oaks onto Robert's car. They clinked as they landed on the roof then slid across its slick surface, scattering onto the ground. The night sounds that had been so serene awakened as a nightmare's far-off screams from the responding patrol car sirens.

From his first glance, Dean knew Robert was dead. He even recognized him. Robert was out on too many EDP calls that Dean had assisted. A couple of attempted suicides, but mainly just repeat psychiatric patients off their medications. If he hadn't been a professional, he doubted he could have recognized him. Dean looked at Robert for just a brief moment, but for years he would remember every detail. Long shadows cast by a distant street lamp. The lack of moisture in the air. The smell of smoke rising from old-fashioned chimneys. The sense that other things seemed to be watching, trying not to be seen or heard. Sometimes giving away their position with the snap of a twig, or the crunch of a leaf. And, of course, Robert. His body lay across the front seat. Dark red, almost black, the blood pooled in the passenger seat and floorboard. Congealing. The muck sat like pudding in the December night air. His left hand around his own neck and his right arm draped across the passenger floor mat. His blank stare pointing at the floor-mounted radio that was trying desperately to reach him. His face twisted into a grisly death mask. Dean wouldn't have recognized his face. It was his dark, wavy hair and the sheer size of the man that gave him away.

Stepping backwards, Dean moved towards the rear of the car, scanning his environment. His skin crawled with the night's chill, as long shadows reached down from the faraway streetlight, leaned and swayed in the driveways, bushes, and behind cars. An old privacy-fence gate creaked slowly on its rusted hinge with the help of the breeze. A cat ran out from under a pile of boxes left stacked in an open carport. Looking at every shadow, every light, and every bit of movement, sound, smell, everything. Leaves danced across the road commanded by the unseen, cold December wind. He slowly made a complete circle of the car, his eyes, and gun barrel darting from sound to shadow. Lump of darkness to tall illumination. Every step or so, he glanced at the trees and buildings lining the street. He returned to Robert's door and stood there shining his light on the lifeless body. Normally, he would look closer. This time, he was close enough.

The sirens drew nearer.

When the officers first arrived, each seemed beckoned to file by, and gaze at the wretch lying twisted in the car. After a brief moment of reflection, gawking, or just plain rubbernecking, they would start to work. Blocking off the length of the entire block, officers were busy everywhere. They gathered the preliminary paperwork, lit the scene with their patrol cars, and encircled a hundred foot radius with barricade tape around the mental health car.

Robert's body lay cold, in the middle of it all.

Other patrol cars buzzed around the neighborhood. Some sat in a stationary position, looking for any strange movement. Others on the prowl, stopped everyone and everything. Officers with flashlights walked through back yards, opened trashcans and unlocked car doors. They checked behind trees and bushes, under cars and over fences, up in overhanging branches and on rooftops. Everywhere they searched, their shadows reached out, their light beams pried and lifted the veil of darkness that blanketed the neighborhood. Signatures of their breath were left briefly as wisps of steam in the cold night air. The movement of their bodies cast dreadful shadows dancing across porches, along driveways, and over hedgerows.

The initial work of the uniformed officers seemed to come to a halt as the investigators from the CID arrived. As crime scene technicians and medical examiner's investigators arrived on the scene, the uniformed officers started to concentrate on assisting with traffic control and gathered to speculate.

It looked like any other crime scene, but one would have to look closely to tell the difference, to pick up the signs. No smiles. No grab ass. No predictions of the fury of a gay lover. No arguments over who gets the deceased's lottery ticket. Just robotic business.

Dean stepped out of the way as the crime scene technicians started photographing the scene, collecting and identifying the evidence.

For a moment, just then, he felt out of place. He discovered the grizzly scene, but now there didn't seem much for him to do. He stepped back, over to the hood of his patrol car, and watched. He thought he could start writing his report, but almost immediately rejected the idea. This report would have to be perfect. A cop was murdered, and he knew the media would make it a real circus. Not to mention the defense attorneys. Any inconsistencies or improper investigation procedures would be highly scrutinized, even if they were just on paper. The cold had caught up to him. His hands began shaking the moment dispatch had cleared the radio channel, but now, the shaking was from the cold, not from adrenaline. He would need a warm office, a hot cup of coffee, and a couple of hours to write this one.

Looking up, he watched an unmarked, Ford LTD, making its way through the rows of blue and whites that lined the street. As the car stopped at the edge of the boundary tape, the headlights went off. Dean knew who it was and walked to meet the driver as he got out.

John Tannerly creaked out of the LTD. A clipboard in one hand and a pen in the other. Both men paused for a moment, looking at each other. Eye to eye.

John, on the topside of fifty had thirty-five hard years of police work under his belt. Twenty-two years in homicide with three different agencies. He was a modest man. Quiet. Most cops would say that *he's forgot more about investigating homicides than most know*. His fellow officers always assumed he had seen everything. He would tell you differently.

Especially this time.

"So, is the sheriff's department going to handle this?" Dean asked.

"Partly. For the most part, I guess. We'd look kinda silly if we couldn't handle the murder of one of our own officers. The Sheriff talked to your watch commander and they agreed, fortunately for us, for ya'll to help us out," John said, as he buttoned his coat.

"Come on, I'll show you. The turd got his gun too," Dean said.

They both headed to Robert's car. John felt like he was in a dream as he glanced briefly around for someone to help him. The lights, and the shadows. He looked for someone to wake him. To tell him it's all a bad dream, so he could go back to sleep. No one would, or could. Then he thought, even if he was asleep in bed at home, there was no one to wake him there, either.

John had known Robert Lassiter for nine years. In that time they took departmental training classes together, and John had even attended a couple of classes Robert taught. Ironically, one of them was Prisoner Transport and Street Survival. John remembered Robert repeating, "If you don't follow these simple techniques, you might find yourself tits up in a bar ditch."

John wondered which technique Robert missed.

They stopped behind a group of crime scene technicians and the coroner's deputies, who were busy at their trade. They were measuring, photographing, and starting on a detailed crime-scene sketch.

Dean said, "We haven't touched anything. The way you see it is the way I found it. Oh, except for the door. I had to open the door."

Hearing the voices behind them, the crime scene techs stepped aside, revealing to John the grotesque sight. John stepped up to the driver's door, squatted down, and started making entries in his notes. "I want pictures of everything. If anyone moves anything, I want a picture before and after they move it. Is the tow truck here?"

"Yeah, it's down the street," a voice said, from a crowd of blue uniforms.

"Tell him I want to talk to him."

Standing back up, John slowly circled the car. He scanned for everything and anything. Anything unusual or out of the ordinary.

Any new external damage that might indicate someone assisted in the murder. An accomplice possibly running into Robert's car, forcing him to stop or trying to make it look like it was some sort of accident. He jotted notes as he went, but saw nothing. The car seemed clean other than the mess inside.

Looking up at Dean, John asked, "Could you have one of your units go by the shithead's house and sit on it until I can get someone from the sheriff's department to relieve them. Have your dispatchers call mine. They have the address."

"You wanted to see me?" a tall, skinny man of about fifty years asked, as he walked up to John. "I got the tow truck."

John stopped what he was doing and looked directly at the man. "After they get him out of there," he pointed to Robert with his clipboard. "You're going to take this car over to the State Patrol laboratory on Lamar. There will be technicians waiting for it there. An officer will follow you. I want both of you to make sure that *nothing* happens to this car. It is imperative this vehicle makes it there unmolested." Looking at the crime scene techs, he continued, "I don't want any latent prints recovered until we get this in some good light. I want every inch of this thing covered. Get the Troopers to use the laser on it. I want the mechanic's fingerprints off the oil filter. Does everyone understand my convictions?"

They all nodded in agreement as John returned to writing his notes.

"So, what the hell do you think the guy did it with? It looks like he tried to cut his head off," Dean said, still observing Robert's body from a distance.

John leaned into the car, "Hard to tell. It wasn't anything too sharp. Look how nasty the cuts are."

More officers arrived at the scene offering assistance, and this was the first time Dean noticed his tunnel vision fading. It was a common problem among police officers in high-risk street situations. Adrenaline induced dilation of the pupils, reducing peripheral vision, and now, with the intense excitement of the discovery passed, his body was once again beginning to relax. He noticed rubberneckers from the surrounding houses. Cameras from local TV stations were adding to the much-needed light, and much-hated confusion.

A group of officers formed a line. With flashlights they combed across the immediate area time and time again looking for anything that may help find answers to what had happened.

Evidence bags were slowly filled. Just about every piece of trash in a 100-foot circle was placed into a container. They overlooked nothing.

As the hours passed, finally, they removed Robert's body. Carefully, the coroner deputies packaged him in the cold, black, plastic bag and zipped it shut. With the assistance of other officers, they loaded him into the medical examiner's van and headed to the morgue.

With the coroners gone, the barrier tape rolled up, and a majority of the responding officers back to their regular duties, John Tannerly headed back downtown. He knew it was going to be a long night and an even longer tomorrow. He would have to stop back by his house and pick up his blood pressure pills, but first a detour to the nearest "stop and rob" for a big, black cup of coffee.

Dean sat motionless in his car looking at what was the scene of a horrible act, now slowly transforming back into a normal, neighborhood side street. One you find yourself driving down any day. A normal place where people live, and children play. He thought how this event would affect their lives. Things on this block would never be the same. People would tell the story. He knew after he left, some people, who watched the whole event, would wander out closer, looking at the orange, spray-painted lines on the street, the ones marking Robert's car tires. They would look for anything left behind by the investigating teams. A piece of blockade tape or stray evidence bag pulled off the hood of the car from the wind. They would look for the blood that dripped over the edge of the door, making its unforgettable mark on the street. In the days to come, children would visit this place. Maybe even children, not from this neighborhood, hearing of the horrible tale from friends at school. He thought of the stories that will be told on this block and of the phantom police officer wandering up and down the street looking for his head. The children would dare each other to touch the blood stains on the road.

It would affect many people in many ways. They will be more conscious of locking their doors now. And the children won't understand why their parents won't let them play out past dark.

So many people.

Dean started his car and adjusted the heater switch again.

Nothing.

He thought about Robert's wife and little girl. Robert mentioned them to Dean a few years ago when they shared a call together. Dean couldn't remember their names, but strangely, felt close to them all the same. After all, he too had a family. He thought of how things like this come to happen. How widows are to go on with their lives, then maybe starting over again. And maybe not. But the worst is how little girls tell their friends they don't have a daddy and their friends wanting to know why and then having to tell the story.

Why?

Dean thought of the husband a wife loses and her feelings of being alone. He thought of his own wife. The one he thought of nearly a hundred times tonight. The smell of barbeque and his would-be grandchildren playing in the back yard. Following them around as they searched for minnows and frogs in the stream beyond the fence, in the woods, behind his house.

Then he thought of his job and the possibility. The real possibility of his own wife being a lonely, gray-haired lady, standing in front of an empty house, with a weathered car on an old street.

CHAPTER NINE

The Crime Scene
"Tuesday, December 17th, 9:24 pm"

Adam was on the far side of town when he heard dispatch clear the radio channel in a frantic search to reach Robert Lassiter. Adam assumed dispatch was calling Robert, and he was out of his car and couldn't hear. Robert did that a lot. He would get out of his car for what he would consider to be "just a bit," and that was always when the calls would come.

That was Adam's first thoughts.

Not now.

Not as he stood watching all the uniforms. All the lights and background noise from radios. The shouts from one officer to another. The sirens all stopped, but still more patrol units were arriving by the minute. The incident commander, a city patrol sergeant carrying a clipboard with emergency instructions laminated to it, barked orders to the arriving patrol cars. They would slow long enough to comprehend the orders and then continue down the street to set up their assigned surveillance or search area.

Organized chaos.

How in the hell did all this happen? Adam thought. A routine EDP call. Psychos kill their families and their coworkers, complacent jailers or court bailiffs, not seasoned mental health deputies. Mental health deputies stay on their toes and they don't turn their backs. And above all, they search them. Thoroughly. That is one of the things Robert stressed to Adam in training. Do a search at the scene. Do a search when you arrest them. Do a search before you put them into the car. When you get out of the car. Search them every time they are out of your sight. Even for just a moment. You're not charging them with a crime, so accusing you of an illegal search doesn't concern a mental health deputy. Search, search, search.

But, sometimes they hid things in the strangest places.

Adam thought of what happened at the apartment. Edward hadn't been taking his meds regularly; that was established, no matter how unorthodox. A lot of people don't, and he had never seen Robert just sack them up like that before. That is, except when influenced by a concerned doctor, politically connected father, or in this case, a persuasive apartment manager. *Female*, apartment manager.

Edward's behavior may have seemed odd, or aggressive, but maybe he just had a bad day. He was obviously eating. All the paper wrappers and pizza boxes attested to that. He had food in the refrigerator. Nothing out of the ordinary. A messy apartment doesn't circumvent the requirements of legal commitment. Robert hadn't even evaluated him, Adam remembered. No, where are you Edward? What day is it? What time is it? Who is the president? What color is the sky? Nothing. Why did he take him? Did Robert know something he didn't? Robert was the kind that liked to keep secrets. He liked little secrets. Secrets that would later make him look good. Smarter. A better investigator.

Half way through the apartment ordeal, Adam gave up on trying to understand what he was doing. Adam specifically remembered Robert doing the same thing on another call that involved the son of a powerful politician. The only thing they could get out of him was that the son reported seeing people in his toilet. No harm there. He could have been seeing them for the past ten years, but that doesn't prove danger or an immediate threat. But when Adam found this out, he understood. If you have money and want a family member to be committed, just say the word. After all, the sheriff's department is a political office too. Things sometime run deep along party lines.

Why this time? Had Robert received other information he did not share? Hell, what Robert did was a borderline federal violation. A civil rights charge. Based on the evidence at Edward's apartment, he had no right to arrest him. At least Adam didn't think so. Even if you know in your heart that a person is crazy, you still have to go through the motions. Not just tune him up and take the ride.

Adam looked around again. He felt he should be doing something. Taking a post or searching the area. All he could do was soak it in. Stand back and watch. He was slowly drawn toward the car of his friend. He could see a half dozen people gathered around Robert's car, and as he got closer, a uniformed patrolman stopped him.

"Hold up," he said. "Are you with the mental health unit?"

Adam looked down at the laminated card that read mental health unit clipped to his left jacket pocket and then at the right side of the jacket where the gold embroidered mental health logo shown.

"Good guess."

"I'm sorry, we need to keep everyone that doesn't need to be here away. Ya know?" he said sincerely.

"I know," Adam said. "I was on the call with him when he picked up the EDP that did this. I know who—"

"They already have the perp's info."

"I know, but I might—"

"Look, if CID wants to interview you, I'll tell them you're at your car."

Adam thought to himself, *I won't be at my fucking car, you prick*, but he had worked with enough city officers to know about the ego problem. The uniform syndrome and mostly the general animosity between the agencies. He decided diplomacy would best prevail here and he would allow the officer feel like he was in charge. Deep down, Adam knew, he shouldn't be there anyway. He knew, being a mental health officer not a detective, he had no business snooping around the crime scene.

Adam had to think of Robert's killer, not just chest pounding. He added, "Look, I might have more than what he put in his report. That is, if he even started a report—"

Another city officer walked up. "You with M.H.M.R?"

"No, I am not with Mental Health, Mental Retardation. I'm with the Mental Health Unit of the Sheriff's Department," Adam answered curtly.

Another group of officers walking by stopped when they heard the conversation.

One asked, "Hey, you work with this guy?" thumbing toward Robert's car.

Adam looked down at the ground and gave an evil little chuckle.

"Were you out on the call with him?" someone else asked.

Adam looked back up at the group of officers. "What the fuck is wrong with you people?"

The barrage of questions stopped and they stood staring at him.

"First, this guy tells me to wait by my car, then all of you start in on me with questions. Any of you writing the report? Recording statements for evidence? Don't waste my time! Who's in charge here?"

"That would be me," a voice came from behind the crowd.

John Tannerly walked through the group.

"Thanks fellas. Appreciate your help. I'd like to talk with Adam here." He looked around the group. "Alone."

The officers dispersed and as they did a couple of them shot hateful glances back. Right then, Adam felt at least two of them would have shot him if they could have gotten away with it.

"I see you're doing a fine bit of networking there, Deputy Thompson."

Adam didn't smile. "Why? Why are they always like that? I would hate to be a victim at a scene with a mentality like that. If they treat a fellow cop like he's trash, imagine what they do to the general public. Especially when supervisors aren't around."

John stood and listened to the young man's passionate observations. He was not only skilled at the art of murder investigation, but in communications as well. And protocol. He answered none of Adam's questions or voiced an opinion. He learned long ago that if there is a problem, don't bring it to the supervisor. Bring the supervisor the solution. And if you don't have anything good to say, say nothing at all.

John rarely spoke in idle conversation.

"You got anything for me?" John finally asked, pretending to jot something down in his notes.

"Yeah. Check in Robert's left breast pocket. There should be an EDP card along with Langtree's picture."

"A Picture?" John asked, astonished. That was something they didn't have. Edward Langtree had no criminal record.

66

"Yep, we take one every time we transport. I normally do it in privacy, when I get to the psychiatric hospital. But Robert doesn't—didn't mind doing it wherever he was. I just thought it was embarrassing for the psycho to be photoed in the middle of a busy waiting room."

"Come on over here." John motioned and turned to go back to the car.

As they walked, Adam continued, "I would be surprised if he started the report already. Most of the Langtree's information will be in Robert's head. I know he works at Micro Invocustics, the big plant up north. I saw a lot of boxes in his apartment marked MI Technology."

"I figure he's going back to his apartment or to his car," John said, as they stopped by Robert's door.

Adam looked in for a moment, and then stood back up. "What the hell did he do that with?" Adam exclaimed.

"I was hoping you could tell me that," John answered, and then leaned across Robert, removing the papers from his front breast pocket. "Yep, the picture's here. Seems like I've seen this guy before," he said holding the picture into the light.

"I thought the same thing when we met. I just can't place him. Yeah, ya see, he took the picture right in the middle of the ER. All those people standing in the background. *Real* confidential."

John looked up. "Maybe Langtree's just got one of those faces."

"I don't think so. I've seen him before. I'm sure of it." Adam nodded.

John was careful when he asked the next question, "You sound as if you didn't approve of Robert's way of handling these people."

"He had his own way, I guess." Adam back peddled a bit. "I just try to protect them more. You know, their identity. Hell most of the time in their state, they can't protect themselves. It's a different sort of police work. A lot of patrol officers just have the mindset that they don't have time to deal with these people. It's kind of sad when you see it happen so much."

"So you have no idea what he could have done this with?" John changed the subject.

"None. I know he was clean when he took him from the apartment."

"You searched him?"

"No, Robert did. If you knew Robert, he would have found whatever could have done that."

John slowly said, "Adam, something did it, and this turd got away with it. Robert might have been thorough in the past, but tonight, something happened. What time did you go on the call with him?"

"We checked out at the residence about five o'clock. I think."

John looked confused. "But he hasn't been sitting here that long."

"No, Robert took him to the county hospital for an evaluation."

"Do ya'll normally stay with them during that."

"Depends how busy they are. I know Robert didn't stay tonight. I heard him check out for supper at Haven Burgers on the drag."

"So just hospital staff was watching this scroat while he was gone? I'm going to send a patrol unit over there and see what they come up with."

Adam thought for a moment. "Dispatch already notified the mental health unit that's on call, and I heard him check on the radio about twenty minutes ago. He's going to be taking my calls. Why don't I go over there? I already know all the social workers and who would have done what. Plus, I'm going to have to write a hell of a report on this anyway."

John frowned. "They'll just want a statement from you, you won't need to—"

"Yes, I will. Even though we're working under a grant, we're still understaffed. We've been trying to get two deputies assigned per car, but they haven't been able to justify it. Not until now, anyway. Still, this probably won't do it either. If I know the system the way I think I do, they will try to blame someone for this shit. That someone will be me."

"No, that's crazy," John said, trying to reassure him. But John knew what he was talking about. He understood the gravitational pull of a dung heap perched at the top of a steep incline.

"Their number one question is going to be," Adam continued, "'Why didn't you ride along with them?' or 'Why didn't you follow them to the hospital?' It won't matter that we have never done that before. Or that if I had even suggested it to Robert, my former training officer, he would have refused. None of that will matter because ultimately I should have realized the potential threat this individual made and I should have acted accordingly. You've sat on a disciplinary board. Are you going to tell me that's not true?" Adam waited a moment. "That's what I thought."

As he turned to go, he noticed a few uniformed officers were listening to him. They glanced away when he met their stares, and he headed toward his car.

John Tannerly watched Adam walk back down the street. He tapped his pen for a moment, still processing everything Adam had said. He was right; they would grill him at the inquiry. But that was all part of the drill. Part of being a cop. Answering to Monday morning quarterbacks giving you the play by play of what you should have done. Whether or not it was actually practical or feasible. None of that mattered. The fact that you have only a few seconds at the scene and are still trying to process the information long after you have acted on it, *usually* not having all the information, didn't matter either. They sit back and compare the officer's split second decision to weeks of hearing testimony and reviewing reports.

Who has the better chance at making the perfect decision?

CHAPTER TEN

The Escape
"Tuesday, December 17th, 9:40 pm"

He crouched in the blackness, peering out between a battered trash can and a scraggly bush. There were still a lot of people on the streets. He wasn't quite sure what part of town this was, but he assumed it was somewhere north of the downtown area. Across the street, he could see a bustling Quick Mart. People made their way in and out of the brightly lit business. A huge, sprawling sporting goods store nestled itself between the convenience store and a self-serve, car wash. Signs and banners, shouting a huge Christmas sale, flapped everywhere in the chilly breeze. Cars jammed the parking lot and overflowed into the car wash area. There, they blocked most of the stalls, but with the inclement weather, everyone was sure the car wash owner wouldn't mind. A rented sky searchlight, beamed its outstretched, long white fingers into the darkness. They swept themselves through the patchy clouds and reached into space. In succession they jetted out, swirled and came back together again. He could hear the whir of the generator that gave life to the beacon.

After putting the pistol in his belt, he pulled down his T-shirt, trying to conceal the bulge. The handcuffs and keys were already in his pockets.

Forcing slow, deep breaths, he made an effort to calm himself. It was a long time since they tried anything like this. Last time, it was in Seattle. North of that river. The river he had forgotten until he read about it in the papers. *The papers were all bullshit too,* he

71

thought. *They're all owned by arrogant liberals, spewing out the bile to fill the pages for their own entertainment.* In his mind, there were only a few newspapers that wrote the truth. And most of that truth was written in code.

North of that river and the bodies, they had found him. That was a long time ago.

Quickly, he stood up and stepped out into the streetlight at the corner. Once in place, passers by would think he had been waiting there for hours.

Edward knew he couldn't remember everything. It came to him in pieces. Bits of information, through the radio, through TV, and magazines. Sometimes the newspapers. News briefs, articles, and small clippings people would attach to the bulletin board at work. They were all messages. He would try to dismiss the message idea. He knew as careful as he was, they would never be able to deliberately put the messages in front of him. Not at work. That was a coincidence. They were just reminders. Words or clusters of words that would put another piece of the puzzle together for him.

Edward waited. *Edward*, the mature one. He considered his options and alternatives, and applied the solution tonight.

The traffic was heavy, even though it was after nine o'clock. The sirens in the distance subsided, and he knew he had made it out of the hot search area. He also knew the taxis would mostly be working the airport this time of year. With evening flights, most would probably be taking travelers home or working downtown. He would wait. His instincts told him to run, to at least call for help, but he couldn't trust anyone. Not right now. The police would never understand. He would have to get proof; he knew that from the time before.

A newspaper fluttered on the ground. Edward resisted the temptation to pick it up, but he did look down at it. His eyes had never been better. His sight never sharper. His hearing and sense of smell. He took in everything. The adrenaline pumped through his veins, and it had been a long time since he had felt this good. He couldn't remember the last time he felt exhilaration like this. He was alive, and his captor dead.

The paper lay sideways, but he could read it. The letters were jumbled, but he had seen this tactic used before. At the Defense Language Institute.

"D-LAB," he said out loud, and then read on.

He could make out the jumbled letters, he thought. An old binary code he assumed.

The loud whir of the bus engine and chirp of the air brakes broke his concentration. He looked up to see the doors to a city bus opening in front of him. A large black man stared at him through dark sunglasses. Edward forcibly held firm to his body's request to remove the gun from his waistband and bore a tunnel through the gloating bastard's head. Split his scull. *Sunglasses at night?* He thought. If that's not a give away, he didn't know what was. It was too obvious though; the driver couldn't be one of them. Plus there were too many people. Too many witnesses.

"Stayin' or gettin' on?" the driver said, in a deep voice.

"Staying," Edward managed, and relaxed the grip on the gun.

The bus headed back down the road before the door closed.

Stupid bastard, Edward thought, removing his trembling hand from the bulge in his waistband. He remembered all the examinations and cross-examinations. They bugged his house in Seattle, Portland too. Then the one in California. Every time, the doctors would ask, "Mr. Langtree, what is it that causes you to believe you're being bugged? There are no traces of any device. No wires. No antennas." But Edward had seen how you could buy a simple kit through a magazine and turn your entire house's electrical system into an antenna. He hadn't told them that. And that is why he threw out all of his electronics that summer. After they let him return home, that is. That didn't last long either. As soon as they discovered he was trying to pull all of the electrical wires out of the walls in his house, he was right back in the hospital.

And there was that one cop who spent an unusual amount of time with him.

"Have you been taking your medication?" they all would ask. "Are you eating?" as they checked the refrigerator. "Have you been keeping your appointments?"

As far as the appointments, they all knew the answer to that.

But that one cop. He had told him everything. They had an understanding.

"Mr. Langtree," Edward could hear him say, "if someone wanted to listen to your conversations, they would simply rent an apartment near yours and use bionic ears—"

A cab was cruising through the intersection and heading toward the bus stop. Edward stepped out and held up one hand.

The cab was warm. It had a smell to it, but not too offensive. The driver listened to Edward's destination and said nothing, just headed back into traffic. Edward liked that. He didn't want one of those talkative cabbies. This one could probably speak very little English anyway. Probably just enough to pass the ridiculous test to get a drivers license. *Hell, it probably wasn't even in English*, he thought.

The cop had told him of bionic ears, synthetic radio wafers, aerial footprints. He ensured Edward there was no need to worry about anything as outdated as radio bugs, when they could do their surveillance from a block or two away.

That had definitely opened Ed's eyes. The next three times he moved, Edward made sure he had a bottom floor apartment and that there were no transmitting or receiving towers in the area. He would even pay for a second cleaning of the apartment. A little personal assurance.

Edward removed the envelope covered with smeared, drying blood from his back pocket. He glanced at the markings on the envelope, "COUNTY HOSPITAL / ER: LANGTREE," before he tore it open. He recovered his wallet with all forty-two dollars, a set of keys, and his admission slip to the state hospital. He dropped the envelope onto the floor, and his foot lodged it deep under the drivers seat.

A block away from the Park and Ride, Edward signaled the driver to pull over.

"But sir, you said you—" the driver protested, with a heavy Eastern accent.

"Pull over here," Edward insisted, his unseen gun, now out of his waistband, pointed through the seat at the driver's right kidney.

Edward could tell the driver was just worried about being robbed. This time of year, a lot of cabs were robbed. These acts of generosity were done so the robbers could buy stolen property from thieves and give the wonderful presents to their ever-admiring relatives. It was a typical ploy. Get into a cab and request to go to a legitimate public area. This would pose no hazard to the cabby, but then they would have them stop before getting to the requested destination where an accomplice was waiting, then do the robbery.

"I'm not going to rob you. I just couldn't get a parking place this morning. That's my car." He pointed. "At the corner."

The cab driver seemed to relax a bit and pulled over.

"$9.20," the driver said.

Edward handed him a ten and stepped from the vehicle.

CHAPTER ELEVEN

The Delivery
*"Tuesday, December 17*th*, 11:03 pm"*

The morgue was old. Small. Morose. Disgusting. There are many other words you could use to describe this dis-inviting place. Hell, toward the end of summer, and the Arctic in winter. Cleaning crews were contracted once a year to remove ceiling tiles and light fixtures to vacuum the piles of dead flies that gathered from maggots introduced to the building during the sizzling weather. Summers so relentless that there is no reason to describe what would happen to a body exposed to 100+ degree heat for any matter of time. Everyone can imagine.

The pale green tile covering the walls and floor, was just one more addition to the building's personality. The washed out mucus color may not be a true fashion statement, but it did make for easy cleaning. A tile in any other color would have made for easy cleaning also however, back in the 1950's the wholesalers to state must have had it on sale; every floor and wall was covered with it. To put it nicely, the building simply needed to be demolished. That was the thing to do, but county funds were short and none of its clients complained, or could complain. And it still served its intended purpose.

It did not, by any means, add any comfort to those who worked there day in and day out. Especially, not to the customers. Each of us, for one reason or another, finds our way to their cold, stainless steel tables. We will have had our innards thoroughly examined, cut, poked, prodded, weighed, and photographed in the process. This has to be one of the most demoralizing places on the face of the Earth. The people who say they don't care what happens to them after they die, have never been there to see it.

Eric Simmons sat at the far end of one of the examining tables. A young man in his mid-thirties lay naked in front of him. His face couldn't be seen, but his genitals could. Something everyone would inadvertently glance at when they entered the room. You didn't want to. It was a sick sort of thing that eyes are drawn to like steel to a magnet. A conscious effort was required to avert your sight. To fight instincts that required you to look at things that were abnormal. Unusual or forbidden. Out of your ordinary, day-to-day picture. The young man's face was covered with the underside of his scalp. The scalp and hair were pulled down to expose his skull. His skull missing its top, became an exposed cavity, now missing the brain which lay next to Eric's elbow, resting on the corner of the table.

Eric had the look of a mechanic taking a break in the middle of an engine overhaul. There were parts everywhere. A *professional* at his trade, he slowly flipped through a day old copy of the local news paper. After losing interest in a page, he would slowly peel it off. Between drags off his cigarette, a sip of his Coke, or bite of his Snickers, he put the paper to use. With one hand, he crumpled it up, taking great care and concentrated strength; it soon formed into a tight ball. Glancing down, he measured the size of the ball, calculated the space in the open cavity, and carefully placed it into the gap the man's brain had occupied just minutes before. Satisfied with the placement, he returned to his readings.

Eric heard about the deputy being killed. He intended to continue with two more autopsy preps, but decided to stop where he was. He knew the investigators would want a preliminary once-over for any possible leads and evidence. Also, the press would most likely be there soon, along with supervisors from the sheriff's department, and God knows who else. Maybe even family members. That always seemed to be the worst. He could handle the smells he told himself. The fluids. The parts. It was the family's anguish that got to him. If he could just stay away from the families, stay in the facility and do his job, processing the folks that came to him. Just do the job and not have to deal with the grief.

He felt, every day, he was in the trenches. Tagging the bodies. Bagging them up. Shipping them out. And some nights he would dream. Actually, most nights he would dream. Blank, colorless faces of families, staring at him, wanting the answers. What happened? Why did it happen? Why did he die? Not just the clinical reasons, the spiritual reasons. Mostly, the spiritual reasons. Okay, he bled to death, but why? Okay, he was stabbed, but why? Why did he have to die? They would search long and deep. He envisioned assembly lines forming uphill. He had to trudge the incline to the next victim, the next body. It was so steep. Table after table. Body after body. Leaning awkwardly on the slope. Never falling off their slabs. They were the double reflections in the barbershop's mirrors he saw when getting haircuts as a child. But these were not the infinite reflections of himself and the barbershop around him. They were reflections of everyone he had defiled in the most scientific manner. They would push closer and closer towards him. Skullcap after skullcap, he removed. Brains oozing. Hearts, livers, lungs, and kidneys lay in pans and suspended under scales. The same weighing machines little old ladies used in supermarkets to check how many pounds of vegetables or fruit they had. White paper tags, smeared with crimson, INSPECTED BY NUMBER 5, fluttered out of their heads and scattered on the tile floor. Red was the only true color filling the visions. Like shucked oysters, sternum after sternum popped under the blades of his bolt cutters as he cracked opened their chests. Blood splattered on his sleeves. Always, he awakened breathless.

He never told a soul.

The doors of the loading dock swung open, and a gurney carrying a full, strapped down, black bag came into the prep room. A young deputy coroner, whose name Eric couldn't remember, pushed the stretcher down the hall. A heavier, older deputy, Harold Chandler followed.

Wheeled in from the winter air, the bag immediately started to sweat. Beads glittered from the sterile whiteness cast from the examination lights. Passing the stainless steel refrigerated lockers where the bodies were kept, they came straight into the cold examination room. The smell of a mixture of alcohol, formaldehyde, and something similar to rotting, molding household garbage greeted their cold sinuses.

Eric stood up. "Table three please."

"You sound like a waiter," Harold commented, dryly.

He noticed they took unusual care and time with handling Robert. In most cases, as soon as the coroners were rid of the spectators and the family, they would start flopping the body like a tote sack, much the way a hunter handles a dead deer. He remembered the many thumps and thuds he heard throughout his career as bodies would be flopped here and there. The sound of a head hitting the steel slab of the autopsy table was a regular tone. Nothing unusual.

Eric supposed the deputies were taking special care of him, out of the respect of a fellow officer. He didn't know for sure and didn't care to ask. He watched as they undid the straps and moved the black bag from the stretcher to the examining table.

He wondered how many times he stood in this very spot, witnessing this very act. How many times he came to work, in this dispassionate place, a place of death, with the day-to-day acceptance of human disembowelment. He couldn't remember. He didn't suppose he really wanted to.

His thoughts were interrupted as they unzipped the bag. Right away, he noticed post mortem lividity and rigor-mortis had set in. The cold night air accelerated the process, he thought. The pooling of the uncirculated blood in Robert's body had turned his whole face and torso into a maze of crimson and purple swirls. He watched the lifeless body being poured onto the stainless steel slab, his face smeared and fingers caked in blood.

Robert lay silently. He stared directly into the glaring, white examination light, eyes fixed and dilated. His throat gaped open like an unnatural second mouth. A look of extreme anguish and disbelief on his face was accompanied by the desolate look of death that no one can duplicate, no one can fake. The dull eyes, huge pupils, mouth askew with every muscle in his face relaxed yet fixed in death.

He could understand why people believe in an eternal spirit. The complete change from a live body to a dead one was physical proof. No, there was no spirit left here. It had vanished and left behind this thing.

"Doc Armstrong should be here in a minute. You want a cup of coffee?" Eric asked as the two deputies turned and headed toward the door.

Chandler looked back with tired eyes. "We have one notification to do, then two more pick-ups. If I start on a cup this early, I'll crash and burn by midnight."

They continued out the door, never missing a step.

The room was silent again.

"Rough evening, aye Mr.—" he examined the bag tag, "Lassiter? Hell of a way to start the Christmas season."

He walked around and stood beside Robert's head. "Let me take a look at you there. Look at your neck."

Eric studied it carefully.

"What did they cut you with, aye? A goddamn chain saw would be my first guess," he whispered.

Whenever he was alone with his *guests*, as he liked to call them, Eric would always talk to them. In his best comedic, Canadian accent, he would clarify just what he was doing. Asking if he could do this or that. Explaining each procedure as he went along. At one point he was doing it for so long, he hadn't realized he was doing it in front of his colleagues. After a counseling session with the medical director, he saved his dissertations for just his cadavers, only when he was alone.

With the sound of the back door closing, Eric turned to see Dr. Armstrong walking in.

"Is that him?" Armstrong asked, skipping any greeting.

"Yes, sir."

Normally, his response was a "yeah," but normally, the Doc burst into the room with a "good evening gentlemen," addressing the living as well as the dead, and "let's get started."

Walking directly over to the washbasin, he continued, "I'd like to give him the quick once-over, just for anything they might have missed at the scene. We'll begin the autopsy in the morning. Let's start early, at say, seven o'clock. That'll beat the media rush and we'll be better prepared for them. We might even be able to do it live."

Eric turned and walked back to his office. "I'll go ahead and call down to the sheriff's office and tell them we're starting early."

The doctor prepared. Knives, scissors, jars and syringes all appeared from the cabinets. He set up the microphone and put a new tape in the recorder. Normally, the deputies prepped the table for him, but with intense purpose, he gathered, organized and assimilated everything with impressive speed and accuracy.

Eric came back to the table and looked on, puzzled as he watched Armstrong actually working. Doing the grunt work, that is. Not complaining or whining like so many of the prima donnas Eric worked with in the past. Those Medical Examiners, who felt life literally flowed from their hands like honey, and everyone should pay homage to them. Intelligence without humility; he felt it was an awful combination.

As many times as Eric worked around this table and many others like it, somehow, this time, it didn't seem right. Strange. He thought if someone were watching, someone from a different place or time, a place not so "civilized," this would seem ritualistic, almost occultish.

His thoughts were broken with the first flash of the camera and the words from Dr. Armstrong were spoken into the microphone hanging above Robert's body, "11:23 pm, December 17th, we have a white male. Thirty-eight years of age. Multiple lacerations to the neck." Armstrong and Eric began removing Robert's clothes.

"Lay something across his waist; I don't want any pictures with him exposed," the doctor said.

"But that's not—" Eric started, and then shut up. Something else out of the ordinary. It just wouldn't seem right, having him exposed to people he knew and worked with. He laid a small hospital towel across Robert's privates.

Armstrong continued, "Post mortem lividity and rigor has set in. Hand me that scalpel."

Reaching across the instrument table, Eric slapped the handle into his hand. Using the handle, Armstrong prodded around the lacerations on his neck.

"Multiple lacerations on the, the right side of the victim's neck. Do you have the weapon that did this?"

"No," Eric answered.

"At this time, an unknown instrument severed the right strenocleidomastiod, leaving approximately an eight-centimeter gash. There are three small puncture wounds to the…the trapezius. None that would have been fatal. Moving around the platysma, there are several lacerations…and puncture wounds. All seeming to be approximately the same size. By the appearance of the trauma to the flesh, the instrument used would seem to be fairly blunt...and jagged."

Turning the scalpel around, he carefully inserted it into one of the wounds on Robert's throat. Moving it around and scraping it on some of the loose flesh and bone, he looked closer. "There appears to be a small bit of foreign matter in the deep wounds around the larynx...thyroid cartilage and hyoid bone. Give me one of those jars."

Repeatedly, Armstrong dug into the wounds. It made a wet, sticky sound and the scraping sent chills up Eric's back. He reached up and slid the back of his hand across his own throat. The doctor burrowed and prodded until he felt he had removed enough of the brownish matter from Robert's neck. He scraped it off into the jar for testing.

"I smell bowel," the doctor said, as he looked up at Eric.

"Wasn't me," Eric protested.

The doctor smirked. "I think this stuff is fecal matter. How the hell did it get in his throat?"

He set the scalpel down and slowly ran cold water into the wounds. Clotted blood, like huge crimson oysters, oozed out and plopped onto the table. One by one the globs followed each other, out of the neck, and onto the table. Then around and around they slid toward the openings of the table drain.

As the water cleared his view, he started again. "It's hard to estimate the amount of—of punctures or slashes here." He looked up at Eric. "Hell, you could fit a racquetball in there."

Eric stared. He thought of an article he read in National Geographic about a Tibetan custom of putting the dead to rest. The article said the bereaved family members would take the body to a high mountain cliff near their village. Then the oldest, competent male, he remembered the word "competent," would start at the job, one-by-one, piece-by-piece, to dismember their loved one. Actually, he thought of the him or her, to be more of a thing or an it. Dismember it. Throwing it, piece-by-piece, to the vultures and other carnivorous birds circling. The birds rode the currents off the cliff, awaiting the spoils. Eric was absolutely horrified by this. Raised Baptist, although not practicing now, he could somehow understand how Christians would consider this act inherently evil. This rationalized why people from the West would lead expeditions to change this kind of barbarism. And if they couldn't change it, they would eradicate it in a similar, yet Christian fashion. Now, Eric felt like one of the vultures, circling. Taking pictures. Nibbling the next piece off the dead. Waiting for the next piece of evidence, the next piece of meat.

"Hello?" Armstrong said, waving his hand in front of Eric's face, "I'm asking you a question."

"I'm sorry, what was that?"

"What time did you say the sheriff's department discovered they lost contact with him?" Armstrong asked.

"Umm—I didn't. I really don't know too much of what happened here. They just called me about an hour ago and said he was murdered. That's about it."

Fumbling through some paperwork the coroner's deputies left, Eric looked back up. "It looks here to have been around 8:30 pm. You want me to call?"

"Not right now; it's not that important. Just note it as soon as you find out. I can still make an approximation of when the death occurred," he said confidently.

Returning to his work, he probed around some more. "Multiple lacerations to the center of the throat. Severing the anterior belly—external carotid artery and submaxillary cervical glands."

Deep red, almost black blood covered his white surgical gloves. He dug his fingers in and around the muscles of Robert's throat. The sound came again. A sticky, gurgle oozed up from the gash.

He was feeling around in there.

Blood ran onto the stainless steel table as Eric reached over and washed out Robert's throat, again. He was trying more to cover the sound with the flow of the water than to clean the area.

Armstrong paused for a moment, looking up at Eric who panicked for a second, but held it well. He assumed the extra water invaded his work and annoyed the doctor. He knew Armstrong discovered his weakness and distaste for that squishy sound. He waited for the doctor to speak.

Turning to the side, Dr. Armstrong reached under the table and brought out a large set of bolt cutters. "I think that about covers the neck wounds. I hate to make a judgment so early, but we all know what killed him, or should I say, the cause of death."

"You going to crack him open right now? I thought—"

"No," Armstrong said. "We'll do it in the morning. I got them out from habit, that's all." He set the bolt cutters down on the table next to Robert's naked body.

"Stick him in the cooler for now," Armstrong added.

The doctor continued with some final preparations and assembled the samples he had taken. Eric didn't really notice. He stared blankly at Robert whose eyes stared blankly at the light.

Sleepily, fixed and dilated.

CHAPTER TWELVE

The Instrument
"Tuesday, December 17th, 11:15 pm"

Adam arrived at the County Hospital and parked his sedan in the police's designated area. He knew everyone in the emergency room listened to the scanner at the nurse's station. He was sure some of the street officers passed the news on to the ER staff, but they would want to hear it from a mental health deputy.

The mental health deputies frequented the ER and maintained a good rapport with the staff, a really close rapport with some of the staff. They were relied upon in dealing with the mentally disturbed, and sometimes, other *problem* patients. They were also invited to attend the frequent parties held by the nursing staff, EMS, and select firemen. Firemen, that on more than one occasion, ended up dancing on tables in nothing more than their helmets, bunker-boots and loose boxer shorts.

Calls to the MHU came from the ER on a regular basis. From attempted suicides and overdoses, to the run of the mill, paranoid schizophrenic, transients, the mental health deputy was sometimes seen as a miracle worker. With the health care system in its current state, sometimes patients suffering from mental conditions would be shunned. No one really wants to deal with them or even knows what to do for them. Many times, answers from the State Hospital admissions physician would be, "I'm sorry, that is considered a mental condition, not a mental illness. We are not capable of providing that kind of treatment."

The laws in the Mental Health code are very specific. Alzheimer's, Parkinson's Syndrome, and many other diseases affecting the brain are not included. Not mental illnesses—*Mental conditions.*

Insurance or no insurance, at that point, it didn't matter. The mental health deputy would need to sort all of it out; are they a danger to themselves or others? Are they having a serious psychotic episode? As if a regular psychotic episode didn't count. Are they experiencing mental and physical deterioration? All of these criteria are considered in meeting the code, a strict code by which all admissions are based. Whether a mental health commitment, drug or alcohol warrant, or any other order issued by a probate judge, the Mental Health Code was the universal guide for the truly downtrodden. In most cases people with money or connections didn't need to deal so much with the preciseness of the code. Money talks in the health care industry. With a doctor's acceptance, a deputy simply arrests the patient on his authority and transports him to whatever hospital the doctor chooses. The deputy would just fill out a 72-hour, police officer's emergency commitment form and be done with it. It was now in the doctor's hands.

With the coming of the Dehospitalization Act, this code was interpreted to the very letter, and it filled the streets with mental patients beyond help and in no immediate need of further care, mainly because it wouldn't do them any good. They were just crazy, and there was nothing to do about it. They were experiencing no serious psychotic episodes, just *living* serious psychotic episodes. No measured deterioration, just existing deteriorated. They were in no immediate danger to themselves or others despite their threats to kill everybody they met. It didn't mean they would carry it out. Guaranteed, First Amendment protection. They talk to themselves, wander around in the same clothes for months at a time, and practice foul habits, many of which normal people do everyday. Only normal people do it privately.

Adam stood outside the sliding glass doors to the ER admissions area trying to gain as much composure as possible since he just learned about Robert's death less than two hours ago.

He also was gearing up, on the off hand chance that Susan was working tonight. He knew her regular days off were Thursday and

Friday, but he was hoping, maybe for some reason, they changed, or she took some vacation time. He hadn't seen her in almost a month and didn't think he wanted to. Maybe, it just wasn't meant to be. She was, in his mind, a teary-eyed, tree hugging, criminal forgiving liberal, with no real perception of the world the way it is. When confronted, she just spoke of the way it should be. He tried to make her understand the reality of it all, that other people make decisions we can't control, and they're the bad ones, not us. Not the police, just because we want to catch them and kick their asses.

"Fuck them!" Adam said, on many occasions after hearing enough of her softhearted delusions. That usually severed the conversation and eventually the relationship. He was verbally aggressive towards her on many occasions. Usually, when things were going really well and he saw her really happy, he would always ruin it, almost on purpose, it seemed. Jealousy, he supposed, but he didn't allow himself to think about her much.

He hated himself for it. He didn't understand it.

He entered the vestibule and immediately saw her standing behind the public services window. She bent over the counter and pointed out some papers to an elderly couple. She smiled and was nodding her head to them. Adam tried to walk past her behind the counter and into the admissions area, but he saw her glance up. He swerved in her direction, trying not to make it look as if he was attempting to get around her.

"Hey, how's it going?" he stammered.

She nodded a good-bye at the couple and turned to him. "I'm fine. I'm sorry about—"

"Well, I knew a lot of people would wonder what happened, and I thought I would come up here first hand and try to settle a few things."

She looked down at her sign-in roster. "Mary Chapman was the one who evaluated—Edward Lassiter, and—"

"So you already know his name?"

"Why, yes. It's been all over the radio," she said politely. "What happened? Why did he—"

"Susan, sometimes people don't need a reason. They just make decisions based on 'I don't give a shit,' and just do it. Maybe after a

89

few more years and a few more bodies you'll understand that," he said, and turned toward the psychologist's office.

It all came out before he could stop it. He couldn't believe he attacked her again. Self-hatred rose in his belly. *Damn fool*, he thought, *stupid ass*.

Susan was as angelic as he remembered. Bright eyes, tanned skin and sandy blond hair. She was beautiful. And her smile, even though he knew he hurt her, she still managed a smile to greet him. Even more impressive was the strength she showed to speak to him. Maybe she just didn't care anymore. *No, that wouldn't be like her either,* he thought. She was a good person.

A beautifully good person.

A month ago, he stood with her at his apartment door. He escorted her that far.

"I don't understand," she said, for the fourth or fifth time.

"That is why you have to go; you just don't understand," Adam said.

"Why?" she sighed. "Two people don't love each other because they are just alike. They love each other because they are different. They gather strength from each—"

"We've been over this," Adam said, firmly. Impatiently.

"Things don't have to be this complicated," she protested.

This was more difficult than he anticipated. This time he decided to break it off. The decision he was carrying around with him for the past two months wasn't fair to her, dragging her on like this. Also, he was not going to let her rule his life, even though he knew she had no intention of doing that. He knew she could rule his life because all he could do was think of her. Her eyes; the softness of her skin; her perfect nurturing, loving, and steady hand. She was the dream lifelong partner, a wife, and he was scared to death. He could think of nothing that scared him more, except very deep and dark water.

He was ashamed.

It was agonizing, and he was furious he behaved so weakly. He wanted it over with her. No more. Make it final, go on, and not think of her. If he thought anymore, it would delay the inevitable. Thoughts of her as his wife, lover, and mother of his children would be too perfect. She was too kind and too understanding. *Too damn gullible and naïve,* he forced his thoughts.

She had looked up at him with tears streaming beside her reddened nose. "Can I just stay, just for tonight? Please."

"No, I'm sorry." He had reached around her and opened the door.

She turned slowly and held her head down, walking toward the parking lot, fighting back the tears. Adam heard her start to sob again, as she got further away. He couldn't stand to hear her hurt anymore.

He shut the door.

He didn't even walk her to her car. But that was the past.

Adam stopped outside the evaluation room. There were no medical records in the file folder rack, so he knew she was not with a patient. He knocked and heard someone say, "Just a moment."

As he stood waiting, he realized his thoughts couldn't escape Susan. If nothing else, what he did to her should have been a first hand lesson for her on reasons to mistrust humans. He gave her no reasons for his decision; he wasn't even sure why he did it himself. Fear maybe. Too nice and sweet. Too lovable. So easy to scare with a hop from a darkened closet or surprise from behind. He usually didn't entertain these thoughts for long; they were quickly dismissed and he would clear his mind. He wouldn't allow her to invade his life, even if he wanted it more than anything.

The door opened and, surprisingly, a uniformed patrol officer emerged in front of Mary. Adam didn't recognize him.

The officer thanked Mary for her time and walked in the direction of the ER exit, not acknowledging Adam.

Typical, Adam thought. "Hey, Mary, is he trying to find out about Edward?"

"Yeah," she answered. "He wanted a copy of everything I had. Why didn't they just ask you guys?"

"That would be too simple; besides, God forbid the sheriff's department and police communicate with one another. Hell, in their minds we already botched this transport. Now, the only thing they're interested in is catching the turd that did it and saving the day for the sheriff. One of those "you amateurs made the mess, we'll clean it up," mentalities. Do I sound disgruntled?" Adam said, sarcastically.

"I'm sorry, Adam."

Ignoring her consoling efforts, he asked, "So, did Robert leave him in the holding cell?"

The two walked to the special room used to quiet problem patients. It was not a comfortable room.

"Yes. It was around 5:20 pm, when he got here, I think. I've been backed up all day. I told Robert I'd get to him as soon as I could, and he said he had some other calls and left him in the cell. I didn't get to him until around 6:30 pm and I had the paperwork ready by about 7:20, or so," she said, trying to refresh her own memory.

Adam's memory was refreshed. He listened to the radio all day, and this was the only call Robert was dispatched. He just dropped Edward off because he didn't want to wait around in the ER. They might have put him to work.

The holding cell was ten by ten, with only a stainless steel commode for accommodations. The walls were sprayed with rubber insulation and painted a light pink. They pulled the door open and immediately, claw marks were apparent as the door swung aside. They were old marks. A big chip of the rubberized insulation was peeled away revealing the white, cinder block walls beneath. Pieces of toilet paper and dust bunnies jumped and gathered in the corners of the cell from the breeze of the opened door.

"So, you and Robert are the only ones who had contact with Lassiter?" Adam asked.

"Yes. Security has been busy with all the other stuff going on around here. I'm sure they didn't have any time for him. The admissions nurse kept an eye on him for me, but I can't think of any reason she would have gone in his cell. Why, are you thinking he got something from one of the staff members?"

"Whatever he used to practically cut Robert's head off, he got in this hospital. He was thoroughly searched before we left his house," Adam assured her.

Mary pointed. "There's Karen now."

A heavy, young woman, wearing pink surgical scrubs saw Mary pointing at her and came directly over.

"Ya'll need something?" she said, in a thick, south Texas drawl.

"I was wondering if you had any dealings with a patient in the slick-cell tonight?" Adam asked.

"Mister Langtree?" she spouted. "Oh, isn't it terrible? To think, a potential murderer was standing right here. I did the usual. Just kept a suicide watch on him. He was quiet the whole time."

"You didn't talk with him, check his blood pressure, or anything?" Adam asked.

"Nope, the only time I ever opened the door was to feed him supper."

Adams eyes widened. "You did what?"

"I fed him some supper," she repeated calmly. "He was admitted and we're required to feed all inpatients at six o'clock."

"Jesus Christ!" Adam exclaimed.

"No!" the woman protested. "We don't give'em any silverware in the padded room, just a plastic spoon."

"What were they serving?" Adam asked curtly.

"Rolls, mashed potatoes—" she glanced up at Mary. Eye to eye. "Green beans—" she continued slowly. She looked around the room nervously, "Apple cobbler—"

"The meat," Adam said. "What kind of meat?"

She swallowed, and searched deep into his eyes. She was searching for a better answer than the one she was about to give. Her hands came up to her face, and she slowly whispered, "Baked—pork chops."

Adam looked down at the floor. "On the bone?"

"Yes, sir."

He shook his head.

CHAPTER THIRTEEN

The Standing Man
"Tuesday, December 17ᵗʰ, 11:30 pm"

Sitting in his car, Adam tried to calm himself. He tried to allow his brain to process what he heard. He looked into the admissions nurse's eyes and saw she fully understood what happened. The words she said, so slowly, "Baked—pork chops." There was no doubt she realized her fatal mistake. The mistake she and Robert made. Adam saw it in her eyes and she knew, if it hadn't been for her negligence, none of this would have happened. It would be something very hard for her to live with.

Adam hadn't said another word; he simply turned and walked to his car. As he left, he thought he heard her start to sob. He wasn't sure. He didn't care.

He also realized, if he hadn't left, he would have torn the woman's head off. Or, at least caused a vicious scene. He knew his limitations, and right then it was best for him to make his exit. Besides, she was the one that would have to swallow it. Deal with her mistake for the rest of her life, not him.

Naive and wanting to help. Just fed him a little supper, that's all.

Driving out of the parking lot, he radioed dispatch, "Unit 1273, I'm en route to the MHU office, hold me out of service."

"County to Unit 1273, I have three mental health calls backed up; I need to hold you en route to 8812 Daffney, on a check welfare call. Meet the complainant at the residence."

Adam knew there was no reason to try to dispute the dispatcher and decline the call. He knew if there was any way they could take him off the street, they would. At this very moment, he would be in C.I.D. helping the detectives try and locate Edward Langtree. But, obviously, the nuts were out in force and the watch commander was doing everything in his power to keep it together.

"Unit 1273, 10-4," Adam surrendered, with obvious disappointment.

He settled back into his seat. The drive to Daffney Lane would take about fifteen minutes, and already the evening had gone by so fast. He had only served one of the three drug and alcohol commitments assigned to him at the office. It was an easy one. The suspect hadn't argued, just made some arrangements at home and took the ride.

Sometimes it was like that.

Sometimes it wasn't.

Susan slipped back into his mind. He saw her as he left the hospital, and he intended to stop and apologize for his outburst, and to say he was sorry. He wanted to tell her he would like to talk to her later. But as usual, that was impossible. She was leaning across her counter talking to a very tall, good-looking man in his mid-twenties. Adam corrected himself quickly, *good looking in a woman's eye,* he supposed. As far as guys went, he thought a woman would think he was good looking. Anyway, the young man was wearing surgical scrubs, like all the other nurses, and Adam suspected he was a new ER nurse. He looked too young to be an intern. As Adam approached them, he could hear the young man say something to Susan like, "I would like you to come over again—"or "something— over again," he wasn't quite sure.

Innocently, Susan had glanced up at Adam, and he shot her a glare that brought tears to her eyes.

Instead of stopping as he intended, he continued by her, looking away, no longer acknowledging her. As he approached the automatic doors, he recalled some of his old military skills and watched them in the reflection. Both stood erect looking at him. The young man was smiling at Adam's back and neither of them were talking any longer. He didn't dare turn around; he was too angry. Angry at the nurse playing waitress, angry with Robert for pushing Edward, angry with

96

Susan for being so nice. Angry at the male nurse and Susan for trying to make him jealous. *That's what it was; they were trying to make him jealous, talking when he was near,* he thought. That would be asking for him to hear them, or allow their conversation to freely enter the rumor mill, knowing that it would get back to him. Or, maybe, they were an item. People around there liked to do those sorts of things, *stir the pot* so to speak.

But, mainly, Adam was angry with himself.

Turning on a side street, two blocks from Daffney Lane, a thought came to him. He was sure the conversation between the male nurse and Susan was a set up. Maybe she asked him to say something or to flirt with her in front of him. She knew it would drive Adam crazy. She also knew Adam was in love with her. He was always so different around her. So guarded. *How could she be seeing someone so soon after?* Adam thought, *and she always said looks didn't matter.*

"Bullshit..." Adam mumbled as he slowed nearing his destination. He parked his car in front of the house and notified dispatch, "Unit 1273, I'll be out at 8812 Daffney, on the check welfare."

"Unit 1273, 10-4."

Adam was confused why they chose him to take the call. Usually, a regular patrol unit could handle a check welfare, especially in the city. Most of the time, it was a family member, overdue from an out-of-town visit. Someone without the consideration of calling and saying they will be late. Or sometimes, a husband or wife not directly home from the bars, for one reason or the other. Usually, the *other*. Dispatch must know more about the call than they relayed to him, he thought.

Adam wouldn't argue about anything right now. He understood, just get it done, and sooner or later they were going to have to let him do his reports and go home. He remembered earlier this same day that he was wishing for the time to go by, so he could get to work. Now, he was wishing the same power would hurry and allow him to go home. That's the way it always was. Every day. A love-hate relationship just about every cop has with his job. A relationship of mental and physical abuse many find so hard to break. Once you are on the streets, doing it, you understand it, but deny it. Most of the time, you can't get it out of your blood. It leeches onto the vessels and breeds. It festers sometimes; eats at you. Many try to get away, and then find themselves hopping from job to meaningless job in search of the escape. A magic word that fixes everything. Most fail, returning like an abused child to the hands of an enraged father. The system also aggravates the condition. It seems to bind your hands making you feel completely helpless as the criminals look at you through the discharge vestibule, leaving the lock-up with their lawyers as you struggle to finish the arrest report.

Sometimes they're laughing.

Adam brought himself out of his trance, noticing a large man walking toward him from the house. Adam removed his flashlight from its mount and exited his vehicle.

"Adam Thompson," he said, as their hands met.

"Doug Attardi," the man responded. He was a clean-cut man in his mid-thirties. Successful looking and polite.

Adam noticed his exaggerated mannerisms immediately. *Obviously gay*, he thought. "What can I do for you, Mr. Attardi?"

"Well, I feel kind of strange calling you out here like this, but this is a strange situation. This friend of mine, Ray Zetner, called the other day and asked if I would come up to see him. I live in Houston and told him I would be busy for the next few days, but I would come up on Friday. Ray seemed kind of depressed, but said he would be here."

Adam strained to keep his eyes from rolling back in his head, struggling to look interested in the story. He fought to keep from shouting, "Get to the point," but he just stood there.

"Anyway, I took care of my business early and got out of there this morning. I tried to call, but his phone has been busy, all day. I got here about two hours ago, but Ray won't answer the door."

"Have you tried to call him, again?" Adam asked.

"Yeah, I tried to call from the pay phone down the street and his phone is still busy. I called a couple of mutual friends and his boss, and none of them know where he is. His boss said he hasn't been at work for the past couple of days."

"Had he called in sick?" Adam asked.

"No, that's the real strange thing. Everybody's said he's been acting weird the last few weeks."

"Weird?" Adam asked.

"Yeah, depressed I guess. He told some of the venders at work he was the president of the company. He even had letterhead printed with his name on it. He hadn't been getting along with very many people, even his family. They pretty much alienated him. I think he wanted me to come down and spend the holidays with him. Lonely, I guess."

Adam walked up the driveway. "Is this his house?"

"A duplex actually," Attardi answered. "He lives in an attachment around back."

Attardi walked Adam around to the back of the dwelling. A security light brightened the side of the house and Adam was able to turn off his flashlight.

The inside lights illuminated Zetner's living room and showed through the thick drapes hanging over the large, plate glass windows. The door was recessed and shadowed from the light. Adam stepped up, rang the doorbell, and pounded on the door with the butt of his flashlight.

"Mr. Zetner!" he shouted.

Attardi looked around embarrassingly, startled by Adam's loud shouting and banging.

It was hard for Adam to concentrate on the task at hand. So many thoughts were streaking through his mind: Robert in the morgue, reports he needed to write, this idiot's boyfriend, Susan doing whatever with the male nurse.

"Mr. Zetner, Sheriff's Department, I need to talk with you for a moment!"

No answer came.

Adam was ready to get this over and his impatience showed. He had more pressing issues than to sit there and try to find this guys boyfriend. *Hell, they probably had a fight and Attardi was panicky and just there to try to patch things up*, Adam thought. *Emotional basket cases, always blowing things out of proportion.* Then he thought of Susan.

Adam tried the doorknob.

"It's locked," Attardi said.

No shit, Adam thought and turned, walking back around to find another entry into the house. Attardi followed and they both surveyed the windows around the residence. All were locked. No other doors led into Zetner's side of the duplex.

Walking back to the door, Adam noticed a shape, illuminated on the drapes in the window. It was long and dark, in the middle of the window, dividing the lighted portion in half. It was too wide to be a freestanding lamp. It may have been some sort of big plant, and the distance it stood from the light source diffused its shadow. That wasn't it either. Adam thought and stared for a moment.

"What is it?" Attardi asked.

"Mr. Attardi, could you go get me my hand-held radio out of the front seat of my car?" Adam looked back at him. "I forgot it when I got out. It looks like a walkie-talkie."

"Uh, sure," Attardi said, then headed back to Adam's vehicle.

Quickly, Adam pulled out his set of apartment pass keys. He had worked security at three different apartment complexes, and each time he was issued a set of master keys. Copies of these keys came in handy, but other people having the knowledge he possessed the keys, did not. He cycled through the ring until he found three matching the model of the doorknob. He slid the first one in and gently jiggled it around. The knob turned, and the door opened, just a crack. Adam smiled. He removed the keys, stowing them away in his waistline, just as Attardi returned with the radio.

Adam looked back and jiggled the doorknob a little, just for sound effect. "Credit cards save the day every time, don't they?"

"You got in?" Attardi said, amazed.

"Lots of practice," Adam added, and stuck the end of his flashlight into his back pocket. It hung out to one side awkwardly, but did not fall. He took the radio from Attardi and switched it on, then pushed the door open a little further.

"Mr. Zetner, Sheriff's Dept—" he shouted, but the stench smashed his face like a solid mass. As Adam recoiled, Attardi let out a little squeak.

"What? What is it?" Attardi demanded.

"I want you to stay right here," Adam commanded. "Right here, do you understand?"

Attardi nodded his head.

Adam raised his radio. "Unit 1273 to county."

"Unit 1273, go ahead," the radio buzzed back.

"Unit 1273, roll an ambulance, my location, notify the city and have a marked unit meet me. Tell them they will need a crime scene technician also."

A moment passed. "Unit 1273, 10-4. Are you code-four?"

"10-4, everything is under control," Adam answered.

He knew the smell. It was practically always the same. The way a certain batch of cookies smell every time you take them from the oven. Peanut butter. Sugar. Oatmeal. Basically the same, just little, subtle differences. Depending on, of course, how long you've cooked them.

Adam took a deep breath of clean, December air and walked into the residence. There was no real hallway, just an entryway. Tile floors and walls adorned with colonial styled pictures. Plantations, with women in white dresses, flowers, and jewelry. The entry allowed only one way of passage, a direct right turn into the living room. Adam continued in. It was hot inside; the heater was on, full blast. He rounded the wall and captured the view of the whole room. Despite the heat, Adam froze. Unblinking, his eyes devoured what he saw. Nothing compared to it. Nothing in Hollywood, anyway. Not Freddy Kruger, not Hellraisers.

Nothing.

He can't hurt me, Adam's thoughts stammered, *he can't hurt me.*

Adam fumbled at his pistol holster; his jacket was in the way. He pulled the cloth up forcefully, exposing the leather case that housed the weapon. His right hand unsnapped the latch and the gun came out. He tore his eyes away from the thing and quickly surveyed the apartment. Was there someone else? Someone who maybe did this? He couldn't imagine anyone enduring the hideous funk in the atmosphere. The rancid odor would now and forever be present in the carpet and draperies. Probably even in the sheetrock. He saw the bedroom door was open, and it appeared to be empty, along with the bathroom. Someone might be hiding in the closet. Or, dead in the bathtub. But he couldn't take his eyes off what he viewed. It was dreadful. Appalling. Yet, it was incredible. Another atrocity you would never wish to see, but when it is presented before you, you consume it and you can't stop looking.

Adam's feet felt like cement. Concrete shoes. Without blinking, he forced one of them from the ground and managed to move it just a few inches in front of the other.

Okay, that's it. Come on. He's not going to do anything, Adam assured himself. The trailing foot came up, then passed the braver one, the one that first decided to advance. His feet took turns, one after the other, creeping toward the wretch. The room was silent, except for hot wind blowing from the vents. The track lights pointed at the thing, standing in the middle of the living room floor. In a puddle of dark, shinny goo soaking into the carpet, the thing seemed to watch him. Both of its feet, planted in a swampy muck. Laces on the high top tennis shoes strained at the eyelets that held them in succession. The tops of the shoes bulged out and ripped the bottom cuffs of the blue jeans. Dark streaks in the jeans marked the path of bodily fluids escaping through relaxed muscles. Atrophied muscles and orifices that once held back the flow. They snaked like drying riverbeds to the floor. Adam found himself standing at the edge of the mire, two feet away from the swollen blob. The top button on the jeans had snapped and his rctreating zipper exposed soiled, Daffy Duck, cotton boxers underneath. The button, nowhere to be seen, presumably engulfed by the ooze on the floor. The torso was enveloped in a yellowing, white T-shirt, looking four sizes too small. It hadn't split anywhere, at least not yet, and it seemed to have shrunk on the body; though the very opposite had occurred. The chest expanded out into a barrel, and a bald belly, pocked with red, and green, and blue bruises protruded out under the bottom of the shirt's seams. Despite the gore, despite the stench, Adam couldn't believe the vivid colors. They were extraordinary. Almost bright. Advanced decomposition did incredible things to an exposed body; only experienced people know such things. The arms hung down, but the swelling caused them to puff away from the torso, as if he was starting to reach out.

"He can't reach out," Adam said quietly. "He's dead." He looked up at the thing's face. "You're dead."

"Officer Thompson, is everything okay?" Adam heard Attardi ask.

"I'll be out in a minute," Adam answered, now having to take his first breath of the fouled air. "Please wait by the driveway."

The gulp went down relatively easy. Easier than he expected. He never threw up at crime scenes, but there is always the first. The smell was bad, real bad, but not as bad as some of the ones he worked in trailer houses. In August. *Texas*, August.

Adam looked closer. The man's neck had expanded to larger than his head. It too, was swept with the various colors, swirling themselves around the throat, and the deep wrinkles the rope made. The head was not slumped over to one side, although Adam was sure it had been, just after the incident when he was still fresh and before he started to rot. Now his head stood erect, bulging green, and yellow, and purple with his eyes protruding. A thick film covered the wide pupils. Adam studied them. He waited for the eyes to suddenly shift their gaze directly into his and the swollen arms with obese, putrid fingers, like greasy sausages, to grab around his neck.

Adam leaned closer. "You're dead; you can't hurt me," he whispered, trying to convince himself.

The thing didn't move. Drying black fluid, like trails of tears, wandered out of the eyes and down the bloated face. Over huge inflated cheeks, and past straining jowls, it made its way to be soaked up by the fibers of the rope. Some tracks bridged off his chin like mini-stalactites, then glued themselves, haphazardly to his shirt. The immense, round tongue, protruded like a purple ballpark frank, out of the gaping mouth. *They definitely plump when ya cook'em*, Adam thought. The lips were torn and peeled back from expanding gases, exposing the inner flesh, and what little fluids vented there. In total, the face was a blur of the putrefying colors. The only color looking out of place, the only color that clashed was the brown rope that allowed this monster to stand in his living room days after his demise. A rope gently tied around the strong, decorative, support beam for the vaulted ceiling stretched down and cinched the soft, vulnerable, fleshy neck of this hopeless man. This hopeless thing.

Adam turned completely around. He stood silently. Waiting. Waiting for the ambulance or the assigned police officer. Waiting two feet in front of the suspended, putrid cadaver, taunting the carcass to reach out and snatch him from behind. Waiting for the arms to wrap around him like a lover's sneaky surprise and pull him back into his bosom. Back hard against the bloated belly, forcing out farts and rumbles of death as the monster ripped into his neck with unclean teeth as green fumes expelled from its mouth.

Nothing happened.

Seeming half disappointed, Adam looked back at him. "See, I told you. You're not going to do anything." Then walked back to the door.

He met with Attardi, outside, in front of the window.

Attardi pointed. "Is that him; I mean is that his shadow?"

The darkness still stretched from top to bottom in the middle of the pane. You could see the outline a little better now. Now that you knew it was the shadow of a man.

"Yes, sir. I just—"

"I know, you don't have to. Did he hang himself? Is that what happened?"

Adam nodded.

"That asshole!" Attardi shook his head.

"It looks like he planned it out fairly dramatically. I think he wanted someone to find him sooner. All three track lights on the ceiling had been moved and were all pointing right at him," Adam volunteered.

"Yeah, he was an actor, all right. That's just the way he would have wanted it."

"Does he have any friends or family living here?" Adam asked.

"None, and I'm not going to take the blame for this or the responsibility to…to…do whatever it is that has to be done. It's not my fault I couldn't get off work sooner. Hell, he always seemed depressed anyway. I didn't notice anything different in his voice."

Attardi continued on, but Adam didn't hear. He just looked at him calmly and thought of his own feelings. Adam wanted to interrupt Attardi's ramblings and tell him what he thought of this kind of suicide, the selfishness of it. Especially when they are young and the ripple effect it has through everyone they have contact with, and the most powerful thing they get out of it; causing the guilt. It had started on Attardi already leaving a lasting impression and a deep scar. That's what Adam thought, but he didn't voice his true opinions. He just let Attardi vent. Let him ramble on about something, he wasn't for sure what.

After a few moments, when Attardi seemed to be winding down, Adam became lucid again. "Could you stay out here a few minutes. The ambulance or a patrol unit should be here shortly."

"Yeah, that's fine," Attardi agreed.

Adam entered and found himself standing in front of the remains, again. He slowly walked around the back of him. He had used the dinner table chair. *When he made his leap, he must have kicked it hard*, Adam thought. It lay on its side, up against the wall. It made a small indentation in the sheet rock. The dinner table stood between the body and the kitchen. A table setting for one sat, half eaten. Adam supposed the supper was the origin of the small chunks protruding around the bulging tongue. A stack of loose-leaf notebook paper lay next to the moldy dinner. He circled the table to better read the writing without having to pick it up.

Just what he expected, an "all you people are assholes," final, undisputed speech of a self-proclaimed martyr. A nine page, I worked harder than you—Studied harder than you—Tried harder than you—Gave more than you—Deserved better than this, bunch of crap.

"That guy's dead!" a voice came from the direction of the door.

Adam stepped around to see a young blond in her early twenties wearing a medical technician's uniform, and pinching her nose closed.

"Your ability to state the obvious is impressive," Adam said. "However, as we all know, I, as a lowly deputy sheriff, am not qualified to make such determinations—"

She did not wait for him to finish and quickly disappeared back out the door.

When they arrived, Adam introduced the responding patrol officer to Doug Attardi and quietly bowed out of the scene. He told the officer he would forward a report over to him by Thursday.

As the crime scene technicians, coroner's deputies, and other essential personnel arrived, none of them seemed too alarmed when Adam said he would be leaving. If they needed anything, they could call the MHU office. It seemed Adam retained a certain bit of odor from the deceased. That happens sometimes. It just seems to weave itself into the fabric. Washing usually doesn't do much good. Most of the time, it is better to just throw the clothing away.

Adam headed home.

It was 2:10 am.

CHAPTER FOURTEEN

The Day After
"Wednesday, December 18th, 7:18 am"

Adam fought through his pillow to get to his screeching beeper. He had been sleeping for no more than a few hours when the office paged. "Call Lieutenant Martin - ASAP," he read from the message screen.

"Jesus Christ!" he exclaimed and reached for the phone.

Lieutenant Martin was a good man. He wanted the best for and from the people he supervised, but he also perfected the skill of crisis management. Everything was a crisis to this man. No doubt, the murder of one of his deputies was a crisis; however, Adam just braced himself for the spasmodic reaction the man would make.

"Mental Health Unit," the lieutenant answered.

"Answering your own phones these days, sir?" Adam asked.

There was a slight pause, "Hey buddy, sorry to wake you."

That was not the reaction Adam anticipated, at all. "No sir, you didn't wake me. What's going on?"

"Bullshit, I can tell by your voice. Look, I'm sorry I didn't make it out last night. My girls and I were in San Antonio. I'm sorry Adam."

Adam could hear his words meant what they said. "Thank you, sir. I talked with John Tannerly and told him everything I heard at the hospital."

"Yeah, I just got off the phone with him. He's been up all night dealing with the crime scene and media." Lieutenant Martin cleared his throat. "Uh, Adam, you know I'll need a report sometime today, right?"

"Yes, sir, I'll get it to you as soon as I come in."

"And victim service called. They want you to stop by their office. Debriefing I assume."

Adam rolled his eyes. "Can I skip it for now?"

"No, but you can delay it until you have time."

He understood what the lieutenant was saying; he couldn't give him the permission to skip it, but if more pressing issues availed themselves, the debrief would have to wait. "Thank you, sir. What's the update on this guy?"

"Have you seen the news?"

"No." Adam hadn't quite had the time.

"It's on every channel. They got the guy's picture up everywhere. As far as I know, the SWAT and Fugitive Teams are working shifts to set up on this guy's house and work. They probably already asked you this, but did he have a car?"

"I don't know."

"Anyway, I think they've got a handle on it. Intel is working on his history and profiling other possible locations the guy might go. That's about it."

"Alright, sir."

"Adam. You okay?"

"It's just a fucked-up deal, but I'm okay."

"Give me a call if you need anything, alright? Working the three to eleven shift, I know you don't get a chance to see much of anyone, but you know we're there for you."

"Thank you. Actually it's kind of nice not having to deal with everybody."

"I understand."

"Thanks again, sir," he said and hung up.

Lt. Martin handled that pretty good, Adam thought. *You never can tell about people.*

He rolled over and tried to get back to sleep. While the sleep did come in bits and pieces, it was not restful. He hated himself for not being able to control his emotions. He couldn't control them with Susan, or in dealing with the condescending city officers. And now he just wanted to calm himself enough to get some rest. As he drowsed, Ray Zetner visited. He was no longer suspended by his rope; he stood freely, on his own two bloated legs, reaching to Adam.

"Shit!" Adam yanked the covers off and paused for a moment thinking he was being foolish. After catching his breath, he got out of the bed and checked to see if he was alone the apartment.

It was going to be a long day.

CHAPTER FIFTEEN

The Plan
"Wednesday, December 18th, 9:12 am"

He wasn't tired. He felt great, strong and alert. The way he was meant to feel. Not the lethargic, drooling wretch they turned him into before. He wouldn't allow it to happen again. The night had gone easy. The cold didn't bother him, nor did the wind. The tree was great cover, fifty feet from the Park and Ride lot and a hundred feet from his car. It was a tall evergreen tree, thick with needles. He was surprised when no one checked on his car. He was careful about being tracked, but was completely amazed to discover they hadn't even made the discovery of the first leg of his trail. He spent most of the morning's daylight watching the buses come and go, the people come and go. He looked as far as he could but never noticed anything out of the ordinary. Now and then a police car would pass by, the officer glancing at the lot, but continuing on. He thought for sure after the police didn't go to his car that they were setting him up by staying back from the vehicle in the hopes he would return there. That's when they would do him. But his vision was so refined, so acute, he finally knew for sure, they had no idea where he was.

He dropped out of the tree and walked straight over behind the bus stand and took his place behind the few people waiting on the next coach. None noticed. It was a few minutes before the bus arrived, and Edward walked around the bench and sat down in the seat just vacated by a boarding rider. He crossed his legs and realized this would give him a much better vantage point to see if they were truly watching. The bus pulled forward, and Edwards's car sat twenty feet in front of him. The overwhelming sensation to get up a run to it was almost uncontrollable. He fidgeted, rocked back and forth a couple of times, and looked around.

"Now, now," he whispered, then stood, and walked normally toward the car. He passed by looking into the front and back seats and continued another twenty feet. He stopped and waited. Nothing. He looked left, then right. Nothing. He turned and moved back to the car. He opened the passenger door, then the glove compartment, and pushed the trunk release. He gathered an old Navy peacoat and a heavy, black backpack, and then closed the trunk and passenger door. He studied the lot one more time just to make sure then headed back toward the tree.

Still nothing.

He kept the peacoat when he left the Navy. It was the only warm coat he had once they released him from the hospital in Seattle. They charged him with criminal mischief and interruption of public utilities after he cut grounding wires on utility poles and threw a dead cat onto a transformer causing it to arc and explode. But after the hearing, everything was dropped. To Edward, all of these things, both in the Navy and in Seattle, were just little experiments.

He passed the tree and turned north onto the sidewalk. Cars passed, people went in and out of businesses, a jet flew high above. Nothing out of the ordinary. Normal. That was the way Edward liked it. Normal. He wished he were normal, not special. *Special people are always treated different,* he thought. He wasn't referring to *special ed*; he meant gifted, like him, on a higher understanding with the special gift to see things the way they really are. *That threatens people*, he thought. *It shouldn't.* Edward felt he could help them, especially the government. He understood what the government was doing, knew the games they were playing, and the dangers technology brought to bear.

They arrested him in Seattle for trying to help them, trying to ensure their safety. Still they refused to believe or truly just didn't understand. Either way, he swore, next time it wouldn't matter. When they put him into the hospital, with all the psychos, he realized they also knew of the dangers. The conspiracies that clouded true thought, pure thought. He understood, to effect a change, to really make a difference, he would have to keep everything together. Refine his thoughts and remember the sequence of how everything goes together. He knew, from all his past experiences, they were not going to listen. They would stare blankly, dismiss him, and go on about their business, doing nothing. As he stood in their waiting rooms and outside the doctor's offices, he heard them say things like, "Thank God *they* can't keep it together long enough to do anything." or "It would be scary if *they* stayed organized long enough to follow through on this stuff." Edward took it to heart, and he was going to follow through. He wasn't going to be a *they*.

He turned and climbed the stairs then entered through the doors of the public library. Stopping in the foyer, he checked the room. A woman was cataloging some books on a cart, and no one else seemed to be there. Edward walked toward the back, following the alphabet, and found what he was looking for. "T" for technology, and stood in front of the shelf.

He would stop the government machine, once and for all.

He would be the example for others to follow.

CHAPTER SIXTEEN

The Candyman
"Wednesday, December 18th, 2:45 pm"

Adam pulled into the side parking lot of the Mental Health Unit's office. The lieutenant's car was parked in its place, but there were apparently no other mental health officers there. That was good. Adam wasn't ready to field any of their questions or accept their condolences. He didn't feel he was the one to get them. It hadn't been his fault, and he shouldn't be the one attached to their pity. *Robert dug his own grave,* he thought, and used his key to get in the back door. He stood in the small hallway leading past a kitchenette and into the reception area. The officer's distribution boxes lined the wall next to the reception desk. The old place was musty, some lights needed to be replaced, and the carpet, early seventies brown had collected remnants of years of smoking, dropped food, and spilled coffee. This was the first time Adam really noticed it. Not much better than the morgue. He was so used to either running in and out or being too busy talking to the other people he worked with that he didn't have time to pay too much attention to his surroundings.

It was quiet and he expected that Lisa, the receptionist, and the lieutenant were over at the courthouse getting paperwork signed. They normally went over after lunch and collected the warrants and commitments in the afternoon. Adam walked quietly up to his box and pulled out the paperwork. He noticed Robert's box was empty with the exception of a single yellow rose. That was Lisa. She and Robert are—were good friends. In the past few years, they spent a lot

115

of their time talking in the office. Nothing strange, just talking, and sometimes lunch. Lisa was partial to him because of the extra attention he gave her. She was in her mid-forties and the survivor of three failed marriages to cops. Her nurturing, caring spirit usually attracted her to the ones in the most danger, the ones she hoped she could save. She couldn't. She felt Robert was special, but didn't realize he spent that little extra attention she found so appealing on most attractive females. Adam stopped his daydreaming, tearing himself from Robert's box, and retreated the way he came.

As he settled into his car, he thumbed through the papers. Two mental health commitments, a drug and alcohol warrant, paycheck stub, a new assignments schedule to cover the days Robert was to work, and a fancy, yellow envelope. Adam was about to tear into the envelope when he realized someone could see him sitting here and would want to come over and talk. Quickly, he backed out of the parking lot and drove down the block. Finding an empty parking meter, he pulled to the side. *Lisa, it has to be Lisa*, he thought as he tore it open. A cream colored card with little birds, bees, flowers, a stream, and some other crap he really didn't notice. Opening it, it simply said, "Thinking of you." Signed, Lisa. He stuffed the card back into the envelope and shoved it among the other fading papers on top of the passenger's side sun visor. He knew she was trying to be nice, but he didn't need nice. Not right now.

"Mental Heath 1273, 10-41, in service," he said into his radio microphone.

"Mental Heath 1273, 10-4, we have no calls holding," dispatched answered.

"10-4." Adam held one of the papers up to read the address. "Hold me en route to Eck Lane on an order of protective custody."

"10-4, 14:45 hours."

Adam set the papers on his clipboard and moved into traffic. He was always glad to see OPC's. Usually, the court issued them the same day as their mental competency hearing and had a good location for the subject. In most cases they were already in the hospital, but cases like this one, on Eck Lane, the family or friends of the person usually testified along with the doctor, that the person needed long term, mental health care. If the probate judge bought it, an OPC was issued. Adam looked back down at the order and noticed, according to the diagnosis on the OPC, Mr. Alan Kovar suffers from depressive disorder.

"Jesus Christ," Adam said, but realized, after working mental health for the past year, depression causes all sorts of problems. He had been one of those people that believed that people with depression should just get over it and move on. But, if it was that easy to do, why did so many people not do it? Adam assumed it was probably part of the natural selection process and if society would stop propping up the weak, people would become stronger as a whole. The weakest would fall by the wayside and humanity would grow stronger. But, he knew Hitler felt the same way and *that* thought diminished his agreement on the matter. It was tough talk, but deep down, he *did* want to help people.

As he turned south on the River bridge, he noticed several police patrol cars blocking the northbound lanes. Apparently, an individual was threatening to jump off the bridge and into Town Lake. It would only be about a thirty-foot fall, but as cold as the air and water were, it would pose a real recovery challenge. As he got closer, Adam recognized the threatening jumper. Glen Leach, a long term, mental health patient, with a flair for the dramatic, stood on the railing shaking his finger at the officers. Adam committed him several times, but he never stayed in the hospital for long. He usually played the game well enough and took his medications long enough to quickly be released. Adam pulled over in front of a street officer directing traffic. The officer obviously did not like that Adam had disobeyed his signaling and stomped toward his car. Adam stopped and rolled down his window. "Hey, I'm—"

"You need to move back into traffic," the young officer pointed in the direction of the southbound lanes.

"I'm with the Mental Health Unit and—"

"You need to find somewhere else to park. I have to clear these lanes for EMS," he said and pointed south again.

Adam gave up. He was used to this, working with the city. He pulled back out and headed south. If they needed him, they could call. He would allow Glenn to entertain them for a while.

Adam worked his way through traffic and finally into "The Hills" addition. The Hills is an older, upper-middle class neighborhood with large yards, lots of trees, and low crime. Adam never made a call here but usually drove through during this time of year just to see the Christmas lights. The Hills association had an annual Christmas decoration competition, and they took their competition seriously. During this time of day, you couldn't really see the decorations. Adam saw plenty of wire reindeer, Santas on rooftops, plastic snowmen, and Baby Jesuses, but he would have to come back at night for the full effect.

He pulled in front of the Kovar residence, and like he expected, it did not reflect the season's mood. It was a large, rock house surrounded by dead or dying grass and bushes. A Cadillac, covered with dust, sat near the garage doors with a flat, left rear tire. All of the windows were shaded by yellowing curtains.

"Unit 1273, on scene," Adam advised dispatch.

"Mental Health 1273, 10-4. 15:10 hours."

Adam grabbed the OPC and got out. As he walked to the front door, he looked around for anything unusual, or for any neighbors watching. They liked to watch. The door was weathered with large water stains and cracks that had formed around the edges. A spider's web clung to the knob and stretched across to the top of the doorframe. It was an old web. The stickiness had attracted far too much dust, long ago, for it to effectively catch insects now. Not that there were many to catch in December. He adjusted his belt, badge and gun holster, and rolled the OPC into a tube, tucking it into his back pocket. Faintly he could hear noise from inside the house. *The TV*, he thought. It sounded like some sort of fight, with a lot of people yelling. He stepped to the side of the door and knocked firmly, twice.

He waited.

He knocked, again. This time, a little more forcefully.

Nothing.

He balled up a fist and struck the middle of the door three hard times and shouted, "Sheriff's department!"

Still, no answer.

Adam left the door and slowly walked around the perimeter of the house. He could tell neither the car nor the door had been used in recent weeks, if not months. The man had to have been getting in and out of the house somehow. The garage carport doors were locked and so was the side door. He walked through a small chain-link gate into the back yard. Leaves covered everything, canopied by scraggly, bare cottonwoods. There the windows were also covered with drapery, old rotting, and torn in the corners. As he neared the wooden back porch, he smelled something. A stale odor. Then it registered.

"Piss," he said to himself and looked down at the ground. The leaves didn't look any different where he stood, but there was a trail from the back sliding glass door to the porch rail. Carefully, so he didn't get near the area where the trail led, he stepped around and up on the porch. The wood was old and it did creak, but he could tell it was still sturdy. He walked to the sliding glass door and looked through its long, vertical blinds. The sunlight glared off the glass and Adam had to get his face right next to it and block the light with his hand. The inside of the house was dim and no interior lights were on; however, the sunlight provided enough illumination to see. Through the separations, there was a kitchen table just in front of the door. The kitchen was off to the right and the living room or den was straight through. A couple of standing gumball machines were just inside the door. They were half full with gumballs and a couple of clear plastic bags of gumballs sat on the floor. There, in the far room, he could see an old, large, cabinet style TV which was on, and once again he could hear the shouting coming from it. In front of the TV was a set of swollen feet protruding out from behind the wall separating that room from the kitchen. The body belonging to the feet, or vice versa, was hidden from sight, but Adam assumed it was sitting in some sort of reclining chair. Gumballs littered the floor under the fat feet. Adam rapped on the glass door and waited.

The feet didn't move.

He banged on the door harder.

Still nothing. It was going through Adam's head that this person was dead for sure. He went to enough calls, just like this one, and was no longer surprised by what he found. At least that is what he told people. He jiggled the door, and it slid open. Just a crack. Just far enough for some stale odor to escape. Piss again, and he recoiled a little.

"Mr. Kovar?" he asked. "I'm with the Mental Health Unit; can I talk with you a minute?"

Adam slid the door all the way open. He felt the warm, thick air passing him as he entered the house. The smell attacked his nose. He wanted to breathe through his mouth, so he wouldn't have to deal with it, but thought that might be just as bad. If particles make up smell, then that meant the particles would end up in his mouth, and that was worse even if he didn't actually taste them.

"Mr. Kovar?" he said again, slowly walking around the kitchen table.

The TV was loud. Some sort of wrestling show was on. He could see it better now. Two men in spandex, grappling with one another, and the crowd cheering. He stopped for a moment and looked around. This was the first time he could actually see the entire kitchen. It was dusty, but there were no plates, pots or pans cluttering the counters. No trash scattered on the floor. Nothing particularly nasty, just a lot of dust and gumballs. But, he knew the particular smell was coming from something.

Adam could now count twelve gumball machines. Some were the small counter kind and a couple were at least four feet tall with spiraling ramps for the balls to roll down to tiny, waiting hands. Then straight into tiny, hungry mouths.

He stepped wide and around to get a better look at the body on the recliner. Stacked around the recliner were more boxes of bagged gumballs. Assorted colors and sizes. Three small gumball machines sat next to them with their tops off, apparently being restocked. Next to them, lying back in stained white boxers, was Alan Kovar, 52 years of age, five-foot-ten inches, 245 pounds. He stared at the TV. In his left hand, he griped a bag of yellow, Tweety Bird gumballs. In his right, he held an assortment of balls that had long since started to melt. The rainbow of sugar ran from his hand and down to his elbow. The melted trail was still fresh but Mr. Kovar was not. He stared at the TV screen silently. Emotionlessly. His body, more yellow than Tweety himself. A mustard yellow that darkened around his armpits, mouth, and eyes. Eyes so bloodshot, the whites were brown. Adam wasn't concerned with his eyes; he watched his hands. Hands are the only things that can kill a man. *His hands are going to be what he does it with,* he could hear Robert tell him. *Watch his hands.* His hands were motionless, but he was breathing. His chest slowly rose and fell.

"Mr. Kovar? I'm Adam Thompson with the Sheriff's Mental Health Unit. Can you hear me?"

Kovar sat, eyes fixed, mouth dry, body stiff.

Adam thought, *This guy's got a lot more problems than depression. Jaundice and probably hepatitis. Great, just great...*

Adam reached around and pulled out his hand-held radio, "Unit 1273."

"1273, go ahead."

"Unit 1273, I need EMS, my location."

"10-4, are you code 4?"

"10-4, I'm okay, I need EMS to check out my subject. Fifty-year-old male. Catatonic."

"1273, 10-4."

Adam checked around Mr. Kovar for any weapons he might be hiding. Other than the kids' gumballs and human feces he was sitting in, he found no standard weapons. Potential biological weapons yes, conventional weapons, no. He walked back into the kitchen and checked the refrigerator. Completely empty, except for three opened Diet Coke cans. The trash can was half filled with empty chili cans and some bread wrappers. He opened the door to the garage and walked around the two, older model Chevys parked within. Nothing strange, the cars were well kept and empty. He walked back through the house and toward the bedrooms. He checked the hall bathroom and found everything pretty much the same. The house was orderly with the exception of scattered gumballs, dust, and human waste. Apparently, in his condition, some time ago, Mr. Kovar forgot to flush, or just didn't care to. All the beds were made, and the laundry was in the hamper.

Adam heard the sirens from the ambulance. He walked to the front door and opened it as soon as EMS pulled into the driveway. He left the door open and stepped out to meet the paramedics.

Adam was grateful to get out of the house. The cold December air flushed the smell from his nose and mouth. The idea of the particles in his mouth came back to him.

"Hey," he said. "I hate to do this to you guys, but he probably needs to go to the hospital before I take him. Looks real jaundiced to me. Frickin' nasty."

As the driver got out, he asked, "Are you with mental health?"

Adam thought the brown, unmarked Ford Crown Victoria, his badge next to the gun on his belt, and brown windbreaker with six inch gold MENTAL HEALTH UNIT lettering answered that question, but he entertained him anyway. "Yeah, I'm with the Sheriff's department," then turned and walked back toward the house. "I got an OPC on him, but he's got some obvious medical issues, and he's catatonic."

The paramedics silently followed Adam. He introduced them to the unreceptive blob on the recliner. Looking around, they put on face masks and gloves, and then started to work: heart rate, blood pressure, temperature, IV drip, and a scan for medications. He had about five small, empty brown bottles beside his chair, but nothing in the medicine cabinets.

As they started to load the big man onto the stretcher, a thinner version of the man on the recliner came walking through the front door. "Hello? They told me you guys would call when you came to pick him up," he said.

Adam stepped over to the man. "I'm sorry, I'm Adam Thompson," then held out his hand.

"Alan Kovar, Jr." He pointed at his dad. "The court said you guys would call, so I could let you in."

Adam pointed at the back glass door. "It was open. They're going to take him to the county hospital first. He's got some medical issues they'll need to clear up before he can be admitted at the state hospital."

"I see, yeah, he hasn't been taking care of himself," the younger Kovar added. "So they didn't tell you I would be waiting?"

"I picked up the paperwork while everyone was at lunch." Adam pulled the orders from his back pocket. As he unrolled them, he immediately noticed the yellow post-it note attached with, *call Alan Kovar at the number listed,* written in red ink. Adam quickly flipped the page over, hiding the note from the son. "The order says to take him to the state hospital, but I know they won't admit him in this condition, so EMS will transport him to the county hospital first. Once he's medically cleared, the OPC will still be in effect, and they will transport him to the state."

Alan Kovar Jr. listened to Adam as he walked around the living room and gathered gumballs off the counters and floor. Once he had too many in his hands to gather more, he placed them back into a plastic bag by one of the gumball machines.

"So your father distributes gumball machines?" Adam asked.

"Yeah, we have a business together. Lately he hasn't done much with it," he said, shrugging his shoulders. "I gotta' get all this stuff over to my place and pick up the slack. I'm almost out of balls and haven't ordered any."

"Hum," Adam grunted, thinking of how many times he bought gumballs from a machine. Maybe one of Kovar's machines. *Great...* he thought.

Mr. Kovar, Sr. was strapped securely to the ambulance stretcher and loaded in the back. They tried to get the gumballs from his fist, but in his state, they couldn't pry his hand open. They left them.

As the ambulance drove away, Adam could still see Kovar Jr. going room to room, gathering the gumballs.

"If you have anything else, give us a call," Adam said. "Here's my card."

Kovar took it and picked up two boxes of gumballs. "Thanks for your help," he said and walked out to his car, loading the boxes into the back seat.

"You gonna use those gumballs in your machines?" Adam asked.

He could tell by the expression on Kovar's face, absolutely, he was going to use them. "No, no, I just have to get them out of here. I'll only use the unopened boxes."

Adam knew he was full of shit, but what could he do? He stood for a moment and tried to think of a law Kovar was breaking, something to stop what he knew was inevitable, the distribution of jaundice-fecesed gum. He shook his head and walked back to his car.

He picked up his microphone. "Unit 1273."

"Unit 1273," radio answered.

"Unit 1273, I'm 10-8, referred to EMS. Hold me en route to the River bridge, assist the PD."

"1273, 10-4."

CHAPTER SEVENTEEN

The Assist
"Wednesday, December 18th, 5:40 pm"

Adam worked his way out of the neighborhood and back into the remnants of the five o'clock rush. Traffic was still heavy he guessed because of the after work shoppers getting ready for Christmas, but he managed to make good time getting back to the bridge. He had to remind—reassure himself, that he was doing the right thing. So often agencies will not solicit help from other departments, wanting to handle, or thinking they can handle whatever is thrown in their direction. Time and time again, it was proven that it simply wasn't so. Just because they survived whatever crisis without a death, no matter how chaotic it was, the supervisors falsely convinced themselves they can deal with anything. The city police did not like calling on the sheriff's mental health unit. Most police patrolmen would tell you not to call Mental Health; they're not going to do anything. In some cases that was the truth. If the suspect was drunk, mental health could not evaluate him, so he had to go to jail and sober up. A lot of patrolmen simply arrested the mental patient for whatever crime they chose, put them in jail, and let the jail personnel coordinate with mental health. He shook his head.

Adam pulled onto the River bridge and, sure enough, the gaggle of police, EMS, and fire rescue were still standing by. Glenn was now squatting down beside a bridge railing pole with two plain clothes officers standing six or so feet in front of him. Adam pulled his car just behind a parked fire truck and got out. He saw at least two-dozen uniformed patrolmen from three different agencies standing around, waiting for whatever was going to happen, to happen.

Adam spoke into his hand radio, "Mental Heath 1273."

"Mental Health 1273, go ahead."

"1273, I'm out with the PD. Has anyone requested us for this call?"

There was a short pause. "1273, 10-74, we've had no request."

"10-4. I'll be out of service for a few."

"1273, 10-4. 17:50 hours."

Adam tucked his radio into his back pocket and adjusted his belt, making sure everyone who wondered, could see the badge on it. He pulled the collar of his brown windbreaker, flattening the stenciled sheriff's mental health unit logo on his left breast and started walking toward the scene. The scene's containment had deteriorated over the past couple of hours. The officer Adam first talked with, the one that forced him back into traffic and along his way, now leaned on the hood of his own patrol car. At this point, he didn't seem very concerned about the traffic situation or the drama in front of him. You could tell that he just wanted to clear the scene. The other groups of personnel were scattered around, telling stories about whatever, smoking cigarettes, or simply complaining about the situation, or the weather, or whatever. The only two who seemed to be paying any attention, were the two plain clothes officers, apparently attempting to negotiate with Glenn on the railing. There was a sergeant sitting in his patrol car talking on a cell phone. Adam walked up and waited for the man to finish his call. After a few minutes, the sergeant set the phone down and stepped out.

"Adam Thompson, Mental Health Unit," he said, putting his hand out.

The sergeant shook it. "Bill King, what can I do for you?"

That was a pretty typical response from any patrol officer. *What can I do for you?* The question at this point was what can mental health do for them.

"I just thought I would stop by and see if I could help."

"We've got a couple of negotiators talking with him now," the sergeant said.

"How long?" Adam asked.

"About an hour, or so."

"Are they making any progress?"

"They're working on it," the sergeant said, which actually meant, *no.*

"I'm surprised. Glenn's a hard man to deal with," Adam said, looking over at him squatting on the rail.

"You know him?" The sergeant looked surprised.

"Yeah, that's what I do."

"Come on over here and let me introduce you to the lead negotiator. You won't spook the dude, will you?"

"He'll know who I am, but that won't matter."

Adam dealt with Glenn enough to know that every doctor he saw gave him a different diagnosis which meant Glenn had what they called in the mental health community, a major personality disorder. Depressive, antisocial, histrionic, paranoid. Whatever the mood, and whoever Glenn's doctor was at the time, the diagnosis changed. They may call it personality disorder in mental health terms; the layman calls it "*asshole.*"

As Adam walked over with him, he quickly thought of a plan. If the plan went bad, the police would have their reason to say how screwed up the sheriff's mental health unit is and to never call them. EMS and the fire department would have a water rescue to do and would formally complain that Adam was a safety hazard on the scene and jeopardized the lives of everyone there. Robert had taught Adam a lot of things, more things not to do than what to do. But, Robert did have the gift at getting close to his suspects, gaining their trust, or at the very least, doing the unexpected with the expected. If the plan went off without a hitch, all of the above would ignore it and they would make up a dozen reasons why they hadn't tried it before.

"Deke," the sergeant said on his handheld radio, calling one of the plain-clothes officers.

"Go ahead," his radio answered.

"Got a MHU Officer, wants to talk with you."

"10-4."

As Adam and the sergeant approached, Glenn pointed from the railing at Adam. "Hey, I know you."

Adam smiled at Glenn and kept approaching. One of the plain-clothes officers turned around and met them with a handshake. "Deke Anderson."

Adam returned it. "Adam Thompson, MHU."

Glenn was still pointing. "You're with mental health. I know you."

That was Adam's cue. If he was going to do it, it was going to have to be now. His chest thumped, and he could feel the blood surge in his face, arms, and legs. He stepped just past the negotiating officers, just enough to put his foot up on the narrow sidewalk separating the railing from the street. He was close enough to Glenn to see he was tired, and the distraction of Adam's approach had thrown him off his game.

Adam looked at him and nodded his head. "Hey, Glenn," Adam said, like they were old high school buddies, and offered his hand. Quite naturally, like anyone would, Glenn met his. That was when the wide-eyed realization took effect. Adam waited, just long enough for Glenn eyes to lock into his. Long enough to see Glenn knew he made the mistake, knew he let down his guard and missed checkmate. Glenn too, saw in Adam's eyes and felt in Adam's grip, the standoff was over. Adam yanked him down and into the warm hugs of the two negotiators. In a matter of seconds, Glenn lay on his stomach, grunting and with a half dozen patrol officers assisting with three different sets of handcuffs.

Adam stepped back from the growing crowd around Glenn. The sergeant stepped around to Adam and Adam waited for his response.

"We could have discussed this," he smiled.

Adam relaxed a bit. "Target of opportunity. I didn't have any other choice."

"No, I don't guess you did. Good job," he said quietly and headed back to his car.

Deke stepped around the crowd. "Hey, can I talk to you a minute."

Adam noticed right away Deke's somber mood. "Yeah," he answered and they walked back toward the fire truck.

"You know, we were building some trust with this guy. You yanking him off like that's going to make our job that much more difficult next time we have to deal with him."

Adam looked at Deke and forcefully calmed himself down. "What kind of trust were you building?"

"We were building a rapport," Deke answered.

"Look, I don't want to get into a negotiation strategies debate with you, but if he hadn't given up anything, come down, at least got off the railing, or something, you don't have a rapport. You have nothing more than a bullshit session. The guy stuck out his hand, and if I hadn't grabbed it, right now you would be asking me why I didn't. Seems any action I take here is the wrong one."

Deke wanted to say something else. He was searching, but he was professional enough not to say what he was feeling. "Alright. You got a card?"

"Sure," Adam said.

As he dug a card out of his wallet, it was the first time he noticed the whole parking lot of the Hilton hotel was filled with news cameras and media trucks. That's why there was no more argument. That's why they weren't more pissed. They didn't want to get it caught on tape chewing the *savior's* ass. Adam had blown their rescue of the poor mentally ill, suicidal wretch, that captivated them for so long. He handed the card to Deke, and without saying another word, walked back to his car.

There were media cameras, now trying to position themselves for a better look at this mysterious tan Ford sedan and its occupant. Adam pulled into traffic and cleared the incident.

"Unit 1273, 10-8."

"1273, 10-4, 10-63, assist other agency," dispatch said.

"1273, 10-4, go ahead."

"Lee County is requesting we respond to 1704 Waterline Drive, check on Kathy Clayton, her parents live out of state and haven't been able to reach her. We have two prior EDP calls at the residence."

"1273, 10-4, en route."

CHAPTER EIGHTEEN

The Breeder
"Wednesday, December 18th, 6:15 pm"

Adam began to wonder what they were doing about Edward Langtree. He hadn't thought of him much today. *Purposefully,* hadn't thought of him much today. He assumed every cop in the area was looking for the murderer. Adam usually checked the bulletin board for new or important information. Today, he simply forgot. He was so concerned about getting in and out of the office quickly, he didn't look. He thought it was strange he didn't have strong feelings on the matter. He was angry. Angry with everyone, but where was the sorrow? Robert Lassiter was his training officer for two months. They spent every day together. The strongest feelings Adam had were not from the fact that some crazy bastard killed his friend, it was that some crazy bastard killed a cop. Adam knew these feelings would most likely change. He knew from his academy teaching there are stages everyone goes through in a traumatic event. He still thought they were strange.

Adam headed northeast, out of town, toward the rural community of Yegua. Other counties without mental health officers often request MHU assistance. Yegua, named by Mexican missionaries, was just on the other side of the Lee county line, and it wasn't unusual for MHU to handle their mental health problems. At the turn of the century, Yegua was a promising, growing township. It had a strong mining industry, several brick mills, miles of cattle ranching, and a slaughtering and rendering house. However, with the invention of the car and the dissolution of company owned towns, the only thing left in Yegua was a decaying community and the Yegua depot. At one time, the depot was the center of commerce for Yegua. The railroad's main line extended from San Antonio to Fort Worth, straight through the bustling little town. The rail provided an excellent market for the strip-mined coal, hard-fired clay bricks, and fresh beef. Now, it was nothing more than a large, half empty red brick pavilion. On one side of the depot, the grandson of the original owner threw up some plywood walls and operated a small country store. The majority of the profits came from the sale of beer, fishing bait for the Yegua Creek, when it wasn't dry, and barbeque on the weekends. In one hundred years the depot had turned from a commerce center to a community center, a monumental step in the wrong direction. Now, the tracks of the railway were gone, the slaughterhouse closed in the early sixties, and all but one of the brick foundries had packed up. The only profitable business left in the area was cattle ranching, and the profits from that didn't come from innovation and progress; the profits came from the encouragement of complacency and governmental subsidies. The ranchers were about the only ones doing well in Yegua since they were the only ones not relying on a prosperous community to support them. They could count on the downturn.

Adam was well aware of the situation in Yegua. He saw the effects when they concluded the last section of mining in the area. That was two years ago, and still many residents had hopes of a section of mining just south to reopen. Some stayed, taking on jobs in some of the small surrounding towns. Some drove all the way into the city and started new career fields in the house keeping or food service industries. Most that stayed were simply socially retarded. They could not exist in any other environment, and they were doing nothing but existing here.

Once outside the city, Adam turned onto a pothole filled blacktop called Farm to Market Road 696 and followed it eastward. FM 696 was the original road leading from Yegua to the city. It paralleled a section of train track owned by the San Antonio Line that branched into the business district. It was shared by several other railways, but most of the commerce came from Yegua, mainly in the form of clay bricks. Adam thought how strange it was that things come and go so fast. How things, business, and life are there one minute and gone the next.

He thought about talking with Robert, just yesterday.

The sun was sinking fast when he turned right, down the gravelly County Road D and saw the first vehicle he had passed in the last ten minutes. An old man in a beat up red Ford pickup, parked in front of a set of rural mailboxes. The old man waved and Adam returned it. He drove on, not remembering how much farther Waterline Drive was. He slowed as the road became a little darker with the setting of the sun and watched carefully as he passed each of the dirt roads off to his right. The road signs in this area were stolen long ago. Some of them were replaced by homemade wooden signs, the street names were scrawled in black spray paint, and some were not. He stopped his car and checked his map making sure he hadn't already passed it. He saw it was two more streets to the right and continued.

Turning onto Waterline Drive, he stopped and radioed dispatch, "Unit 1273."

He waited a few seconds and repeated himself, "Mental Health Unit 1273."

Still nothing. He realized he hadn't heard much radio traffic in the past few minutes and assumed his radio reception was weak in this area. He continued on and found the house on the left side of the road. He stopped in front of the lot next to it and turned on his cell phone, but gained no reception signal.

"Unit 1273," he said, once more in the radio.

Nothing.

"Shit," he said, and shut off his car. He had two choices: backtrack out of there until he could get out on his radio or cell phone or try to make contact with the person in the house and hope they had a phone. And also hope they didn't kill him and repeat the same fiasco Robert put everyone through.

Adam got out of his car.

It was almost dark now and the wind was starting to pick up. The leafless trees swayed and clattered around him. A dog was barking down the road but that was about all. No cars, no lights on in the house, nothing.

Adam checked his flashlight, adjusted his gun belt, and looked down at his silent, hand held radio. He tossed it onto the driver's seat and closed the door. He was alone.

The house was a typical farmhouse, white, one story, surrounded by a porch and scrubby bushes. A detached two-car garage sat a few feet to the right, obviously built long after the original house. Its half acre yard was contained by a wavering four-foot chain link fence and had signs of recent dog activity, but the gate was open and there was no sight of a canine. Adam approached slowly, deliberately. He stepped through the gate and walked on the cracked concrete walkway to the porch. He hadn't used his light yet; he didn't want to give himself away too soon, in the case of an angry homeowner ambushing him as he approached. A bald flower garden stretched its way around the house, and a few remnants of rawhide chew bones littered the porch. He stepped slowly onto the porch and to the side of the front door.

Take a deep breath, think about what you're going to say, Adam thought, and knocked on the door. Bam-bam-bam. "Sheriff's Department."

He waited. He was used to waiting; it was part of his job.

Bam-bam-bam. "Sheriff's Department, come to the door please."

Adam was a little irritated that the Lee County sheriff's department hadn't sent a deputy to meet with him. But he also knew Lee County only employed less than ten deputies total, and they might not have any to spare at the moment. He waited another minute, then clicked on his flashlight. He checked the doorknob, but it was locked. He studied the windows on the front of the house, but the occupant had taped aluminum foil over them. He reached to see if they were possibly unlocked, but noticed all of them were painted over. He walked down, off the porch and around to the garage. The building had two garage doors and one side door. He circled the entire structure and then checked the side door. It was open. Adam took his flashlight in his left hand and pulled his pistol out with his right. Pushing the door open, he sent the beam of his light in first. He paused. There were stainless steel stacks of cages from the floor to the ceiling. Rows of them apparently filling the whole two-car garage. He stepped further to the side to shine his light more toward the front of the garage; more cages stood in double rows. Then the smell; Adam pulled back. He turned his face toward the December winds.

"Shit," he said, literally disgusted. "I am tired of this *shit...*"

It took a second to regroup and look all around to see if anyone was sneaking up on him. No one. He seemed alone. He walked through the threshold and made his way around the cages. They were canine pet cages, the kind pet stores keep animals in while they are for sale. Professional pet cages. Each of the cages contained what Adam believed to be the remains of a breeding pair of Chihuahuas. At least fifty pair lay in their cages, all in different states of decomposition. Adam worked his way through the maze of metal frames and decaying flesh. All the food and water bowls were completely empty. He circled through and had to remind himself why he was here. Why he had been called. It was not a cruelty to animals call; it was a check welfare call. And if this was the outcome of the subject's pets, what was the condition of the subject?

Adam stopped just before he stepped back out the door. A stack of Naturezyme dog food sat just a few inches away from the first set of cages. The corner closest to the cage was torn open and a few pellets of food spilled on the floor. The dogs must have scratched at it with their little paws to tear it open, but didn't have any way to grab it out. There was enough there to feed them all for two months. A water hose lay stretched out on the floor, swollen from the pressure the spray nozzle held in. A tiny trail of water escaped from the nozzle and darkened the concrete floor next to the cages. It snaked down the middle of the aisle and teased a turn toward one cage then another, never coming close enough to grant relief. He imagined the little dogs looking at the trail, scratching and digging at the bottoms of their cages straining to reach it. He walked back out into the fresh air.

Just outside the garage, he remembered no one knew where he was. He had to be careful and stay on his toes. If the subject was still alive and able to allow this to go on, or not able to keep it from happening, he was very sick; possibly very dangerous. He relaxed the grip on his pistol and adjusted it. His hands were sweating and he tried to let some of the December wind cool his palms. He forced himself around to the backside of the house, checking all the windows. Some had foil, and others had the Taylor newspaper taped in them. Adam continued to the back door and stepped up on a small wooden porch. He was about to check the door when an idea came to him. *Investigate,* he thought, *Mental Health Investigators, investigate.* He stepped off the porch and walked back to one of the windows with the newspaper.

"December 8th," he read aloud. It was clearly printed in the margin. *The dogs were dead longer than ten days. Someone's here,* he thought.

He walked over to the back door again. This time he checked the knob. It was locked but there was a gap between the door and the frame, and the door bolt was plainly exposed. He pulled out his pocketknife, and with practically no effort at all, slipped the bolt and the door squeaked open. Like before, Adam allowed his light to venture in first. He checked the small entryway and mudroom. It was clear. He stepped through, took cover behind the door, and adjusted his beam to search down the hallway to the kitchen. Nothing seemed strange. No blood, hanging bodies, screaming maniacs, or gumballs, he felt fairly good, so far. He walked slowly down the hall and into the kitchen. He saw the light switch on the wall, but decided against turning it on. He felt the dark would mask him as well as anyone else in the house, but he had the flashlight. The living room had a fifties style décor, dusty but straight. There was only one more way to go, down the hall and to the bedrooms. He tried his best to walk carefully, but the old floors announced every step. He stopped. *Identify, or not to identify, that is the question,* he thought. If he announced himself, that would definitely give away his location and possibly endanger his life. If he didn't announce, anyone in the house might think he was a burglar and shoot him anyway. He contemplated.

"Sheriff's department," he made his choice. "I'm with the mental health unit. I just need to talk to you."

He stalked down the hall, up to the first door, and listened. The knob was closest to him making it easy to reach out and turn it. It unlocked and he pushed it open, letting it freely swing and lightly strike the wall on the other side. Using his light, Adam slowly worked his way into the room. It was a common bedroom decorated with yellow flowered wallpaper, a bed, dresser, and nightstand. He checked inside the closet and under everything, periodically glancing back at the door. Nothing. His chest thumped and he started breathing again.

He stepped back into the hallway. The second door was directly across. He stepped to the doorknob side, grabbed the knob with his flashlight hand, and opened the door, that's when something moved. Adam let the door swing open, but it stopped when it bumped into something soft and swung half closed again.

"Sheriff's Dep—" Something moved again, shuffled around, just inside the door. He tried to calm himself, to be in control. "Sheriff's Mental Uni—Sheriff's Department, is everything okay?" He stammered.

A long silence passed. He tried to breathe deeply and force his body to settle down. As it did, his hearing became shaper. He thought he could hear someone breathing. Someone or something else. *Maybe one of the dogs*, he thought. He definitely heard a mattress spring squeak. He knew what that sounded like, and smiled a little, until he forced himself back to reality.

"Sheriff's Department," he repeated. "I'm going to come into the room, okay?"

The bed squeaked again.

He positioned his pistol in what he thought was the direction of the sounds. If something happened, he could fire off some rounds through the wall if he had to. He took the flashlight and reached around the door jam to shine it in the direction of the sound, just to see if there would be any reaction. There were more quick squeaks from the bed.

"Sheriff's Department," he said, as he tried to force the door open wider. "Sheriff's Department," as he stepped through the narrow doorway. "Sheriff's Dep—" he said as he saw the thing balled up on the bed. "Kathy Clayton, Ms. Clayton?"

The thing on the bed barely resembled a human, not to mention a female. Piled in clothes she had apparently not washed in weeks, Kathy Clayton burrowed into a nest created in the middle of her queen size, antique brass bed. Only her shoulders, head, and hands protruded from the pile of sheets, clothing, and newspapers she had gathered. Her eyes tore into Adam's with fear, paranoia, and hatred. Her hands and face were filthy, covered in dirt and scabs. Her mouth was completely crusted over from dehydration, and her eyes were caked with sleep and infection. He could tell by the condition of the bed and floor not only had she not washed, she hadn't left the room in weeks.

For anything.

Empty water bottles littered the floor along with assorted food wrappers. Every time Adam moved a muscle, she wiggled herself in the nest, like a rattlesnake, warning to keep your distance.

"Kathy, I want to—"

She grabbed the sides of her head and covered her ears. Her eyes clinched and her mouth opened wide in silence.

He stopped and just looked at her. *How in the hell am I going to get this bitch out of here?* he thought. *No way to request back-up. No rubber gloves. Restraint straps in the car. Great, just Great…*

He looked around the room for water. He tried to keep the light on her as much as he could, but there were things he had to do. The light seemed to be upsetting her, so he tried to keep it out of her face. All the bottles were empty, so he holstered his pistol and reached down for one of the big gallon jugs. Kathy recoiled, but didn't go anywhere, just rooted around in her nest. He stepped back into the hall and went to the kitchen. He felt uncomfortable about leaving her in there, but decided if she wanted to ambush him or run away, she would have already done it. He paused to see if she was going to follow him but her room was silent. He held the jug under the kitchen sink and turned on the water. As the jug filled, Adam stood facing the hallway waiting for her. He saw the phone hung on the wall and he picked it up, but the line was dead. Had he expected anything else? The jug started to overflow as Adam shut off the faucet, then walked back into the room. Kathy shuffled around and shielded her eyes from his light. Adam stepped over and set the jug on the bed. Immediately, she lunged for it and it fell over spilling water onto the mattress. Adam instinctively tried to help her recover it and not spill any on the bed, then remembered where he was. What difference would it make? It might get the dirt wet?

She pulled the jug to her lips and gulped the water. He almost told her to slow down, but, once again, what difference would it make? He reached for the light switch and flipped it. She gave out a half-hearted gasp, and then when the lights didn't come on, continued to drink. He shined his light to the ceiling and saw someone or something had broken the light bulb. He looked at the lamp on the nightstand, its bulb, too, was broken. While she continued to drink, he stepped over to the window, trying not to step on or in anything and reached up to the paper. She stopped drinking and started rocking vigorously on the bed. Like an angry monkey, she added yelping shrieks. Adam pointed at the newspaper. She calmed down for a second and stared at it. Adam had seen this before. Certain fixations the mentally ill can develop; correlations with the physical and emotional world. Ties, whether right or wrong, that solidify their thinking, and totally control their behavior. For Kathy, obviously it was light; she had to keep it out. Adam tore the paper quick enough to where she could not divert her eyes and was forced to see, there was no light outside. It was dark. She jerked, surprised at his quick movements but continued to stare out the window. He could tell she was thinking. She took another drink of water, slower this time.

"Kathy, can you tell me what night it is?" He asked.

She scowled at him, a glare that stabbed.

He held his pointing finger to his lips, "Shhh."

She looked back at the window.

Adam knew dispatch would soon be trying to call him to check his status, and he needed to get her out of here. They would be trying to find out why he hadn't checked out on his call. He was surprised they hadn't paged him yet, and looked down to check his pager for sure. He found no messages.

He stepped a little closer to the bed and whispered, "Kath—"

She glared again.

He motioned with both hands for her to come toward him. She leaned forward some, but was entangled in her nesting materials. Adam reached out and touched the blanket. She fidgeted in it, and it came loose, dropping from her shoulders. In the dark room, Adam saw her body. Her body above the waist. A picture straight from a Nazi concentration camp. Her skin was shrink-wrapped bone with every rib, every tendon, animated in full detail. Also, he could now see the fleas. They apparently had infested her house from the dog kennels. Hundreds of them, jumping all around her, crawling on her, seeking warmth and moisture. He tried not to think about that. He had to get her out of here. Over and over in his mind, he tried to think of a better solution. A safer, more sterile way to transport her. She needed to go to the hospital. She needed medical attention. She needed a lot of things, but he wasn't going to call EMS to transport her, even if he could get out on his radio. An ambulance crew would be down for the rest of the shift, trying to decontaminate. He reached up and touched her shoulder. He waited, but she didn't react. She was becoming exhausted. He thought about the stress of his coming in and her lack of water and food took everything out of her. She looked directly into his eyes as a drunken lover would. She flopped half toward him, her eyes half closed. He didn't dare say anything. He gently took her upper arms and pulled her to the edge of the bed. There was no resistance left in her, or she just capitulated and was easier to work with now. He pulled the blanket completely free from her and pushed away the papers and soiled clothes. A white cotton robe with little yellow kittens hung in the closet next to the bed. Adam reached over to get it and Kathy almost fell to the floor. He caught her before she went and she made no attempts at her own rescue. He pulled the robe down with one hand and draped it around her like a cocoon. He picked her up and carried her through the house like a groom with his bride as she curled and tucked her head against his shoulder. He retraced his steps and carried her out, back across the threshold. Adam walked in the darkness to his car, carrying his little one. He didn't think she weighed more than eighty pounds. He tried to hold her out, away from his body, but it didn't seem to matter. He could feel the fleas jumping from her and lighting on his arms, neck, and face. He ignored it. He knew he would probably be spending the rest of his shift decontaminating himself and his car. That was one way he could get a break from all of this. When he thought of it that way, he didn't mind the bites. It seemed a small price to pay for a few hours of freedom from all this loveliness.

He settled her in the back seat and got in. The seat was cold. He hadn't noticed how cold it was outside or how the wind was still so strong. He started the car, set the heater on high, and headed back down the road. Through the darkness, over gravel and sand, he searched for pavement once again. It took about ten minutes before his cell phone registered a signal and dialed the number to dispatch, but was cut off before they could answer.

"Mental Health 1273," he tried his radio.

A scratchy voice responded, "Last unit on county, re-identify and go with your traffic."

"Mental Health 1273, I have one in custody, en route to the county hospital, white female, beginning mileage, 324."

"10-4," and there was a long pause. Adam knew why; they were trying to find out what time he had checked out on the scene, but they couldn't, because he couldn't. "Unit 1273, you have one in custody from Waterline?" dispatch asked.

"10-4, and have a Lee County unit respond to that location, clear the house and take pictures for me," he asked.

"10-4, what will you want pictures of?" dispatch asked.

"They'll know when they get there."

"10-4," dispatch announced. "20:05 hours."

CHAPTER NINETEEN

The Evening Stroll
"Wednesday, December 18th, 8:35 pm"

Adam's trip to the county hospital was uneventful; Kathy slept the entire way. Even when they arrived and he wheeled her into the bright interior of the emergency room, she barely moved. He placed her into the mental health holding cell, not only because of her mental condition, but because it would be much easier to control the flea problem that way. Immediately, the triage nurse put down everything she was doing to concentrate her efforts on Kathy. It wasn't that the hospital staff cared that much about her, they just wanted to hurry and get the nasty wretch the hell out of their emergency room.

Adam went to the psychiatric services office to find out who was the duty psychologist, when he saw Vicky Becker, the Sheriff's Victim Services Specialist on the office phone. She looked up and covered the mouthpiece with her hand, "Do you have a minute?"

Adam nodded.

"Never mind, I've got a mental health deputy right here, thanks," and she hung up. "I was just calling dispatch to see if they could send me some help. And by the way, you're supposed to go to a critical incident stress debriefing," she scolded.

"I know. I told the lieutenant I would catch up to ya'll next week. Anyway, what's going on?"

"I've got one of your," she made circles, pointing her index finger at her head, "people in the family room who just lost her four month old baby."

"What do you mean, lost?" Adam asked.

"Died. They were coming to town for the holidays, and she put the kid in the back seat with the three older ones. When she got to the river, she realized the baby wasn't breathing. A little girl. She's been in there with her for the last hour, and we just moved her to the family room. They said it might be SIDS; she's lost two others to SIDS."

"It could be suffocation too," Adam added.

"There is a detective from the city working on it."

"So why isn't the city victim services handling it?"

"When they found the baby wasn't breathing, they were driving in the city and came to the hospital, but the grandparents live in the county and called the sheriff's department. So I came with them."

Adam seemed satisfied with the explanation.

"Anyway," she went on, "the mother is freaking out, wanting to see the kid again. Could you go in there with me to see if we can calm her down?"

"Where is the kid?" Adam asked.

"Still in the emergency room intensive care."

"You say the woman's crazy?"

"Not crazy, her sister says she's slow; retarded I guess."

"Great...Okay," Adam paused. "Why hasn't the coroner come to pick the kid up?"

"The hospital called them, and I called them. They're just busy and said it might be an hour or two. They're not real concerned since the body is at the hospital anyway. They are more interested in picking up bodies in town, I guess."

Adam thought for a minute. "Let's do this, I'll get the release and take the kid over to the morgue myself, while you try to console the family. That'll take care of her wanting to see the kid again since the kid won't be here. She simply won't be able to."

"You think?" Vicky asked.

"You said she already saw the kid, right? Said her goodbyes?"

"Yeah."

"Well, the closure issue is out of the way, so let's eliminate the problem and see what happens."

"Alright," she agreed. "You can transport a dead body?"

"Not usually, but the hospital is connected to the morgue, and I don't think anyone will mind."

Vicky folded her arms. "It is not. The morgue is a block away."

"Oh ye of little faith. There is an underground corridor that leads over to the coroner's office. I'll simply walk the kid over there. What's the name?"

"Crawford," Vicky answered and proceeded back to the family room to try and do her duties. She would have much rather had Adam come back to the family room with her. Deep down, she felt like he was trying to get out of going, and that is why he suggested transporting the baby. And her suspicion was right; he didn't want to deal with the family. He would much rather deal with a quiet, little baby.

Adam walked down the hall, through the double doors and to the emergency room nurse's station. The whole area was bustling with activity. All of the treatment areas were full, the stretchers bearing patients and medical staff were all moving in controlled confusion. A charge nurse sat behind the round nurse's station desk, shuffling clipboards. Adam stood in front of her for a moment when an ER doctor stopped near him to hang a chart.

"What can I help you with?" the doctor asked.

"Yes sir, I understand you have the baby-Crawford waiting for the coroner?"

"Yeah, she's in there." He pointed at one of the intensive care rooms.

"I was wondering, if you would release her to me, I'll take her to the morgue."

Adam was prepared to explain why a mental health deputy was going to do it, but it seemed as long as Adam was going to free up the doctor's intensive care room, he could care a less.

"Sure, here's the paperwork, and she's ready to go," he said, handing Adam a regular-sized envelope bulging with papers.

Before Adam could unfold the discharge order, the doctor was gone, heading for another table. Adam tucked the papers into his back pocket, and walked over to IC3, the room with the baby. He looked through the small window above the door handle and saw a little object lying on the gurney, wrapped in a light blue, hospital sheet. Adam opened the door and walked over to the child. He looked around for a moment taking in the whole scene. Stainless steel instruments, tables, pans, shelves, and stacks of clean, white linen.

Bottles of substances he had never seen and could not pronounce. The antiseptic in the air and the white of the medical lights seemed to clean every surface. He reached down and clumsily picked up the baby. This was only the second time Adam had ever held a baby. Being the youngest of his family, he was never afforded the opportunity of a little brother or sister.

In order for him to make it through the hospital and to the elevators without causing a scene, he decided to carry her the way he saw other mothers and fathers carry their children. It was his intent not to cause attention to himself and to look as natural as a proud, new father would, walking his daughter through the hospital. After all, he had just practiced carrying his bride across the threshold, why not practice with a baby?

He saw the child was wrapped as any baby in a sheet or blanket; they just added an additional fold over her little face. Adam peeled the sheet back some and looked at her. She would have looked like she was asleep, except for the reddening of her eyelids, gaping, slack-jawed mouth and the purple, spider webbed lines of post mortem lividity across her pale cheeks. He folded the sheet back over and lifted her up, so her head could rest on his shoulder. He turned and looked at himself in a stainless steel cabinet. He thought he did look like a father and felt confident with his plan. As he walked through the emergency room and out into the hallway that leads to the main entrance of the hospital, no one took notice of him. He looked like a real natural. Hospital staff walked by, patients, concerned family members, and a couple of police officers were all just going about their own business. The whole area was busy with people walking in what seemed every direction. As Adam entered the front hospital foyer, a large group of people came into the front doors looking for the ER. It appeared to be a whole family along with a now, half pregnant young girl. The girl apparently couldn't wait to start the delivery of her son while they were rolling her up the sidewalk in a hospital wheel chair. They passed him in total confusion, hurrying down the hall. He thought for sure he was going to make it to the elevator, then four ER nurses rounded the corner.

"Adam!" one shouted, playfully. "What are you doing?" and poked at his stomach.

This caught the attention of the other people walking in the hall.

Adam smiled and tried to walk around the group of nurses; the elevator was only ten feet away.

"Not so fast," another nurse said. "What do you have there? A little baby!" she squeaked.

"No, I, it's a—" Adam shuffled, trying to get around them.

"Let me see," the third nurse said, in her best little baby voice.

Now the whole crowd of people was watching and smiling, and waiting to get a glimpse at the proud father's little angel.

"No you don't—" Adam didn't know what to do when the fourth of these devouring, motherly mad women reached up and pulled the sheet aside.

At that very moment, time seemed to stop. Everything slowed and was quiet. Silent. Adam saw their faces. All of their faces. The nurse's faces as they realized what they had done. His mind seemed to take a picture of each of them. The two teenagers standing by the front door, mouths opened, eyes wide. A lone woman carrying a vase of yellow, white, and purple flowers. The blank stare of the cop across the hall. The old woman in the wheel chair, whose cataracts were so bad, she still wore her excited smile imagining the beauty of the darling little tot. But everyone else clearly saw what Adam was holding.

Adam stepped to an open elevator and the three people who were waiting to go up, quickly exited, leaving him alone. It seemed to take the doors forever to close, but when they did, his panic left him and was replaced by sheer relief. But then, the elevator moved, and it was going up, 2…3…4…5…then it slowed and opened on the sixth floor. Adam waited but no one entered, then the doors closed, and once again he was alone.

"Thank you," he said to God. It was the one break He gave him this week.

Adam reached over and pushed the basement floor button, 5…4…3…2…then it slowed and opened, once again, in the main lobby. Most of the people were there as if they never moved, still looking at him. Adam stood staring straight ahead, waiting for the doors to close. They did, and the elevator sank to the basement below.

He didn't say anything to God, that time.

The doors opened and Adam found himself stepping from the elevator into a dusty, concrete tunnel, lit by what appeared to be a single sixty-watt bulb. He stared down the corridor into the darkness and saw a single light, glowing on the other side of the black hole. He looked on the walls for a light switch, but found only cobwebs and dead crickets. The hospital was apparently using the corridor for the storage of outdated hospital equipment. Stacks of old beds, chairs, and patient monitoring equipment lined each wall.

"Great..." he said. "Things just keep getting better."

He wished he was in the family room with the mother.

Adam pulled the baby off his shoulder, cradled it in front of him and headed through the tube. He estimated it was about a sixty or seventy yard walk. It was hard going at first; he had to let his eyes adjust to the darkness. As he walked, he stumbled over some of the scattered hospital junk on the floor. Cobwebs dangled from the ceiling and startled him as they tickled across his face. He found himself walking faster than normal and had to consciously slow his pace; fast in the dark was not necessarily better. Dead baby jokes skittered through his mind. Dracula. Night of the Living Dead. It's Alive. He heard a sound behind one of the old, broken wheel chairs. There was a movement or he thought there was a movement to his left, behind some leaning bookshelves. He thought if there wasn't a movement there, there was about to be one in his pants. He forced himself not to look down. Not to look at the little thing he cradled in his arms. Forced himself not to look and see if she was looking back at him. Looking up to him.

As he arrived at the other end, he greeted the light and stepped gingerly up the flight of stairs to the morgue office. A single bead of sweat slipped off his brow and dotted the baby's blue sheet.

A clerk Adam hadn't seen before, looked up from his desk. "Hey, that the baby?"

Adam decided not to be a smart ass. "Yep."

"You should have called over here. I would have turned the corridor lights on for you."

Adam forced a smile. "That's alright. It's cool."

"Just set her down, over there." He pointed to a small prep table near the refrigerators.

Adam handed the man the paperwork. "You need anything else from me?"

"Naw, that's it."

"Thanks," he said, and headed out the front door.

The cold night air felt great. He inhaled deeply and savored it as he walked across the street and around the side of the hospital to his car. He didn't think he had any more adrenalin left in his body; he was ready to go home. He prayed he wouldn't receive another call.

Not tonight.

Reluctantly, Adam checked back on the radio, "Unit 1273, 10-8."

"Unit 1273, 10-4. Hold you en route to 1273 Pascall Lane. CID is requesting a mental health unit."

Adam shook his head. "10-4. En route."

CHAPTER TWENTY

The Accident
"Wednesday, December 18th, 9:33 pm"

Since the beginning of the month, the coroner's office worked fourteen suicides. Mental health was usually not called out on the scene of a deceased person unless, of course, there were circumstances of a highly unusual nature. Adam was called out on maybe ten this whole year, but so far, this one would make it three this month.

As he drove he checked his map book to make sure he was close to Pascall Lane. He confirmed his direction and made the next left onto Green, and the following left onto Pascall which was located in one of the cities first suburbs. The houses were all built in the late fifties on half-acre lots. Most of them were sprawling single story homes with lots of trees and separated by chain link fencing. The streetlights illuminated the brown leaves that covered the shoulders of the roadway, concealing any hints of gutters or curbs. About mid-way down the block, he could see two sheriff's patrol cars and a crime scene van.

Adam pulled behind the van and stopped. "Unit 1273, hold me out on Pascall."

"Unit 1273, 10-4, 14:52 hours."

Adam got out and walked toward the house's front porch. It was all brick but long ago had been painted over in white. The shutters on the big windows were trimmed in light blue, and white drapes hung heavily inside. Adam noticed the front door was opened but he saw no signs of sheriff's personnel.   He paused before he entered. "Hello?" he called inside the house.

A uniformed patrol deputy stepped into the front foyer from what was apparently a front living room. "Hey, Adam."

Adam had seen the deputy before but couldn't remember his name. Even so, he smiled like they were best of friends. "Hey, man, what have you been up to?"

"Same ole, I heard they were having you come; the sergeant's back there waiting on you." He motioned a thumb down the hallway.

Adam wiped his feet and came in. "We got family on scene?"

"No," the deputy said. "The minister from the church came by and picked up the mother about thirty minutes ago. I don't think the father lives in town."

"It's a kid?" Adam asked.

"Nineteen, I think she said. I don't know if they're divorced or just separated."

As Adam walked on down the hallway, the deputy sat back down in a living room chair and continued filling out the form on his clipboard. Adam passed a bathroom to his right and could hear some voices coming from the bedroom at the end of the hall. As he approached the door, he could see the crime scene technician taking flash photographs of something just to the left of the door inside the room. He stopped at the door and waited for someone to recognize him and give him instructions. He could see most of the inside of the room. Hard rock posters covered most all of the walls. There were clothes practically covering the floor and empty packs of cigarettes everywhere. It was a complete contrast to the rest of the house, which appeared to be in order. He leaned in just a little and could see Sergeant Craig Milam squatting down, using a tape to measure the distance between a bedpost and something in the closet.

Sergeant Milam looked up. "Hey, Adam." Milam was Adam's sergeant on patrol for a short time, before he was transferred to mental health.

"Hey, Sergeant. Is there a detective working this?"

"No. I had enough time in CID to handle this one. I just wanted you to come by for your *professional* opinion."

Adam knew what he meant by *professional* opinion. He could have just said *nutty* opinion and that would have got the idea across.

"What do you have?" Adam asked.

Milam stood up and swung his hands toward the closet. "Taa-Daa," he said, like an amateur magician revealing an illusion. Unfortunately, this was no illusion.

Adam stepped into the room and immediately noticed pornographic magazines littering the floor in front of the opened closet doors. Each one of them were opened to a large foldout picture of woman; most were spread-eagled on the page. Adam didn't count them individually but he estimated there had to have been at least twenty scattered around the floor. Adam looked back at the closet but still couldn't see inside; the folding shutter doors guarded either side of the opening. Adam stepped further around, trying not to step on anything on the floor and saw a set of bent, naked knees protruding out from the closet. There, hanging from the clothing rod, was the nineteen year old, completely naked, would-be lover. His face was bright purple from the necktie constricting his throat. It looped around the clothes rod and was tied with two large knots on either side of his Adam's apple. His knees were bent so far, he could have easily stood up and saved himself before passing out. His arms hung down by his side, and by the condition of his penis and the viewing materials on the ground, it was quite obvious what he had been working on.

"You seen one of these before?" Sergeant Milam asked.

"Yeah, did he tie the necktie to the rod?" Adam asked.

"No, it was looped around and looks like it just got tangled," Milam answered. "Apparently, while he was getting busy, he was putting more pressure on his neck by bending his knees. Supposed to choke you or some goddamn thing and get you off better."

"Yeah," Adam agreed.

"They don't supposed to use anything that would normally support their own weight or tie it off in case they pass out, right?"

"Right," Adam said.

"I guess this guy slowly put pressure on the necktie and it just held there when he passed out."

Adam looked down. "Oh, he did finish, didn't he."

"Yep," Milam said.

"Shit..." Adam added. "Hell of a way to go."

"Yeah, almost makes you want to stop jackin' off in the closet," Milam added.

They looked at each other, shook their heads in unison and said, "*Naaah.*"

"Anyway, could you write me a supplement, just describe the situation and explain what you know about it."

"Yeah, no problem," Adam said.

"Auto-jackoff-jizm? What's it called?" Milam asked.

Adam smiled and slowly said, "Autoeroticism."

"Yeah. That. Write that in there." He smiled. "I'm going to process everything like a homicide but unless there's some toxicology thing or other injuries we can't see, I'm pretty sure this was an accident."

"Probably. I'll send a copy of the report to you through inner-office mail."

"Thanks, Adam," he said, "and say, I sorry about Robert. I know ya'll were friends."

Adam just nodded his head and walked back out. He knew Milam's condolences were genuine, not just an attachment to be a part of the situation and a precursor to asking more questions about what happened that night.

Adam got back into his car and notified dispatch he would be out of service to clean up. Everyone listening thought they knew exactly what that meant. Either someone had puked, defecated, or urinated in his car. This time, after checking the back seat, it was a combination of the latter two, with a side of bug infestation. The poor girl from Yegua had made her presence known.

He started off down the block. He forgot he had wanted to call Susan tonight. He pushed the thoughts of Robert clear out of his mind. He didn't think about the mother who one hour ago had found her dead son, hanging in his closet, suspended in time at the end of a successful masturbation.

In reflection, he didn't even remember driving home.

CHAPTER TWENTY-ONE

The Catharsis
"Wednesday, December 18th, 10:40 pm"

Adam was only two days into his week and he felt like he had been working for a month straight. In only three more days he would have his weekend to rest, that is if they didn't make him cover Robert's shift on Sunday. With a couple days off he felt he could clear his head and get himself back on his game. He knew he needed the rest. Robert's murder happened only yesterday and it seemed like a year ago. He knew in the next few days he would have to go by the funeral home to show his respects. In the mean time, he would need to get as much rest as he could. With Robert gone, there would be no extra time off or coverage for vacation until they had another officer selected and trained to replace him. The coverage was thin enough and with the length of the selection process and the three months time to train, it could be four to five months before the mental health unit was totally back to full staff. Robert lay cold in his box and Adam was thinking of his vacation time. Adam didn't know how he should feel about that. Bad he supposed.

In two days Adam went from a predatory lust for his next call to wanting to cower at every crackle of his radio's speaker. He was twenty-six years old and for the first time in his life, he was tired.

He always carried a can of bug spray in his glove box, Robert had taught him that, also. When he pulled into his apartment complex parking lot, he got out and opened all the car's doors. He got a bottle of Formula 409 and paper towels out of the trunk and the can of bug

155

spray from the glove box. It was apparent that most of the fleas stayed on Kathy, burrowing in for the transport, but he wasn't going to take any chances. He sprayed the entire interior of the sedan with the insecticide and did his best at disinfecting the back seat. He left the windows a quarter of the way down to let it ventilate overnight. That would pretty much take care of everything, the bugs and the smell. The bugs that didn't die would hopefully jump out the windows. It wasn't a perfect plan, but it was *a* plan.

He put his cleaning equipment back into the trunk and headed to his apartment. He wondered what Susan was doing, and then he stopped himself. He walked around to the back porch and hopped his fence. He slid the glass door open and flicked off the porch light. After making sure no one was in the courtyard, he stripped down to his boxers and dumped his clothes in the green garbage bag with the ones Ray Zetner had contaminated the night before. Grabbing his badge, pager, cell phone, and gun, he quickly let himself in and ran to the shower, hoping no fleas or other things fell or jumped off into his home on the way. He looked over himself in the bathroom and was pretty sure he was clean of the infestation, but jumped into the shower anyway. After a long suds from head to toe, he dried off and threw on his robe. He tossed the underwear out the back door with the rest of his clothes and walked over to the refrigerator. There was a small frozen pizza in the freezer and he threw it into the microwave. As the pizza thawed, he opened a canned Coke and sat at his kitchen table. He liked his apartment. Everything in its place, dishes put away, sink clean, towels hung evenly on their bars. The paper towels fed over the top and outward instead of along the wall. Everything the way he liked it. The way the Army had told him was so important. So different than the way Susan would do things, or not do things, or allow them to become. One of their biggest arguments was over not letting anything sit in the sink. Adam wanted it washed now and relax later. Susan wanted to relax now and maybe wash it later. She was the one who really understood what was important: forging relationships, not washing dishes.

Adam wouldn't find this out until much later in life.

He looked up at his ceiling fan and thought of a straining rope, bulging eyes, and fluids. The buzzer sounded for the pizza and Adam jumped, kicking the table with his knee. "Shit!"

He got up, rubbed his knee, then removed the pizza and brought it back to the table. He stared at it cooling for a long time as the cheese turned a jaundice yellow. The red dripping sauce, little bits of scabby pepperoni, and a crispy brown crust did nothing for his appetite. He managed two bites before it slid off the plate and into the trash. He walked over and tossed some fish flakes into the aquarium and then headed toward the bedroom. It was the first time, *ever*, he didn't sit to watch his fish eat.

Flopping onto the edge of the bed, he set his alarm for 7:00 am, knowing he wouldn't get up; it was 12:01am now. He shut off his light and turned to start his descent onto his back when his pager screeched.

"Shit!" He was too exhausted to come up with any more creative expletives. He snatched it off the nightstand. The number of the apartment answering service was in the pager's view screen. He reached over and dialed the number.

"The Villas, my I help you?" a young woman answered.

"Yeah, this is Adam, on-site security, I got a page."

"Yes, sir, a lady called from 104 and said there was a strange man sitting on the walkway in front of her apartment and wanted you to check it out."

"Okay, I'll take care of it," he said and hung up. He couldn't believe it. He hadn't received a call in over three weeks, and now tonight. *Great*. He thought he might just call the city police and have them come and check it out, but quickly dismissed it; it was his responsibility. He threw on a pair sweat pants, a t-shirt, and running shoes, grabbed his gun and cell phone, then went out the door. He was half way over to the apartment when he realized the caller was the new girl, Michele Blackmon, in apartment 104. He specifically told her if she saw anything suspicious to call the answering service and she did. It only took two days.

He came around the corner in front of her apartment, but saw no one. All of the security lights were illuminating the sidewalk and parking lot like daytime. If there was anyone in the immediate area, Adam would have seen them. He checked around the apartment building and back to her door. He didn't see anything. Her lights were out in the windows and as he turned to leave, he saw her door open, just a crack. He walked over and she opened it enough to stick her head out.

"Is he gone?" she asked.

"Yeah, I checked around the entire building, I didn't see anyone. What did he look like?"

"I didn't get a good look at him, white guy in dark pants and a shirt."

That was Adam's first clue. With the bright security lights, you could practically tell a man's religion. Since the lights went up, they had several complaints about them being too bright.

"You didn't get a good look at him, huh?"

"No," she still craned her head around, as if scanning the parking lot for him. Her face was glowing from fresh cream, and her almost white hair was pulled back into a ponytail. Face flawless, eyes, ice blue, pink lips.

He pulled himself away. "Okay, well, I'll check around here a couple of more times, but if you see him again, make sure you call."

She leaned out of the door a little more and he could see she was wearing nothing but a white laced teddy. "Okay. Uh, you been busy? Work and all?"

"Yeah, pretty busy," he said, as he started to turn. "I'll check around the back again, before I head home."

She opened the door enough where he could see her from head to toe. Legs long and slender, pink toenails; one foot on top of the other.

"Would you like a beer or something?" she shyly asked and bit her bottom lip.

Adam stopped. "Yeah, I'd like a beer." They went inside.

She didn't have any beer.

CHAPTER TWENTY-TWO

The Escape
"Thursday, December 19th*, 10:22 am"*

Slowly, Adam's left eye opened. He focused on something purple in front of him. He raised his head off the frilly, pink pillow and rubbed his eyes. A big, purple teddy bear sat on the edge of the bed looking down at him. Adam sat up and pulled off the note taped to the bear's hand. It read, "Thank you for my house warming present. I can't believe how happy you made me."

"Shit," he whispered.

The letter continued, "I had to go to work, so I let you sleep. I'll call you when I get off and we can go do something. Your Love, Michele." Two little hearts were drawn playfully in the corner.

"Shit." He rifled through the pile of stuffed animals that were displaced off the bed during the night's festivities, looking for his MIA clothing. Quickly, he pulled on his sweat pants, grabbed his shirt and made his way to the front door. Michele had set out a bowl of Frosted Flakes adorned with another little note, "Sorry I couldn't cook breakfast, but Tony the Tiger will have to do. See you after work." Little X,O's and hearts.

"Ah, Got to get out! Got to get out!" he repeated in his best Homer Simpson voice. He wrestled with a green monkey hanging on the doorknob, as if it was fighting his attempted evacuation. *Great, just great, good call Thompson, good frickin' call,* he thought as he pulled the door open and fled from her lair. She was absolutely gorgeous, athletic, accommodating, and everything, but he could tell

159

this added to his problems. She added to his problems. She helped him forget, and forget he did, just for a few hours, everything that happened in the past two days. For the past few months for that matter. But, ironically added another dynamic to his accumulating pile. Mainly, a dynamic that lived only four doors down and he would probably see everyday. *God you are a genius Thompson, a frickin' genius*, he thought, while he walked to his apartment, still adjusting his clothing. As he pulled down his t-shirt and rounded the sidewalk to his front door, Susan appeared, almost colliding with him.

"Oh, hey, ya scared me," Adam stammered.

"Sorry," Susan laughed. "I was just—" she looked at his wrinkled clothes. She knew how particular he was about his clothes. She stood in silence; her mood immediately altered.

"I was just going running and had to put up my gun," he smiled.

"I see," she said curtly, stepping around him. "I just dropped something off for you. I hope you like them," then continued walking toward her car. She may be a gullible liberal, but not stupid.

"Uhm, thanks. Been busy at work?" He tried to make small talk to relax the tension.

She stopped and turned toward him. "Yes, and I'm late now. Goodbye Adam," and she left.

He stood there, watched her get into her car and pull into traffic a little faster than she normally would. She didn't even look at him while she drove away. No smile or wave. No mouthed curses or giving him the middle finger. Nothing was sometimes worse than a full-blown go to hell. Was this what he wanted all along, he wondered. Didn't this take care of the Susan problem? Wasn't this an indication of a severance of the relationship? Finality. He could tell that she knew what was going on. She wasn't stupid. Adam never dressed like that to go running; he certainly never had his cell phone and gun. Was there a Susan problem or was it an Adam problem? He walked to his door and found a small wicker basket covered by a red and white-checkered cloth. Inside, she hid a dozen blueberry muffins and a small card. The note simply said, "Thinking of you."

Adam picked up the basket and let himself into his apartment. He stripped down and turned on the shower. Turned it hot. When the steam spilled over the curtain, he grabbed a muffin from the basket and got under the water. He anointed himself letting the shower flow over his head and down his body taking everything with it. He took pauses from the water to get bites of Susan's blueberry muffin. His eyes began to water, mixing with the streams over his forehead and concealed in the steam.

CHAPTER TWENTY-THREE

Last Respects
"Thursday, December 19th, 2:10 pm"

Adam spent the rest of the morning and afternoon around the apartment, feeding the fish, laundry, dishes, all the things he would normally do on his days off. The phone rang a couple of times, but he let the answering machine pick it up. He listened to the message his mother left checking to see if he was all right, and Lieutenant Martin explaining he would need to make an appointment with internal affairs for sometime next week. Martin said there was no real hurry since they would probably want to conclude the criminal investigation before the administrative investigation. Adam erased the messages and reset the recorder. He was stuck. He didn't want to stay at home, and this was the first time he could remember not really wanting to go to work. It's not that he didn't want to go; he was just ambivalent. After working through the last Christmas season, he knew what to expect. It was call after call beginning late November through mid-January. The busiest time of the year, by far. Statistics from the coroner's office told them one suicide every day. Three-times the normal rate. Suicide becomes the sixth major cause of death during the *jolly* season and that was hard for him to believe, at first. That is until he worked a season. You just don't hear that much on suicide unless it is a homicide/suicide. Even then, the media lets the story die quickly.

Adam got into his car and didn't notice any of the bugs from the day before, but there was a strong odor. One of armpits and insecticide. As he pulled into traffic, he rolled down all the windows. It was only 2:10, but he felt like getting out. He drove to the county fuel station, topped off his gas, and checked the oil. There were other county cars coming in and out, but no one from the sheriff's office. No one recognized him and he was somewhat relieved. But there was also a side of him that resented those people all around him who didn't recognize him and didn't want to know what happened. Irritated that they would bother him and irritated that they wouldn't. He understood and didn't understand. Being a friend of Robert's and Robert having been murdered made Adam important. He didn't want it to be, but there it was, still.

He decided to go to the county hospital and see what has been going on down there. As he pulled into the parking area, he checked on the radio, "Unit 1273."

"1273," the radio responded.

"1273, put me on duty, and out at the county hospital."

"1273, 10-4, when you go 10-8, I have two calls holding."

"1273, disregard, go ahead with your traffic."

"Emotionally Disturbed Person, 3578 Ditmar Court, meet with the store clerk, reporting a transient doing criminal mischief to the property."

Adam turned back into traffic. "10-4, en route."

Adam knew what he was in for. Transients typically do only one kind of criminal mischief. At least EDP transients typically do only one kind of criminal mischief; fecal smearing to mark their territory. It is a fact, if you want to stake an area for your own, take a dump and smear it everywhere. No one will dispute your claim. Adam did not care for these calls and they were all too often.

He headed south on the expressway, and just as he was settling in, the radio interrupted, "Unit 1273, 10-63, suicide in progress."

Adam grabbed the microphone, "1273, go ahead."

"1273, 1705 O'Kelly Road, received a 911 from the suspect's son at his work, says he just spoke to his father who took an overdose."

"1273, 10-4, do you have a cross street?" Adam asked, hoping dispatch could assist him in getting there faster, instead of having to pull over and use his map.

"10-4, I-35 to St. Elmo, to Murry, to O'Kelly."

"1273, 10-4, en route."

Adam was only about a mile from the house. He missed the exit ramp, but decided to go through the median instead of going to the next overpass and backtracking. He cut across the frontage road and onto St. Elmo. He turned left onto Murry and right onto O'Kelly, looking for the numbers, 1612, 1642, 1701, then 1705.

Adam keyed his mike. "1273, on scene."

"1273, 10-4, 14:55 hours," dispatch acknowledged.

Adam grabbed his hand-held radio and jumped from his car. Quickly, but cautiously, he walked to the front door and listened. The house was about thirty years old, but in fine shape. Yard groomed, walks and porch free of leaves. Shades drawn with no apparent interior lights on. He heard nothing.

He spoke quietly into his radio, "Unit 1273, have you tried to make contact with the suspect?"

"1273, 10-4, the phone has been busy."

Once again, Adam was forced into making a decision. He reached out and rang the doorbell. Immediately, a muffled gunshot thumped the windows of the house.

Adam stepped to the side of the door. "Sheriff's Department!"

The house was silent again. He couldn't wait. If he waited and there was any chance at saving the man, time would steal that away. *Bam-bam-bam*, he struck the door. "Sheriff's Department! Come to the door!"

Still nothing. He tried the doorknob, but it was locked. With everything he had, he kicked the door next to the knob and it flung open. In front of him was a darkened entryway, then a hallway apparently leading to the living room. A hall branched off to the right just after the entry, possibly leading to some front bedrooms.

"Sheriff's Department!" he announced, then drew his gun. He didn't have his flashlight this time. In the middle of the day, he didn't think he would need it. He stepped into the entryway and turned on the first light switch he came to. The lights in hall and entryway came to life. He heard something down the hall to his right. Cautiously, he turned and made his way through. There was a hissing noise and some sporadic, light thumping coming from a closed bedroom door.

"Sheriff's Mental Health, I'm here to make sure everything is okay," Adam assured the resident of the house. He stood to the side of the door and reached out to check the knob. The hissing and thumping was louder. Slowly he turned the knob, and satisfied it was unlocked, pushed the door open. Causiously, he peered around the opening. He could see the far wall, shelves packed with books, a leather chair, and a dark wood desk. He pulled his gun tight to his side to get a better angle on the room. Leaning in, he saw a man's elbow in a red and black checkered, terry-cloth robe. The elbow bounced rhythmically, thumping the hard bone on the desk.

"Sheriff's Department," Adam repeated. He stepped slightly into the threshold and saw the chest of the man and the swivel chair he was seated in. He could see pens and pencils scattered on the desk. He could see the notes, a glass paperweight, and chrome letter opener. He could see the man's leather, slippered foot wiggling under the desk, luring Adam closer. He could see the pack of cigarettes, ashtray, bottle of scotch, and little red, and orange, and blue pills. He saw the oxygen tank, overturned, with the plastic hose hissing the gas into the air. He stepped in and saw the man. His head tilted straight back and mouth gaped, as if he had fallen asleep. But he hadn't fallen asleep. Adam stepped into the room and smelled the spent gunpowder; he saw the gun sitting in the man's lap, his left hand still gripping the handle. He walked around the desk and saw the flap on the back of the man's head; a back door for the bullet's hasty exit. The man's eyes were half open, or half shut, depending if you are an optimist or pessimist. Adam, at this point, was the latter. The man's body jittered and convulsed, trying to keep itself alive. It tried to suck in air, past broken teeth, torn gums, and blood. Adam thought he could see some brain matter in his mouth, but he wasn't for sure. It was a mess. Blood pooled onto the floor, as he fought for life.

"Unit 1273, checking status," the radio crackled.

Adam was aware they were checking his status, but the requests seemed so far away. Distant, and out of reach. He thought of the young woman he had saved from her fiery death and the fact that she was still in a coma in a burn unit in San Antonio.

Quickly, he walked out of the room and through the rest of the house, searching for anyone else, an asleep family member or a possible suspect who murdered him, but the house was empty.

"Unit 1273, checking status," dispatch repeated.

Adam held up his radio, "1273, stand-by," was all he could think to say.

He didn't want to request an ambulance too soon. He went on too many calls where the paramedics saved some poor son-of-a-bitch like this so his family could take care of him another ten years while he sat drooling and crapping on himself. Adam understood it was the paramedic's job and respected that, but he didn't want to make it that easy for them. Not this time. For the next five minutes, he didn't feel guilty at all. This man made a decision to take his own life and if he felt that life was that bad, then Adam knew he would feel it was a lot worse without half his brain, missing most of his teeth, and breathing through a tracheotomy for the rest of his drooling and slobbering life.

As his spasms slowed some, Adam said, "Unit 1273, roll EMS, I have one white male with a gunshot to the head."

"Unit 1273, 10-4, are you code 4?"

"Unit 1273, 10-4, I'm okay."

Adam stared at the man, who reminded him a little of his own father. He recognized the pills on the desk and oxygen bottle. This man was already dying of something, anyway. Cancer most likely. A slow, painful, delayed death. Agony. Adam hoped the man would have approved that he waited. That Adam wasn't a part of the machinery that forces others into prolonged agony. Adam did it for him and hoped the man would respect him for it. After all, he was not only sworn to protect, but also to serve.

Adam stood by him, making sure he didn't disturb the crime scene or step in anything. He patted the man's shoulder reassuringly and waited until his breathing ceased. Adam stood guard there, for what seemed a long time, until he heard the wails of the EMS sirens.

"I'll be right back," he said to the man, who probably wasn't listening, and walked to the front door.

He met with the paramedics in the yard and escorted them back into the room. After setting their equipment down, one immediately checked his carotid pulse and said, "I've got activity." This set everything into motion. As they pulled the man from his chair, Adam recovered the gun and set it on the desk. The paramedics pulled him to the floor and began their resuscitation efforts. Adam could tell by the way they went about their business; it was all protocol. All for show. Neither of them expected a save, but they had to go through the steps.

As they worked, Adam stepped from the room. He witnessed the same scene only a few months ago, minus the suicide part, when his father died of heart failure. He was surprised this was affecting him so strongly. He squinted his eyes and shook it off, running baseball batting averages through his mind. He never understood how they determined batting averages, but that didn't matter, it always helped him disconnect. Batting averages helped prolong other activities also, and he thought of that too.

His emotions passed.

Standing in the front yard, he raised his radio. "1273, go ahead and roll Criminal Investigations and Crime Scene."

"10-4," dispatch said. "The son is en route to your location. Do you want Victim's Services?"

"1273, 10-4," Adam answered. He really didn't feel like dealing with that also.

Adam was out in the yard for about ten minutes when the paramedics came out. One walked over to Adam and handed him a paper. "We left everything we used on him inside. Here's the patient sheet for the report. I got his name off his license on the desk. He had a contact wound in his mouth and it looks like he took an overdose of his prescription medication. You got anything for us?"

Adam looked for their names on the sheet. "Are your names here?"

"At the top," he answered.

"No, I think that's all. Thanks."

"No problem, take care," he said, then returned to his ambulance.

They spent a few minutes getting their equipment back into order, then left, leaving Adam once again, alone. He wished he had a cigarette. He hadn't smoked since he was a kid, but this was one of a few times he really had the urge. He thought of the cigarettes on the man's desk and knew he wouldn't mind, but decided against it.

Adam didn't go back in.

Soon a district patrol officer came to secure the scene, then two detectives from CID, then the crime scene technicians. Victim Services met with the man's son when he arrived and Adam was glad he didn't have to deal with the him too. It wasn't that the son was out of control, he just didn't want the extra work.

He got back into his car. "Unit 1273."

"Unit 1273," dispatch responded.

"1273, I'm back in service, change this call to a Deceased Person, and I'll be doing a supplement to CID's case number. Go ahead with the next call."

"1273, 10-4, I don't have anything holding for MHU."

Adam paused, wondering what happened to his criminal mischief transient, then said, "10-4, I'll be available on pager," not wanting to remind them of it.

"10-4, 16:32 hours."

Adam drove down the neighborhood street and back into traffic. He was going to just drive around for a while. Not go to the office. Not go to the hospital. Not go to anywhere in particular, just cruise.

He relaxed, turned on the car stereo, and thought about the last time he went fishing with his dad.

CHAPTER TWENTY-FOUR

The Bag
"Thursday, December 19th, 5:42 pm"

Adam spent an hour driving around the city. He looked at the darkening streets and the way the lights sparkled on his windshield. It seemed to him, the streetlights were clearer, crisper, during the winter months; during cold nights. He had just begun to relax when his pager went off. "PHONE LT MARTIN ON CELL" is all it read.

Adam turned on his cell and dialed the number. On the first ring, Lieutenant Martin picked up. "Adam?"

"Yes sir, you paged?"

"Yeah, did you deliver the stuff?"

"What stuff?"

"Did you go by the office?" The Lieutenant sounded annoyed.

"No sir," Adam was going to make up an excuse but decided to leave well enough alone.

"Are you on a call, right now?"

"No, sir."

"Go to the office, right now and pick up a bag of personal items beside your mail box and deliver it to the victim's father. You know that high school girl that did herself a month or so ago. CID released the clothes she was found in, I spoke to her Dad, and he wants them back."

"Yes, sir, sorry about that."

"Don't worry about it; it is still early, just get it done. Everything else okay?"

"Yeah, just chuggin' along."

"Alright, if you need anything I'll be on my pager," he said.

"Thanks." Adam hung up.

He really didn't feel like taking the clothes of a dead girl to her father's house, five days before Christmas. Because it was the death of a seventeen-year-old girl, the sheriff's department handled it just as if they were conducting a major homicide investigation; even though all evidence suggested otherwise. Adam read part of the report a month or so ago when he was hanging around the office waiting for a call. According to the witness statements, early in October she started giving away things that were very dear to her. Teddy bears to friends that really showed interest in them, some clothes, dolls, and other childhood toys. Her parents took notice of it and just assumed she was growing out of them and becoming a young woman. What they should have noticed was when she returned letters to people who had written them to her. Birthday, holiday, and special occasion cards, from friends, grandparents, and other close family members. Letters to her when she was at twirler camp and band camp. Pictures of her with family and friends, all returned with the explanation that she didn't want anything to happen to them. These are not things a healthy young girl does.

Adam swung by the office and was in and out with the bag in less than a minute. He had checked his box, and it was empty; Robert's was stuffed with more flowers and ribbons than before. He thought it looked like people were using it to build a shrine.

Adam headed north to meet with the girl's father. He found himself unusually nervous, anticipating their meeting. How would he express his condolences? Did he need to express his condolences? Adam suppressed enough emotions this week to last him a year, to last most people a lifetime and he didn't know how much more he could take. He reached over in the seat and checked the brown paper bag, the same type of bag you receive at the grocery if you request paper, except this bag was worn. It looked old, wrinkled and rolled down from the top. He rolled the top up enough to confirm the address written in black marker on its top edge, 9812 Russell Lane. Under the address were the words DECEASED / POSS. OVERDOSE in hastily written scrawl. There were some stains around the bottom of the bag from when they removed the clothes still moist from her relaxing muscles. Adam found it hard to believe how insensitive cops could be. They were just going to return the little girls clothes in a dirty brown paper bag and think nothing more of it.

Adam pulled to the side of the road and slammed the gear shifter into park. He shut the car off, got out, and breathed in the cold, crisp air. He walked to the back of the car, opened the trunk and rifled around in a black plastic tub where he stored his extra paperwork and forms. He found a new, folded brown paper bag and brought it back to the driver seat. He unfolded it and sat it in the passenger floorboard. Using his pen, just in case there was something surprising inside the bag he didn't want on his hands, he started lifting out the items, one by one. First, there was a pink button up shirt, with little white bunnies hopping across it; he set it down in the new bag. Then a pair of white running shoes stuffed with one sock each; they went into the bag. A pair of blue jeans with pink flowers embroidered on the left thigh went into the bag. And finally a white cotton, under-wire bra and pair of bright yellow panties. He put the bra into the new bag, but held the panties on his pen, looking at them. He crushed down the old bag and sat the panties on top. He thought of what he should do with them. He knew what he wanted to do with them, but the father might wonder why all the other clothes were returned, except for his daughter's panties. Maybe, he thought, he could return everything except the panties now, and just give them back to him later, after he was finished with them. Adam finally concluded the best thing was to apologize for their condition and ask the father if he wanted the sheriff's department to clean them before they were returned. Sometime after death, she apparently lost her bowels and the coroner's office hadn't felt it necessary to rinse off all the residue. He put them in the bag with the rest.

He pulled back onto the street and continued to her house, wondering what he was going to encounter.

He turned onto Russell Lane and looked for 9812. It was a new neighborhood, with many houses still under construction. Some of the residents had strung tiny, cheap Christmas lights on their doors and eaves, but most yards looked like the owners were busier at work trying to make the mortgage than spending time decorating their barren front yards. As he stopped in front of the residence, he saw a man in his early forties adjusting a human-sized plastic snowman in the front yard. The snowman looked ridiculous standing in the bald yard, with no snow or even grass around him. The man stopped what he was doing and stood watching Adam get out of the car.

"Mr. Steager?" Adam asked.

The man walked toward him. "Yes?"

"I'm sorry to bother you. I'm Adam Thompson with the Sheriff's Department."

The two men shook hands. "Those Anna's things?" he asked, looking down at the bag in Adam's hand.

"Yes, sir," he said. "I was wondering if you would want me to take care of these for you, before you get them back?"

"What do you mean?" the man asked.

"We just got them back from CID, and I was wondering if you wanted us to launder them for you?"

Steager looked at Adam and he knew what he was getting at. "No. That's okay."

"Well," Adam added, "they're not in the best of shape. She...when..."

"I changed her diapers hundreds of times Deputy Thompson. I think I can handle this."

"Yes, sir," Adam nodded. "I understand."

"Do you?" Steager said, as he took the bag from Adam.

"No, sir," Adam said.

Steager nodded toward the snowman. "Got it for half price, last January. She practically threw a fit for me to buy it. She said she couldn't wait to see it lit up this Christmas."

Adam was silent.

"I don't know why I'm putting it up," he looked back at Adam, as if he was going to give him the answer. "I told some people I was going to put it up, and they said she'll be able to see it."

"Yes, sir," Adam agreed, out of politeness.

Mr. Steager looked down at the ground, completely defeated. "You and I both know that's bullshit."

David Steager, took the last remnants of his little girl, contained in that brown paper bag, back into their home and closed the door.

CHAPTER TWENTY-FIVE

The Messenger
"Thursday, December 19th, 8:15 pm"

Adam continued his roaming around the city. He thought about going by Langtree's apartment, but he was afraid he might scare him off. He knew CID and the fugitive unit, and who knows all else, were working on locating him. He forced himself to relax and calm his mind. He stopped at a convenience store and got a bottled Dr. Pepper, but that was the only time out of his car. Sometimes he liked going into stores or restaurants just because people looked at him. They wondered what he was or what he was doing. Wearing plain clothes with a gun and badge on his belt. The only real clothing restrictions for mental heath were no blue jeans, different colored jeans were okay, no ties that looped around the neck, clip-ons were okay, and nothing bright red. The real psychotics didn't like red. They didn't like it, *at all*. As far as the neckties, it was too easy for someone to get a hold of it around your throat and choke you to death; the clip-ons simply snapped off. Adam had heard Wayne Davidson, another mental health deputy on the radio earlier. He apparently took care of the fecal smearing transient call and was checked out at the county hospital with the subject. Adam was glad Wayne was busy. Wayne had been around for a long time and Adam was sure he was just waiting for the chance to talk to him to give him his advice on how to handle the Robert crisis. Wayne's advice, while usually entertaining, was usually wrong and Adam didn't feel like dealing with him just yet. Wayne seemed to wake up in a new world everyday, never having learned anything from the prior day's events. Adam was content just admiring the Christmas lights.

Adam's pager suddenly beeped and jarred him back into reality. He looked down at the tiny screen and it read, "PHONE DISP. 4 CALL."

Adam chose his radio instead, "Unit 1273, do you have a call for Mental Health?"

"10-4," dispatch said. "10-63, deliver message."

"Go ahead," Adam replied.

"2410 Gaston Avenue, contact Bonnie Curtis, inform her to call the New Mexico Highway Patrol. She has had a death in the family. I'll send you a text message in your pager."

Adam shook his head. "10-4, en route." He hated this part of mental health. Whenever victim's services or the coroner's office was too busy, they always deferred to mental health. They assumed since mental health dealt with emotionally disturbed people, they would automatically be able to handle emotionally distraught people; this is where family death notifications came in. That simply was not the case. Mental heath had a general idea for how to break it to them slowly. Prepare them, so to speak, for tragic news but they were never really trained for it. It was hit and miss, on-the-job training. Disturbed and distraught were two totally different things.

His pager beeped and he pulled it from the clip on his belt. It read, "HAVE CURTIS CALL SGT. RALSTON NM HIGHWAY PATROL REF. DEATH 16 YEAR OLD SON, JAMES CURTIS 1820 HRS. THIS DATE."

"Shit."

Adam looked up Gaston in the map-book and started that way. It was in a nicer neighborhood than most. West of the city a few miles, nestled in a hill country gated community. Most of the homes were in the three to four hundred thousand dollar range and housed some of the city's most prominent figures. All of the houses were elaborately decorated with not only lights on every eave, but full productions in their yards. Grazing electric reindeer, Santa and his elves, sleighs on rooftops, Jesuses and mangers, wise men and camels. The whole community in complete, fervent Christmas competition. Adam pulled onto Gaston and noticed cars parked on both sides of the street. He drove slowly halfway down the block looking for number 2410.

There were a lot of people wearing dark suits and long dresses, walking to and from the lines of parked cars carrying Christmas packages. He got a strange feeling in his stomach. As he slowed in front of 2410 Gaston Avenue, his fears were realized. There was a Christmas party at 2410. Bonnie Curtis was having a Christmas party. Adam drove on up the street a few houses and then pulled into an empty driveway. He sat contemplating, *what do I do?* He couldn't just leave. Come back later or maybe tomorrow. This had to be done now. Not on the phone, in person. He thought about calling a supervisor, but he knew what they would say. "Deliver the message."

"Unit 1273, hold me out on Gaston," he said to dispatch.

"1273, 10-4."

Adam got out of his car and straightened his clothes. Adjusted his badge and gun, and checked his face in the car's side mirror. He wanted to look as professional as he could; he didn't want to go up there with a big zit on his face, or with a booger showing. This was going to be difficult enough as it was without looking like a slob that's been doing nothing but riding around in his car for the past few hours. As he approached the house, he felt the general stare he received whenever he went anywhere. People slowed down to watch what he was doing. Gawking and making the same ole joke as he got near, "I didn't do it," holding their hands up. There was a gathering of finely dressed people on the front porch as Adam arrived. Most of them looking, trying to see why there was an "undercover" cop at the door.

"Sorry to bother you, but is Mrs. Curtis here?" Adam asked the crowd.

A bit of confusion moved across the porch as the partygoers looked among one-another to find Curtis. Finally, after a lot of talking, one of the men stepped through and laughed, "Did we get a loud music complaint already?"

The crowd broke out into laughter and this encouraged the newly elected comedian of the party, "Or are you here because were are double parked?"

Adam smiled flatly. "No, I'm here to speak to Mrs. Curtis."

Bonnie's name was being repeated throughout the crowd as more people were arriving in the yard and gathering behind Adam.

Another man came out of the crowd, "Are ya shutting us down already?" Then another added, "Come on in an have some nog." Laughter. "Are ya'll so busy they have to send out detectives to investigate loud parties?"

"Will someone find Mrs. Curtis for me?" Adam asked again.

A well-dressed man in his mid-fifties stepped from a sea of people. "I'm Gary Whitehead, Bonnie's husband. What can I do for you?"

Adam shook his hand. "Adam Thompson, Travis County Sheriff's Office. May I speak to you in private, sir?"

Gary looked concerned, then addressed the people on the porch, "Go on in. It's cold out here, go on," and pointed at the door.

The two men stepped farther out in the yard. "Mr. Whitehead, do you and Mrs. Curtis have any children?"

"We both have, from previous marriages, why?" he said.

"Is James your biological son?"

"No, James lives with his father, he and his mother don't get along too well. Is he in some sort of trouble?"

"Well, Mr. Whitehead…" Adam was going to explain, but was cut off from the crowd still on the porch.

"Officer—Officer, Bonnie is right here," someone said.

A woman in a long, glittering, red dress sporting a Santa hat walked through the crowd. She was smiles from ear to ear, apparently very pleased with the turnout of her gathering. She called out to her husband, "Darling, are we being too loud?"

"No, the officer wants to—"

Adam panicked; he wanted the man to shut-up.

"—talk to you about James," he finished.

Adam walked toward the woman. "I'm sorry to bother you, I am Adam Thompson."

"What has James done?" she crossed her arms.

More people were arriving at the party.

Adam stepped closer to Mrs. Curtis so he would not have to shout over the noise of the crowd. "Is there somewhere we can talk?"

"Right here is just fine Officer Tomas, what has he done?"

Adam didn't have the heart to correct her, and continued, "Mrs. Curtis, James hasn't done anything. Is there somewhere we can talk in private?"

"As you can see I am in the middle of a party. James lives with his father in San Leanna and he's in New Mexico for the holidays, so if there is a problem, you need to contact him."

"No, ma'am, please is there somewhere we can talk?"

It finally registered to her. Adam was not there for suspicion reasons. Something was wrong with James. "What's wrong?" she asked. "Did something happen?"

The crowd was now strangely quiet.

Adam thought of what to say, "Is there some where we can talk?"

"Right here," she blurted. "What's happened? Is he all right?"

Adam was committed now. He didn't seem to have any recourse. She was obviously not going to accompany him anywhere, where they might talk in private. She was going to force him to say it. Right here, and right now.

"Mrs. Curtis, James was in a car accident this evening."

A woman behind her came up and put an arm around her shoulder. "Is he alright?" she asked again.

"It was a bad wreck," Adam said.

"Is he okay?" she asked a third time.

"The ambulance and doctors worked very hard," Adam continued. He was trained to give them a little at a time. Let them absorb it in stages, not all at once.

"Where is he? Is he okay?" She demanded.

"No, ma'am, he is not okay. Is there somewhere we can talk in private?"

The crowd gathered completely around them now.

Her face scowled as she hissed, "Tell me where he is!"

"I have a telephone number for you to call with the State Police."

"You tell me right now. Is my son okay?!" she shouted.

"No, ma'am, they couldn't save him," Adam answered.

Gary walked over to her and tried to put his arm around his wife, but she pushed him away. "Stop it! What are you saying?"

Adam didn't want to say it. He had a huge lump in his throat. Every face that stared at him for the answers to her questions reflected her same anger, and the more pressing question that ran through their heads, *why had this cop come to ruin our party?*

She stepped toward Adam, "Tell me!"

"Your son died this evening." There, he said it. It didn't seem as hard as he thought. It just came out.

She stood, shocked by Adam's words and then pointed her finger toward the street. "Get out of my yard! Get out of here!"

A woman behind her struggled with her for an embrace. At first Mrs. Curtis resisted, but the other woman was a good friend and pressed harder. Then Bonnie Curtis broke down, collapsing into the arms of the angry crowd.

Adam turned to her husband. "Here is the contact information." He handed him a mental health card with the names and numbers on the back. "Is there anything I can do?"

"I think you've done enough," a woman in a blue dress said, scowling. Most of the crowd looked like they were going to start throwing rocks any minute.

Mr. Whitehead took the card. "I don't know, I don't think so," he said reading Adam's writing. "They'll tell us what we need to do?"

"Yes, sir," Adam said.

He and Mr. Whitehead shook hands again, and at that very moment, Adam could tell in his eyes, he understood what a bad position they had forced him into.

"Thank you," he said, and returned to the crowd to find his wife.

Adam turned and headed back to his car. He watched the ground, not making eye contact with anyone he neared. More and more people passed him, walking toward the party, looking forward to the food and fellowship. A gathering most of them are only afforded once a year and Adam had just shattered it. Adam knew it wasn't his fault. He didn't have anything to do with the wreck or choosing when to deliver the message. But still, he couldn't help feel somehow responsible about how the message was delivered. Was there a better way to do it? Had he been assertive enough to control the situation, or did the situation control him. If he tried to force her someplace where they could have talked privately, would he have caused more problems? None of these questions could be answered, but his mind wondered anyway.

He drove his car back up the street and out of the community. He felt weak, his hands were shaking and his mouth was dry. It was a feeling very common to him, but not yet a comfortable one. Maybe with a few more years of experience, he would graduate to the numb, veteran status.

He never wanted to do that again.

Adam picked up his microphone, "Unit 1273, message delivered, back in service. Do you have anything holding?"

"Unit 1273, 10-4," dispatch said. "1618 Buckner—1618 Buckner, EDP, reported to the 911 call-taker he was going to kill himself if we did not send someone out to speak with him."

He reflected on the beginning of the evening and appreciated his few hours of calm. He also knew he had only been lingering in the eye of the storm.

"1273, 10-4, en route."

CHAPTER TWENTY-SIX

The Reaction
"Thursday, December 19th, 9:45 pm"

Buckner Road was in the middle of old town. The main section of the housing development was built in the late forties to accommodate the oncoming baby boom. These old houses had half acre yards that today's developers could only dream of and huge trees, completely vacant from most of the city's absorbed farm lands. Adam slowed, trying to read the street numbers, either on the curbs or houses. Most of the trees in the front yards loomed over the street giving it an archway effect. Many of the street lights were above the sparse tree limbs and blocked the lights from reaching the pavement. They left dancing shadows as the wind moved through them. About halfway down the block on the left, Adam could see a figure standing by the road. As he approached, the figure turned and walked slowly back toward the darkened residence. Adam used his side-mounted spotlight and brightened the curb, 1618 Buckner. He pulled his car to the side and stopped.

"Unit 1273, I'm on scene," he reported to dispatch.

"Unit 1273, 10-4."

Adam got his flashlight and stepped out of the car. The night was getting much colder. He reached in the back seat and got out his official mental health jacket. The brown windbreaker was unmistakable; a large yellow sheriff's department badge on the left breast pocket, and huge, gold letters on the back, SHERIFF'S MENTAL HEALTH. He pulled it on, adjusted his belt and walked to

183

the dark figure who was now sitting on the steps of the house's front porch. He turned on the flashlight and held the beam down at the man's feet, as not to blind him, but for Adam to be able to see anything strange or any weapons. The shadows from the tree limbs reached across the yard and the night was quiet, except for some sirens in the far off distance.

"Good evening, I'm Adam Thompson with the Mental Health Unit," he introduced himself.

The man on the steps just sat, staring at the ground. He was a small man, thin and weathered. Adam guessed him to be in his mid-twenties, even though he physically looked to be forty; mental illness sometimes does that to a body; the stress and medication seem to compound the years. He was dressed in a pair of old, dirty Converse tennis shoes, faded blue sweat pants, and a thin flannel button-up shirt. His hands were trembling, and he kept reaching up and pulling at his face as if there was a spider web tickling it, and he couldn't wipe it away. Adam scanned around with his light and didn't see anything unusual or particularly alarming.

"What's your name?"

"Randy."

"Did you call the Sheriff's Department?" Adam asked.

"Yeah," he grunted. "No, I called," he thought for a moment, "911."

"What can I help you with?" Adam asked. It was pretty obvious the man was confused, but sometimes people put on an act for some unknown motivation or manipulation. The fact that he called on himself could be an indicator there is more to the story, and Adam was going to find out.

"Nothing. Everything. I'm not on my meds. My mom's driving me crazy."

"Is your mom here?"

Randy threw a hitchhiker's thumb over his shoulder toward the front door. Adam pointed his light up and sure enough, Randy's little gray haired mother was peeking out.

She saw Adam's jacket and leaned out of the door. "Are you here to help him?" her feeble voice quivered.

"Yes, ma'am," Adam answered.

"He's not taking his medicine and—"

Randy blurted, "I just told him that, Mom!"

She recoiled back into the door.

"Are you okay? Everything inside okay?" Adam asked her.

"Yes, sir. Just help him; he's a good boy, he—"

Randy snapped again, "Go back inside Ma!"

The door closed.

Adam waited to see if Randy would initiate a conversation, but after a minute he decided to begin where he left off.

"So why did you call us?"

"I don't feel right. My mom says I ain't actin' right." He rubbed at his face.

"Tell me what you mean by right."

"I keep hearin' things, things they say ain't there. Things crawlin' on me. I can't hardly stand it. I need to go back. I know I do." He rubbed up and down his foot.

"Let me take a look at you, Randy," Adam said, as he moved closer. He took his light and shined it on Randy's face. By the look of him, he could actually have something crawling on him. Adam looked for bugs or anything else that might be giving him these feelings. He didn't see anything.

Randy looked up at him, "What's all that?"

"What?" Adam asked.

"Them sirens, they're getting loud."

"I don't know; they sound only a block or two away. So do you think you want to hurt yourself?"

"If I don't get no help, I know I will," Randy assured him.

"Are you willing to sign yourself into the Crisis Stabilization Unit?"

"Yeah, I need something; it ain't right."

"Come on over here and I'll have my dispatch make sure they have a bed for you, before we get going," Adam said, motioning toward the car. "You don't have any weapons on you, do you?"

"Naw," Randy said, getting up from the step.

"Turn around and let me check, okay?" Adam instructed.

Randy turned around and put his hands up; he knew the drill. Adam checked around the top of his shirt, his sleeves, around his waist, then down to his shoes; nothing.

"Okay, come on over here," Adam said, and the two men walked back to his car. Adam retrieved the microphone and called dispatch, "Unit 1273, contact CSU and see if they have a bed for one male subject."

"Unit 1273, stand-by," dispatch said.

"It'll be just a minute, Randy. Have you done a voluntary commitment before?"

"No, they usually arrest me. But I'm tryin' to do the right thing. I know somethin's wrong," Randy said, as they both stood in the yard near the car.

Adam looked down the street and saw lights coming from some police cars running their sirens. "Looks like they're coming this way."

Randy looked up and watched.

"Unit 1273, CSU is saving a bed for you," dispatched advised.

"10-4, I'll be en route shortly."

"Randy," Adam asked, "is there anything you need to get out of the house or take with you?"

"No."

"No medication or anything?" Adam asked loudly, as the speeding, screaming police cars got closer.

"What?" Randy asked.

Adam motioned to him to wait until the cars passed by to resume their conversation. However, that wasn't going to happen. More police cars came up the street from the other direction followed by an ambulance. All of them were slowing and converging on Randy's house.

Adam and Randy stood motionless in the yard as the officers screeched to a halt and came bounding out of their cars, pistols drawn. Three of the officers ran directly over to them, guns trained, shouting assorted commands, "Get on the ground!" "Put your hands up!" "Put your hands where I can see them!" "Don't fucking move!" "Step away from the car!"

Adam held his hands in the air and one of the officers shined a light in his face, "Who are you?"

"Deputy Thompson, Mental Health," Adam answered. He could make out Randy's silhouette in the light and hear another officer asking Randy his name. Randy got half of it out before several other officers grabbed him by his arms and forced him to the ground. Randy started screaming, but there was nothing Adam could do for him. There was a lot of yelling behind him, around Randy's house. Adam could see several more officers had surrounded the residence and two were knocking on the front door.

"I talked with his moth—" Adam tried to say, but was cut off.

"Just hold on. Stay right where you are!" said the officer, holding the light in his face.

Adam stood there with his arms in the air, flashlight still in his left hand, blinded by the officer's flashlight. He was getting a little pissed. He could hear the officers interrogating the poor old woman about what happened here, tonight. They asked if anyone had been hurt and to search through her house to see that everything was all right. After a minute or two things seemed to calm down and the officers' pistols returned to their holsters. He heard an officer call out, "Code 4," and all of them started gathering around Randy.

"May I put my hands down now?" Adam smiled.

The officer took the light out of Adam's eyes, but didn't answer, just turned and walked over to Randy.

As his eyes adjusted to the darkness, Adam could see Randy face down in the yard with his hands cuffed behind him. Randy was sobbing to the point of hyperventilation. The officers surrounding him were all questioning him at once. "What is your name?" "Do you live here?" "Did you call 911?" "Hey look up here."

Adam looked at the crowd of officers and asked, "Hey, what's going on?"

They stopped asking Randy questions and looked at Adam. One officer, a short fat woman in her mid-thirties asked, "Are you with MHMR?"

"No, I'm with the Sheriff's Mental Health Unit," Adam answered, as if talking to a child. He knew most city officers didn't know the difference between mental heath investigators and mental retardation caseworkers, but he was going to be as difficult as they were.

Then a barrage of questions assaulted him. "Why are you here?" one officer asked. "Did you talk to his family?" another said. And other questions were asked too, but Adam didn't hear them clearly. He couldn't believe the situation.

"Who the hell is in charge here?" Adam asked.

It caught them off guard, but silenced their attempts at cross-examination. Adam looked around at the officers surrounding him and Randy. Slowly, an older sergeant with a gray handle bar mustache stepped through his ring of uniforms. "I guess I am," he said, after taking a long, Clint Eastwood drag from his smoldering cigar.

"So, what the hell's going on; what has this guy done?" Adam asked.

The sergeant stepped up and took another drag. "He called 911 and said he had just killed his whole family and was going to kill himself."

Adam looked down. "Is that what you did, Randy?"

"I called the sheriff," he sobbed. "And no one came, so I tried to make them hurry up, and called—" he huffed, "911 to make them hurry. I wasn't going to, but I wanted you to hurry."

"Well, you're obviously in control of this situation. Do you mind me asking what you're going to do with him?" Adam asked.

"He's going to jail," a short, little muscled-up officer said.

Adam searched the darkness for the man who spoke. "For what?"

The tiny Hercules answered, "False report."

"You've got to be shitting me. False report because he didn't kill his family or because he didn't kill himself?"

One of the other officers joined in, "He's going to jail because he called 911 and mobilized half our shift for no reason."

"I can understand that if this was a prank, but this man is a mental patient off his medications. Do you actually think you can get a conviction on a mental patient for a misdemeanor?"

"You can beat the rap, but you can't beat the ride," the fat little female said.

Adam laughed, "That's fucking beautiful."

"What do you propose, deputy?" the sergeant calmly asked. He knew things were a little out of control, but he wasn't about to admit it, just calmly rein it in.

"To serve and protect, for one."

"What does that suppose to mean?" another officer from the crowd asked.

"The man is mentally ill. You're going to waste everyone's time and through him in jail to teach him a lesson? That makes absolutely no sense. A judge is not going to allow the prosecution."

"And if we don't file charges, what then?" the sergeant asked.

"I've already arranged a bed for him at the Crisis Stabilization Unit and we were about to be en route, but we were delayed."

"Why don't you go ahead and do that, deputy," the sergeant said.

One of the arresting officers stepped up. "Let's go ahead and change out cuffs."

"That's okay, just uncuff him," Adam said.

The officer shook his head and reached down to remove the cuffs. Adam assisted the terrified man to his feet. Randy stood there, snot and slobber dripping to his belly. His breathing came in gulping spasms.

Adam took his shoulders and forced him to look into his eyes. "Randy, I want you to calm down. Calm yourself down."

The crowd of officers watched.

"Look at me. You're okay. It was a misunderstanding." Randy diverted his eyes. "Look at me. Will you go get in my back seat? Randy. Go get in my back seat, okay."

Randy turned and stumbled over to Adam's car. It seemed like an eternity for him to get there as Adam reached into his wallet and pulled a business card, pretending not to be paying attention to him. He silently prayed Randy wouldn't freak or turn and run. Adam so much wanted to seem the ultimate professional and be totally in control. To give the appearance he knew exactly what he was doing, although once again, he chose to roll the dice. He wanted the other officers to see his confidence. No one could know what someone was going to do at any given moment. Especially a season ticket holder to the disorient express, but Adam could still hope.

As Adam wrote the case number on the back of the card and handed it to the sergeant, Randy silently tucked himself onto the cold, vinyl seat of Adam's car.

Adam looked at the crowd. "Is there anything else I can do for you?"

A couple of the officers huffed and turned to leave, and the sergeant looked at the card. "No, I think that's it."

Adam returned to his car and started it.

"It's cold in here," Randy stammered, through his sobbing.

"Yeah, I'll get it heated up here in a sec."

"Why did they do that?"

"Hold on Randy," Adam picked up his microphone. "Unit 1273, I'm en route to CSU with one."

Dispatch answered, "10-4, I'm on the phone with PD. Are you going to be assisting them on this call?"

"10-4, Yeah, I'm *assisting* them."

"County's clear, 22:30 hours."

CHAPTER TWENTY-SEVEN

The Concealment
"Thursday, December 19th, 11:23 pm"

Adam dropped Randy off at the Crisis Stabilization Unit without incident. They went in admissions, filed the voluntary commitment, and Randy signed it; end of story. After wishing him luck, Adam headed home and was looking forward to a calm evening where he could relax and maybe watch some late night TV. That was a rarity for him. Usually he worked too late or was simply too tired to stay awake. Not tonight though. Tonight he would have to wind down some. He had a bottle of vodka and thought about making a big drink.

He hadn't thought about Robert much today. The news reports kept reminding him of Edward Langtree, and that he was still, as the media said, "on the run." There were reported sightings of him around town but no real leads. Adam was thinking he skipped town. Since he was such a traveler, he thought Edward might have moved on. He at least *seemed* to have moved off into obscurity.

Adam started to pull into his apartment's front lot where he normally parked, but saw Michele's Mustang next to his normal space. He swerved back onto the road.

"Shit."

He pulled around to the back lot, behind the dumpsters where he hoped she wouldn't look and pulled in. Now, it was just a matter of getting inside his apartment without being detected. A stealthy operation under the cover of darkness. While being an irritation, it was also a challenge, and he liked that. He crept along the back walkway, all the way to the side of his front door. He looked toward her apartment before he moved. Her lights were on, but he didn't see any activity. He went for the door and fumbled with his key, trying to get it into the lock. In the dark, he had chosen the wrong one and searched through the bundle again. Getting it right this time, it easily slid in and the door opened. He zipped in and closed it back, standing in darkness. He reached for the light, but decided against it, letting his eyes adjust to the darkness. The side streetlight helped some, illuminating the windows, and soon Adam was able to go about his business in secret. After changing into just a pair of sweat pants, he went to the refrigerator to fix the long awaited screwdriver, but there was no orange juice. He looked under the cabinet and found a single plastic bottle of cranberry juice. That and the vodka would have to do. It wasn't something he would ever order in a bar, but after mixing it, he thought it was one of the best drinks he ever tasted. He walked over, got his apartment pager off the desk, and turned it on to check the messages. Michele's number came up first. Then second, third, fourth, and…

"Shit."

Instead of turning on the TV and sending the blue light signal that he was home, he turned on the stereo, very low, sat back on the couch savoring his drink.

Robert's funeral was going to be Saturday. He thought all the mental health officers would have to be bearers sitting up front during the ceremony. That would only be natural. He was dreading the whole ordeal. It was a terrible thing, Adam knew, but he couldn't help but think Robert really caused a lot of problems. Adam knew being a pallbearer was simply an inconvenience to him, but it was also the loss of a husband and a father to someone else. Total devastation to someone else. He was never close to Robert or Marla, but felt guilty for not calling or stopping by the funeral home to pay his respects. He was sure everyone wondered where he was and why he hadn't come by. He just didn't want the attention. He didn't want to be the focus of their sympathies and they would need to show their sympathy. He would be the likely target with everyone wanting to tell him it wasn't his fault, but deep down imagining he could have, should have done something more. Adam knew it wasn't his fault, but they didn't.

Growing up as the youngest child, Adam hadn't needed to share time with anyone, work out a schedule, or be responsible to anyone other than himself. It was much simpler that way. Much more convenient.

Adam woke up around four in the morning. He staggered to his feet and put the empty glass in the sink. After turning off the radio and relieving his aching bladder, he crawled under his wool blanket passing the rest of the night.

Adam slept soundly except for the dreams of a stretching rope, a jaundiced eye, and being trapped in a stainless steel kennel with no water or food.

CHAPTER TWENTY-EIGHT

A Phone Call
"Friday, December 20th, 9:12 am"

Adam pulled the phone to his ear, "Yeah?" The ringing still continued in his head.

"Are you awake?" the voice asked.

"Who is this?"

"Drew. What are you doing?"

Drew was Adam's old patrol partner. They had attended the same academy class and started out on the street together. Drew was promoted to detective two years ago and Adam went to mental health shortly after. They were like brothers on the street, but now kept in touch only through the periodic dial of the phone.

"I'm trying to sleep; what do you want?" Adam growled.

"Just checking if you are still alive. Everyone keeps asking me about you and I don't have anything to tell them."

"Tell them to stick it," Adam said, half in the phone and half in his pillow.

"What?"

"Tell them I'm fine," he said.

"Hey, you know in mental health, be direct and people will believe you are taking them serious, so, are you thinking of hurting yourself?"

Adam laughed, "Fuck off."

"No, I'm serious, man," Drew changed his tone. "You doing okay? Seems like you've been avoiding everybody."

"Are you serious?" Adam asked, sitting up in his bed.

"Yeah. I'm just checking."

"Okay, let's see, yeah. I'm okay. And no, I'm not thinking of hurting myself. I am thinking about killing you for waking me up, so that means I have future plans, thus eliminating any immediate threat to myself and disqualifying me for an emergency commitment!"

"Okay—thanks—nice talking to you—bye," the dial tone quickly replaced Drew's voice.

Adam blindly returned the receiver to its housing and dove back into his pillow.

CHAPTER TWENTY-NINE

The Appointment
"Friday, December 20th, 2:50 pm"

Adam pulled his car into the busy afternoon traffic. It seemed that today everyone was getting off early from work. Four days before Christmas, they were all doing their last minute shopping. Adam could see sacks, boxes, and wrapped packages in the commuters' cars. Everyone seemed to be heading someplace quickly to do something important. Not only was it four days before Christmas, it was only one day before Robert's funeral. Adam didn't want to deal with Robert. He didn't want to deal with the emotions. He didn't want to deal with the grief and the impending hugs and condolences from friends and strangers that should be directed at his family, not Adam. He had effectively avoided most of these good intentioned utterances by staying on the road, out of the office, and keeping busy. It was partly due to working the three to eleven shift. The majority of his avoidances had to occur for only two hours, until these emotional supporters decided eight hours in a day was enough and went home at five o'clock sharp. He was still waiting for the unavoidable statement some well-wisher was going to make, assuring that it wasn't Adam's fault. Adam practiced his response over and over, in many different ways, in different tones, and with assorted emotions. He could hear them say, "I so sorry, Adam," then imagine them putting their arm on his shoulder. "It wasn't your fault." Adam knew damn good and well it wasn't his fault, but he still hadn't perfected his response. Sometimes, when he thought of it, and he thought of it a lot, he would get mad and scold the sympathetic idiot with a series of reasons why he knew it wasn't his fault. Usually, this retort contained a series of colorful adjectives not suitable for the situation. Other times his fantasies were a calmer and more calculated justification for why he didn't feel guilty or in the least bit responsible. There were, in the past two days, a couple of times Adam thought he should have stayed with Edward and helped Robert check him a little closer. Run some out of state background investigations. That wasn't the protocol in the past, but maybe now the mental health unit should adopt a new set of procedures to avoid this situation in the future.

"Unit 1273, assist complainant," the radio called.

"1273, go ahead," Adam answered, already knowing what they wanted. As a mental health officer, there are an assorted, but limited number of calls you are dispatched: emotionally disturbed persons, check welfare, deliver message, and the occasional assist complainant. The mental health assist complainant call was usually dispatched due to one of the dispatcher's favorite, and well known, emotionally disturbed people. The EDP that constantly assaults 911 call takers with the reports of attic noises, bombarding radio waves, poisons sprinkled in their yards and water sources, and the various other paranoid delusions such persons entertain. These EDPs are usually the uncommittable kind, that while being a day-to-day nuisance, do not meet the criteria for protective custody and cannot be charged criminally for false report because they actually believe what they are saying.

"1273, 1505 San Leanna Drive, meet with Myrtle Cowan in reference to paratroopers landing in her back yard."

Adam imagined the laughter of the people around the county that were listening to the radio on their scanners. "10-4, en route," he said and headed south toward the outskirts of the city and to San Leanna.

Adam knew Myrtle Cowan well. She was one of the first EDPs Robert introduced to him. Myrtle was a wonderful woman. She had been the dutiful wife of an Air Force long-range bomber pilot, mother to three boys and one girl, a Sunday school teacher, a piano player, and the survivor of the random deaths of her entire family. To begin, she lost her husband in Vietnam, but preferred to believe he took up house keeping with a gay lover and retreated to France. Her first son died from cancer, the second to a car accident, and the third to AIDS, and her beautiful baby girl to toxemia during her first pregnancy. She was a woman left utterly alone and that didn't sit well with her, and wouldn't sit well with most. It effected a change in her.

Adam pulled into Myrtle's apartment complex and around to her front door. An old-fashioned cardboard Rudolph and Santa were taped to the door and mistletoe adorned the threshold.

"Unit 1273, 10-23," he advised.

"1273, 10-4, on scene at 15:15 hours," dispatch responded.

Adam drew his pistol and slid it under the seat, slipped off his badge and holster, and got out. He scanned the area, just to make sure she wasn't out making her regular security checks for unauthorized spaceships or other suspicious activities. She had learned reconnaissance techniques from her husband. The sidewalk was clear and everything looked normal, whatever that was. He walked to her door and listened for a moment. Myrtle was never violent, but as a mental health officer, one can never be too careful. He knocked on the door and immediately the door creaked. Adam could tell she was looking at him through the peephole.

"Adam?" she said.

"The one and only," he answered.

The rattle of chains, the clack of opening dead bolts and the jiggle of the knob preceded the slow opening of her door. Her grandmother's hand reached out, gripped him by the jacket and pulled him into the house.

"Hurry, hurry, come in," she squawked.

Adam stepped into her entry and she immediately went back to securing the door. Adam looked around at the apartment. She lived in a nice apartment, had expensive things, and kept the entire place spotless. Adam saw the white shag carpet and couch, a tan leather, overstuffed chair, her coffee table, end tables, and television. Everything looked perfect except one little matter of concern; it was all turned upside down. The couch, the leather chair, the coffee table, end tables, and television, *all* upside down. Adam turned back to her as she set the last lock and started to say something, but he immediately forgot what it was. She turned and smiled. She was a sixty-year old, mirrored refinement of Lauren Becall, tall and blond with elegant streaks of gray and delicate lines pointing to green eyes that held back the sea of her emotions. She stood before him in brown leather shoes, a forest green jacket and pants, wearing a stainless steel colander wrapped with aluminum foil on her head.

"Did you see them?"

"Myrtle, there are no paratroopers in your yard," Adam said calmly. "You don't even have a yard; you live in an apartment." Then he pointed at her helmet. "Why?"

"You know damn good and well, why," she said and walked into the kitchen.

"Aircraft?" Adam asked.

"Of course. You know he tells them to point their lasers at the house and they go straight into my head. Him and his lover, point them right into my head," she tapped on the colander.

"Myrtle," he said, sitting down at the bar separating the kitchen from the living room, "you live in the flight path of the new airport. *They* are not shooting lasers at you, at least not from there."

She pulled the lid off the pot of stew boiling on the stove and stirred it. "They are watching, and they've been coming through the medicine cabinet. It opens into an entire operation command post!"

Adam pointed to the couch. "Why?"

She got out two large bowls, a can of Coke, and began ladling out the stew. "I had to go to the store and I didn't want those bastards to come in here and be comfortable. If they want to come in here, they can sit on the floor. Look—" she set the ladle down and walked down the hall to the bathroom. Adam followed. "In here," she said, and opened the medicine cabinet.

Adam nodded his head. "Yep, big command post, large enough for an entire squad of green, plastic army men between the aspirin and Pepto-Bismol."

"Smart-aleck!" she snapped, moving the bottles around and checking if the back wall of the cabinet had a hatch door. "It was a room!" She turned and stomped back into the kitchen. "CIA bastards."

Adam followed and sat back down at the bar as she placed the bowl in front of him. He stirred the steaming clumps in the broth and waited as she cut the cornbread. "It smells great."

"Thank you," she said, as if expecting the compliment before now. She slid the hot buttered slice onto a small saucer and joined him at the bar. "Eat, eat, eat," she pointed with her spoon.

Adam shoveled and enjoyed. She always prepared something different. He had known her over a year now and followed this routine religiously, once a week. *Except* for the few weeks she spent in the Caravelle Hospital, it was a ritual. There was one good thing in her favor, her husband had taken care of her. She wasn't rich, but he arranged enough money for her to live on the rest of her life, and she had good health insurance. That made all the difference in the world in mental health care, health insurance. Without it a person is a number at the will of a state paid psychiatrist, and seven dollar-an-hour ward keepers.

They didn't talk until the last of their bowls were drained and the cornbread had disappeared. She taught Adam that there was no room for talking if you are eating good food.

"They came through the attic, too," she said.

"The attic?" Adam pointed up.

"Yes, I know you never believe me, but they came through the attic."

"How?"

"You're the detective, you tell me?"

"I'm not a detective, remember?"

"Whatever. I took the rest of my flour and sprinkled it up there. Go look for your self; you'll see the footprints…In the flour."

"Myrtle, you did that six months ago."

"I know when I did it," she reached under her colander and scratched her head. "Go look."

"Isn't that thing hot?"

"Don't change the subject and go look."

Adam checked it for her, every time he came over, but he still liked giving her a hard time about it. Sometimes, he thought she might know better. Know that her delusions were just that, delusions. But sometimes he believed it was easier for her to go with them, than fight them. That way she avoided her past and postponed the present. Adam thought about how he handled Susan, his avoidance of Michele, and his disassociation with Robert. Was hers as easy as his? Just disconnect?

Adam walked back to her laundry room and pulled down the attic stairs. Myrtle moved her clothesbasket out of the way so he could work. He climbed up, pulled the string for the light and looked around the attic.

"What the—Hey, let me see your hands," Adam commanded. "Get them up!"

Myrtle stumbled back then started to run out of the room, then looked back at him as her colander-helm fell down in front of her eyes, "Are you, if…"

Adam looked down to her. "There's a whole platoon of paratroopers up here, call the Pentagon!"

"You jackass!" She pointed up at him and scowled. "Get down from there, get down this instant!"

Adam made his way back down, never taking his eyes off her. She adjusted her colander and kept her finger pointing at him. "You, you…Oh, you think I'm full of crap!"

"No, ma'am," he smiled.

She stared straight at him, and they both broke out into laughter.

"You're a little shit!" she said, and walked back to the kitchen.

Adam folded the stairs back into the attic and went and found her putting away the dishes. He sat back at the bar and watched, sipping on his Coke.

She glanced up. "You're a jackass," she said and closed the cabinet doors.

Adam asked, "Are you taking your medicine?"

"No! It makes me feel like crap."

"You know, I will put you in the hospital if you get worse. If you scare me."

"I'm not going back to the hospital," she said.

"I'm not saying now. I only mean if."

"I know. And I'm saying, I'm not going back to the hospital."

"You know," Adam changed the subject, "in another time and another place, I would have given George a run for his money."

"My dear, young Adam, Mr. Cowan would have kicked your ass." She sipped her Coke.

Adam smiled, then stood. "Thanks, I've got to get going. Do I need to write a report on this heinous incident?"

"If you do, I will tell you where to file it," she smiled.

He turned toward the door and saw the newspaper sitting on top of the bottom of her end table. Robert's picture covered half of the page. He looked back at her.

"When is the funeral?" she asked.

"Saturday."

"Are you going?"

"I think I have to," he said.

"I might take a taxi."

"You can ride with me, if you want," Adam said, then couldn't believe it came out of his mouth, and he couldn't take it back. He knew the three of them, were—had been, the strangest of friends. Robert wouldn't mind it if she came. He spent extra time with her but not for the same reasons he spent it with other females. With Myrtle, it was so others could admire him for helping out an old widow. But she never knew that and didn't need to know.

"I can?" she said.

"Do you want to?"

"Of course not," she paused, "but apparently, it's what I do best."

"Are you going to freak out?" Adam smiled.

"No," she said. "Are you going to be a jackass?"

"No, I'll see you at eleven o'clock. The family is having a private service and the procession starts at noon."

"You're not going to be a pallbearer?" she asked.

"No," he said gratefully. "They're going to use the honor guard."

"Thank you, Adam."

He smiled and she watched him from the door as he drove away. It was a strange situation, mental health officer and mental patient, together at a funeral. It was almost like they had a date. Each of them looked forward to the time they were going to spend together, but dreading the reason, and each of them needing the other to help lessen the burden. Adam couldn't think of any policy violation or rules against it. Still, he would tell Lt. Martin just in case.

"Unit 1273, I'm back in service, no report."

"Unit 1273, 10-4, 16:31 hours," dispatch advised.

There was a short break in radio silence, then dispatch called again, "Unit 1273, 10-63, assist city department."

"1273, go ahead."

"1273, 275 Capital Circle, meet with city officers, reference family violence."

"1273, 10-4, en route."

CHAPTER THIRTY

The Frustration
"Friday, December 20th, 4:41 pm"

As Adam pulled onto Capital Circle, he saw the scattered patrols cars accompanied by an ambulance. He slowed and pulled behind the closest car.

"Unit 1273, on scene," he advised dispatch.

"1273, 10-4."

He got out and to his surprise, a patrol officer standing in the suspect's yard smiled and walked over to him.

"Mental Health?" he asked.

"Adam Thompson," Adam said, shaking his hand.

"Alan Salter, thanks for coming by so quick; they said it might take you a while."

"Normally it probably does. I just so happened to be in the area. What happened?"

Alan waved him toward the house. "She's still inside, talking to another officer. We got the call from a neighbor who heard screaming from the house. We responded with two units and found the husband stumbling around in the front yard with his front teeth knocked out." He pointed at a trail of blood snaking its way through the grass. "He's over in the ambulance and I think he's going to refuse treatment. Anyway, she's apparently been in the state hospital a bunch of times and supposed to be crazy."

"Do you know what happened?" Adam asked.

"Supposedly, Mr. Spence," he looked down at his notes, "Albert Spence, he works nights, and Wanda his wife, she's accusing him of sleeping around on her. He has to be at work at six in the evening and according to him, she usually wakes him around four. This time she did it with a roofing hammer in the mouth." The officer pointed to the ambulance. "There he is now."

Adam turned around and saw a black man in his mid-fifties stepping down from the back of the van assisted by two paramedics. He was barefoot, wearing a faded pair of loose jeans and a white t-shirt, splattered with drying blood. The man had two rolls of gauze protruding like tandem cigars from either side of his mouth and was trying to say something to another black man in a business suit beside him.

Salter said, "The guy in the suit is the family preacher. He's been trying to excise the demons from the house since he got here."

"Great, demons. Just great…"

"Officer—Officer," the preacher shouted, as he walked toward Adam. "This man's wife has been afflicted by the devil. She don't need no jail time, she don't need no hospital, she needs to come to the church and we will rid her of this evil!"

Adam looked back at Officer Salter. "The evil did it."

Salter smiled, but remained silent.

Adam spoke to the preacher, "Sir, I'd like your help in a minute, but let me talk with Mr. Spence."

The preacher continued as if Adam never said a word, "She don't need no police. She is under a spell!"

Adam stepped around him and addressed Mr. Spence, "Sir, could you step over here for a moment, so we can talk?"

Mr. Spence walked with Adam to the side of the ambulance, and the preacher followed. "God will reward your suffering, Brother Albert, God will—"

Adam turned and winked at Officer Salter and said, "You said your public information officer is still over there?"

Salter caught on; he knew he hadn't said anything to Adam about a PIO. "Yeah, he's waiting on the news crews to show up."

The two officers were right in tune. "Sir," Adam said to the preacher, "could you accompany Officer Salter over to their media area so they can get your information for the news?"

"Yes sir," the preacher smiled. "Lead the way."

Salter smiled at Adam and they headed toward the far end of the yard.

"I know you've already told everyone, but can you tell me what happened?" Adam asked the nearly toothless man.

Mr. Spence spoke surprisingly well with the swelling of his gums, gauze rolls, and the new holes in his mouth. "I ain't pressin' charges," he said.

"Okay, I understand that, but can you tell me what happened?"

"I was asleep, and she hit me in the mouth with a hammer, that's it." He shook his head.

"Is she on any medication?"

"Yeah, she's schizophrenic; she's been takin' all her medicine. I been makin' sure. She's been fine. She's just pissed. She thinks I'm goin' round on her."

Adam looked over at one of the paramedics. "Can you watch him a minute, I'll be right back?"

The medic nodded and Adam walked to the house. He found Wanda Spence sitting calmly at her kitchen table talking with three uniformed patrolmen. The conversation was casual, like anyone would have with a stranger. They were talking about the weather, about food, and what they were going to do for Christmas.

He stepped up and addressed her, "Mrs. Spence, I'm Adam Thompson with mental health."

"Hello, I know most of you mental health deputies, never seen you before, though."

"No, ma'am. Your husband—"

She cut him off, "Albert?"

"Yes, Albert," Adam continued, "said you've been taking your medication?"

"Yes, sir."

"Can you tell me what day it is?"

"Please deputy, you don't need to go through all that. It's Friday, December 20th, around five o'clock, money is green, sky is blue, I don't see no little green men, and don't hear nothing that no one else cain't hear."

Adam smiled and looked at the other officers. "Has anyone read her, her rights?"

One of the officers smiled. "Can I talk with you outside a second."

Adam followed him onto the porch.

"This woman is a fucking nut; we get called here all the time for shit. Call your other guys. They will tell you that she needs to be locked up," the officer advised, in his *professional* opinion.

"I don't doubt she needs to be locked up," Adam agreed. "It just doesn't seem like the hospital is the place she needs to go."

"Jesus Christ," the officer exclaimed. "Alan, come over here a minute."

Alan Salter left the preacher with what he thought was the PIO and joined them on the porch. "What's up?"

"This guy doesn't want to take her," the officer said, thumbing to Adam over his shoulder.

"I didn't say that," Adam corrected. "I said, she needs to be locked up, but not necessarily in the hospital."

"But she's an EDP," Salter said.

"She's obviously a danger to others and has a history," the other officer added.

"Look, last night I was on a call with you guys and they wanted to take a psychotic man to jail for saying he was going to kill his family then didn't do it, charging him with false report. Now today you guys don't want to take a lady to jail after she has committed aggravated assault family violence, which by law, mandates a peace officer in the state of Texas to make the arrest." Adam shrugged his shoulders. "I don't know what to tell you guys."

That pretty much ended the smiling demeanor of Officer Alan Salter. "Thanks for your professional observation."

The other officer added, "He don't want to press charges."

"I'm not trying to be difficult; I'll take her to jail, but she needs to be filed on, whether he wants to press charges or not," Adam said. "It's family violence."

"That's alright, we've got it," Officer Salter said, starting to walk into the house.

"Alan," Adam said, using his first name, trying to defuse the situation. "Family violence mandates the arrest to be made, and as far as the assault, mental illness is a defense to prosecution, not an exemption. She's got to go to jail."

Alan Salter knew it. He knew it before he called the sheriff's department to request the mental health unit. He simply had a brain cramp and didn't think family violence and EDP went together. He knew the arrest was mandated by the family code, but just saw the big letters, EDP, and called the mental health unit.

Adam walked back to his car knowing this would be one more of those stories circulated around by patrol officers, that the MHU doesn't do anything. And how there is no reason to call out mental health, it will take them too long to respond, and when they do, once again, nothing. Most officers did feel this way, mainly because they never heard about most of the calls mental health answered. And even if they cared to share their exploits, the mental health deputies could be charged with releasing information under the Privacy Act, thus further facilitating the lack of information exchange.

Adam had made a friend in Alan Salter one minute and lost him the next. He thought if things had been a little different, he and Salter might have developed a good working relationship but that was gone. He noticed how the officers around the scene were, once again, not making eye contact with him. He was used to that. On most occasions they went about their work without ever even acknowledging he was there. At first it mattered to him; he wanted them to like him. To trust him. To respect him. Now, he was just going to do his best with his knowledge of the law, even if he hurt some feelings. It was their problem, not his.

Adam settled into his vehicle. "Unit 1273, back in service, no report."

"1273, 10-4, are you available for a call?"

"10-4, *I am in service*," he said sarcastically.

"CID wants you to meet them at 7204 Sand Finch, they're out on a deceased person call and requesting you stop by."

It was pretty unusual that homicide detectives would be asking for help from a mental health deputy and this was the second time this week. It usually meant they suspected suicide on the victim's part and just wanted another opinion, that's all.

"1273, 10-4, en route."

CHAPTER THIRTY-ONE

An Expectation
"Friday, December 20th, 5:15 pm"

As Adam drove, he turned on his cell phone and it immediately alerted him to seven missed calls. He hit the forward button and the screen read, ONE NEW NUMBER. He hit enter and there it was, Michele's. He needed to call her. Had to call her. By this time she had to be sick worrying why there were no flowers, cards, or candy on her doorstep. At the very least a telephone call. Adam was getting to the point where he waited so long to call, now it made it almost impossible.

He dialed the administrative number to dispatch and a tiny voice answered the phone, "Sheriff's Department."

"Hey, Cindy, this is Adam, what's going on?"

"Oh, hey, guy, not much, what can I do for you?"

Adam and Cindy had two liaisons at patrol shift parties when Adam worked the street. However, neither of them wanted to give up their current squeeze for a regular boyfriend, girlfriend thing, so they just treated each other as a potential future convenience.

"What's been going on with Langtree? I never hear shit working three to eleven."

"Nothing," she said. "I know the fugitive warrant team has been trying to set up on him at his apartment and work. The detectives have been doing their thing, but other than that, we haven't heard anything either."

"Alright. Well, I'm about to go out over here on Sand Finch, just thought I'd call." He was waiting for her to say it, and she did.

"Hope to see you soon."

He knew what it meant. "Me, too. Talk to you later."

Adam shut off the phone as he turned on Sand Finch. One sheriff's patrol car, a detective's car and a crime scene van were parked in front of 7204.

"Unit 1273, on scene," Adam advised.

"1273, 10-4, 17:24 hours."

Adam got out of the car and zipped up his jacket. It was noticeably colder and the weather report predicted the possibility of freezing rain. Adam always looked forward to bad weather. He enjoyed having someplace warm to go to; shelter from the cold. Protection from the rain.

It was an upper-class neighborhood with large yards, lots of trees and the houses were all brick. The subject's house was a long, white one story with big picture windows. It had a flag pole near the walkway, stacked with the United States flag on top, the Texas state flag in the middle, and the Dallas Cowboys football team logo flag just underneath. There was a tinge of chimney smoke in the air and he noticed someone had been raking leaves in the yard; an abandoned rake lay by the flag pole and piles of leaves scattered around. Adam could hear a small dog yapping constantly from the back yard.

Detective Bill Grossman met him at the front door. "Hey, Thompson."

"Hello, sir."

Like many of the detectives at the sheriff's department, Bill Grossman was a cop for over thirty years, worked with half a dozen different departments, and had done his time.

"I'm not going to tell you anything, just yet. I want you to look around at everything and just write a supplement to my report."

Adam trusted Bill's wisdom. "Okay," and walked in.

The house was dim but absolutely immaculate. The foyer adorned with tapestries, oriental carpets covered hard wood floors, oil paintings, sculptures, and vases with fresh cut flowers.

"What does this guy do?" Adam asked.

"High school football coach." Bill smiled.

"Must pay them pretty good these days."

"His wife has money," Bill added, then pointed down the hallway toward some bedrooms. "All the way down on the left."

Adam looked into the other rooms as they passed. They all looked like they were straight out of a furniture showroom, everything was in its place, bed comforters folded back for easy access and candles burning.

Adam stopped at the opened door to the last room.

"Don't touch anything," Bill said. "We still haven't photographed it. The crime scene van was out of film."

Adam looked back at him and smiled. "Great."

Adam studied the room before going in. It was obviously a teenager's room; posters of rock bands splattered the walls, stereo equipment, and a television with some type of electronic game hooked to it. On one side of the room was a draped window, and on the opposite was a door leading to a bathroom. Adam could see several model airplanes hanging from the ceiling, but it was what was on the bed that caught his eye. He stepped in and walked up to the bed. There was a navy blue suit placed in the middle of the bed, as if someone had been wearing it, laid down, then simply disappeared. The jacket encased a white shirt with a gold tie, and the pants protruded from the jacket, leading to a black pair of socks and leather shoes. Adam could only imagine the black leather belt around the top of the pants, indicated by the lumps under the jacket. Next to the jacket, where a left hand would be, was a report card. Adam leaned closer and saw it contained straight A's. He looked back across where the right hand would be, and there was a hard covered book entitled, *No Good Deed Goes Unpunished.*

"Wow," Adam said, to no one in particular. Then he looked back to Bill. "Where?"

He pointed to the bathroom.

Adam walked over to the door and carefully looked around the corner. There was a marble topped sink, toothbrush, paste, hairbrush, and a dryer. He stepped a little farther in and could see the toilet, a towel rack, the waste paper basket, and a pair of shoes sticking up from the end of the bathtub. Adam walked over to the tub. It was the kid. A sixteen or seventeen year old boy lay on his back in the bottom of the tub. The tub itself was a little too small to accommodate the entire length of the boy's body, so probably, when he pulled the trigger, an involuntary reflex kicked his feet out of the tub, and he slid down to where he laid now with what was left of his head pushed over to one side and his spine twisted grotesquely in the confined space. A 20 gauge, single barrel shotgun rested on top of the body. As Adam's brain was processing all of this, he realized, there was something else. The boy was wearing a bright red pair of workout sweats with the Washington Redskins logos up and down the sleeves and pants legs.

"Do you think this kid was trying to make a statement?" Adam asked.

Bill huffed, but didn't answer; he didn't have to.

Adam turned and walked out of the bathroom. "Anything else you care to brighten my day with?"

"Yeah, sunny isn't it?" Bill followed.

"Not that he really needed to. I think he got his message across, but did he leave a note?" Adam asked.

"Several," Bill answered. "Not all of them written by him. Come on."

Adam followed Bill to the far end of the house and into the kitchen. Bill pointed at a stack of scattered notebook-sized papers on the counter. "The one on the Tiger's note pad, that's his Dad's rival team, was written by the boy. All the rest, the other fifty or so, were written by the Dad. You don't need to read them all. They all basically say the same thing."

Adam looked down and read one, "Come see me in my room."

"Shit..."

"Apparently, his dad left him these notes whenever he was in trouble, and by the looks of it, the kid kept every one. For posterity I guess."

Adam looked up. "I can think of other things to collect."

"Yeah, the kid even picked out the Tiger's colors for his suit, blue and gold. His Dad's team is maroon and white."

Adam asked, "Where are his parents?"

They're both down the street at a friend's house. Victim's services are with them."

"I don't think you need me on this one," Adam said.

"Well," Bill added, "according to the neighbors, the boy and his father fought a lot. You saw him; he's pretty small for his age.

Anyway, it's the Dad's shotgun, and his fingerprints will be all over it. The notes and everything will most likely be turned over to the Grand Jury."

"You're going to try to file on the father?" Adam asked.

"No, I don't think he actually pulled the trigger, but just because of all the circumstantial stuff, I want the grand jury to no-bill it."

Adam still did not understand. Normally, a case like this would be handled by the detective and closed.

Bill noticed Adam looked puzzled and added, "Who knows, maybe he found out his son was gay, and in a fit of rage…"

"Who knows," Adam agreed. "You want me to inner-office mail my report to you?"

"Yeah, that will be fine," Bill said, as the crime scene technician walked into the kitchen. "Thanks, Adam, and I'm sorry about Robert."

Adam nodded and decided not to say the response he had been practicing. As he walked back into the front yard, he could see a man standing next to a victim's services car that was parked in front of a big green house, half way down the block. Adam assumed it was a neighbor rubbernecking, but couldn't help think it might be the boy's father, standing alone in the yard grieving over his son's passing. Maybe regretting the harshness he had dealt towards his son. Or maybe, the man was wondering if he had forgotten anything.

Adam backed his car down into a neighbor's drive and turned around. He was just about to advise dispatch he was back in service when the emergency tone warbled over the speaker, "All units, clear channel two, standby to copy broadcast. Disturbance in progress."

Adam pulled out his pen and waited for the information, just in case he was close and could assist.

"Back to all units, suspect wanted in capital murder of a peace officer, reported to be at 23045 Canty Drive, Micro Invocoustics complex, causing a disturbance. Possible EDP. Possibly armed with officer's service weapon. Responding units meet security at the front entrance. 18:25 hours."

Adam accelerated his car; he was only five miles away.

CHAPTER THIRTY-TWO

The Contaminate
"Friday, December 20th, 6:15 pm"

Edward waited by the bus stop for what he hoped would be a larger group of Micro Invocoustic employees to arrive. The stop was only fifty feet or so from the front door to the plant, and he knew if he sat on the bench facing away from the doors and the cameras, they wouldn't recognize him. That is if they were even looking for him. When he first arrived on the bus, he planned to join the group entering the building, but he didn't feel there were enough to mask his presence. The group was simply too small to hide in.

As the next bus arrived, he sat patiently. In the past two days he effectively hid from all law enforcement. He picked up police bulletins on his Walkman and saw his picture in the papers and on the news, but not once did anyone take notice of the real him. No one ever did a double take or study his face trying to discover why he was familiar to them. He was in and out of four public libraries, had gone back to his car for a change of clothes and his Walkman twice, rode the bus, his bicycle, withdrew money from his ATM, and ate at McDonalds. No one questioned his identity or suspected him of anything other than just existing. Everyone in the city seemed to be just going about his or her own business, not minding anyone else's.

During his readings in the library, he came to understand that he was what they called, at least what the experts called, an anarchist. He liked that; it seemed to legitimize his actions. He always had a calling against the establishment. Against technology and everything

217

it represents; its de-humanizing of the world. A path clearly away from nature and the things God had intended.

Edward saw a large group of riders standing in the bus, waiting to exit. He knew this would be his chance. He was calm, like he thought he would be. The day he threw the dead bird, a rotting seagull, into the main deck fan room of the ship, he was shaking. He hadn't been able to eat for two days prior to dumping the carcass; his stomach just wouldn't hold anything down. He had watched the bird be devoured by the spinning blades. Now he realized why it was so important. It had been a test. A test for what he would need to do today. What he was required to do today.

What he was called on to do today.

As the group poured from the bus, Edward picked up his backpack and slid in among them. He maneuvered himself into the middle of their pack and held his head down. As they passed through the doors and into the lobby, he got into one of the four lanes to pass through an automated identification card analyzer. Edward looked up and saw there were four security officers present, instead of the normal two. This didn't surprise him; he knew they would be taking extra precautions, until he was caught anyway. The presence of the officers didn't discourage him; he would just have to move faster. Think faster. He knew the Invocoustics building as well as any employee. He was first hired in maintenance after leaving the Navy, then promoted to board assembly, and then to the clean-rooms and microchip wafer technology. That was his target, the clean-rooms; they were the center of Invocoustics' power. Edward knew, Micro Invocoustics supplied almost one third of the world's semiconductor and microchips used in industrial applications. He also knew one contaminated atomizing filter had shut down the wafer manufacturing line for two weeks and cost the company over two million in lost supply and productivity. That was from one tiny puff of dust atoms, and he concluded, if dust particles could do that much damage, imagine what an entire dead bird could do, or even something a bit larger.

The woman in front of him was having trouble getting her identification card to swipe, so Edward stepped up and asked, "Could I try?"

218

"I always have trouble with this thing," she said, half moving out of the way.

Edward took the card from her hand, turned it over, and swiped it. "The strip has to be down," he said.

"Thanks," she smiled, and they stepped through together.

This is truly beautiful, he thought. *The right place, at the right time,* and no one took notice. He moved with the flow of employee traffic down the hall toward the locker rooms. He looked straight ahead, not wanting to seem suspicious and give himself away. He was proud of himself, pleased he had beaten their safeguards, breached their security system. He had covered the bases and executed his plan according to schedule, but there were things Edward Langtree forgot. And even more important things, he didn't know.

In the dark camera room, a security officer eyed monitors one and four. "That's him, I'm telling you!" he said.

"Pan left, camera four," another camera officer said. "Replay three, the lobby—the lobby."

Both of the officers were adjusting levers and turning dials, trying to get a better look at the man they thought was Edward Langtree. They had a color photo of him taped to one of the shelves supporting the monitors. The faint blue light from the black and white viewing screens illuminated them working like robot zombies at their consoles.

The first officer picked up his radio.

"Not yet, what if it's not him?" asked the second.

"What if it is?" he answered. "Camera room to internal security. We have a possible breach, possible wanted subject walking from the proximity scanners down the main hall, toward the locker rooms."

There was a long silence.

"Camera room to internal security, did anyone copy?" he asked.

A series of 10-4's flooded his radio and both camera operators could see on their monitors the front security officers moving from their assigned posts to pursue Edward down the hall.

"Are we supposed to stop him?" one of the front officers asked the camera room.

"No!" he responded. "Just observe, he's supposed to have a gun."

Before Edward came to the locker room, he paused at a maintenance access door. As he looked over his shoulder, he saw the security officers had left their post and were walking his way. All of them looked directly at him.

He opened the maintenance access door and stepped inside the long narrow hallway. Quickly, he reached down into his backpack, past his extra shirt, past the bundles of wires and assorted computer parts. Past Robert's pistol and a small dry chemical fire extinguisher, all the way into the bottom, and grabbed one of the many big nails he had collected. He pulled it out and managed to wedge the pointed end into the door latch, jamming it shut. The corridor was lit with the same artificial florescence as the rest of the building, but this corridor, and others like it, tied the entire complex together. Like the nerves and veins through the body, the tubes and wires transported power, fuel, nutrients, and communication signals that allowed the machinery to function. He was going to become a living virus to this abomination of global influence. Edward studied the walls and ceiling of the corridor. The entire network of computer filaments entangled themselves through this maze of cables and fiber optics. Edward was tempted to reach again into his backpack and pull out his wire cutters and begin work on them, but he knew he couldn't waste any time. Cutting the wires here would be nothing more than a nuisance for them. In a matter of hours they would have the system up and running again. His hit would have to be more pointed, more strategically based than a random act of mischief. His mission was to bring down the company's network servers and then contaminate the clean-rooms. He knew others would follow. With bringing down Invocoustics, hackers and other anarchists would see the signal to bring about a new beginning. He began jogging down the corridor, but all the equipment he gathered was making too much noise and he decided to walk instead. He knew there were no cameras in the access corridors, so they would not be able to detect his movements, unless he went back into the main hallways. He turned down the first right he came to and followed the largest of the fiber optic conduits. He came to a T-intersection and here was his first target of choice; the back panels of the network servers that facilitated the transfer of information to millions. Down the corridor he heard the security officers trying to gain entrance into the door he jammed. He worked fast, looking around the panels, wires and cards, looking for the fire suppression system. To his amazement there were none; however, at either end of the bank of servers, there were manual fire fighting hose reels. Edward assumed the designers didn't want to rely on machinery to decide the fate of their computer systems and wanted a real person to assess and decide whether water was needed. He reached over and pulled a nozzle from its holder and spun the reel, dumping the hose to the ground. Edward knew water, while damaging, could dry-out and the systems could be saved if their breakers tripped before the circuits shorted out. What he also knew was if he added dry chemical fire extinguishing agent with the water, it would have a caustic effect and eliminate any attempts at restoring the equipment. Edward pulled down the handle and charged the hose with water. He positioned himself at one end of the computer bank and released the nozzle to a full stream. Sparks flew and alarms sounded. In a matter of a few seconds, Edward soaked the entire bank of computers, all of which immediately stopped humming and blinked out. He could imagine the employees monitoring the systems on the other side of the wall, getting sprays of water in their faces, just before their screens went dark. Edward shut off the water and took the fire extinguisher from his backpack. He pulled the pin and squeezed the handle, making one run past all the panels and covering the entire system with a white powder. As the extinguisher ran out, he dropped the bottle and ran back down the corridor, heading toward the clean-rooms. As he made it back to the main access corridor, he turned and followed a set of pipes mounted to ceiling brackets. He knew the pipes contained liquid nitrogen and other chemicals used in wafer production which would lead directly to the production control room. The corridor turned left and the pipes disappeared through the wall into the production facility. Edward found the ladder that extended above the ceiling into the air filtration system and conditioning service area. The system was huge and responsible for forcing air throughout the entire manufacturing complex. He walked along the catwalk above the production facility and located the main fan. It was a huge metal box the size of a diesel truck, sitting in the center of the attic area. Huge silver tubes reached out of its sides like octopus arms to direct the high-pressure air being pushed by the fan to different areas of the facility. The rumble of the fan vibrated the entire floor of the catwalks and was deafening. Edward looked for the maintenance access panel and located a red hatch that read,

Environmental Controls, DANGER HIGH PRESSURE AIR PUMP, Secure electrical before removing panel. He realized that there would be no way for him to get into the system through the intake vents; there were too many safeguards and filters to enter that way. It would have to be through the service hatch. He took out his wire cutters and snipped the metal safety band from the hatch's handle. He knew once he opened the hatch, he would have to be careful; the suction of a fan powered by 20,000 volts would be as significant as that of a jet. He laid his backpack down on the catwalk then turned the handle. He stepped to the side of the panel and pulled it towards him, avoiding standing directly in front of the opening, exposed to the suction. The panel slid effortlessly, releasing the scream of the fan motor. With the hatch open, Edward had a three by three-foot entrance directly into the fan. The fan's vacuum was incredibly strong and he slowly peered in to see a whirling bladed barrel, forcing high velocity air into the facility.

Edward had made his decision days before. He had no doubts of his responsibilities and no questions whether what he was doing was right. Before Micro Invocoustics security could even imagine where Edward had disappeared, he cast himself into the spinning fan and sent parts of himself through dozens of air vents throughout the manufacturing facility. Immediately, the fan blades screeched out a noise like ice in a blender, and the motor slowed down slightly, but it only lasted a few seconds. Edwards's body was processed by the machine and distributed like foliage through a wood chipper. Throughout the facility, employees standing near air vents were sprayed and pelted with bodily fluids, bone fragments, and warm chunks of flesh. The three main vents in the wafer manufacturing facility adequately dispersed Edward across every square inch of the production line.

The entire sterile white environments of the Micro Invocustics clean-rooms were speckled with red and pink.

CHAPTER THIRTY-THREE

The Funeral
"Saturday, December 21st, 10:00 am"

Adam didn't sleep well and at six in the morning he found himself staring at the ceiling. Last night was one of the strangest nights in his life. It took him less than five minutes to arrive at Micro Invocustics. But the police had already secured the building and Edward was already dead. He had sat in his car watching as the detectives and crime scene personnel arrived and worked the scene. It was a while before he realized there was nothing for him to do and decided to go back to the office and complete his reports.

By 9:00 am he had showered, shaved, dressed and had nothing else to do. He didn't need to pick Myrtle up until eleven and he had an idea. He grabbed some things from his kitchen and headed to a clothing shop near her apartment. He arrived at fifteen before ten and sat in his car, waiting patiently for the shop to open. He spoke with Lieutenant Martin late last night and received all the instructions for where and when he was supposed to report for the funeral. The lieutenant expected the funeral procession to be extremely long, not only in distance, but also in time. Adam was going to be the third mental health car in the procession, directly behind the family. It was a great burden off Adam's shoulders when he found out, for sure, they were going to use the honor guard as pallbearers instead of members of the mental health unit. In another time, and in another place, Adam wouldn't have had any trouble with pallbearer duty, just not this week.

He and the lieutenant talked quite a while before he mentioned wanting to take Myrtle Cowan to the service, and he thought the lieutenant was going to blow a tube.

"Bring an EDP to the goddamn funeral! Are you crazy?" a poor choice of words on his part.

"Sir, she doesn't have anybody else. They were friends and I was just thinking that it wouldn't hurt anything."

There was a long silence on the phone and Adam realized the lieutenant was deep in thought. He was thinking of what the mental health unit's real mission was, assist the mentally ill. He was thinking that bringing Myrtle to the service would not only help Myrtle with the coping process, but it would also serve a purpose for the department. It would show they actually worked with the mentally ill, not just committed them. It would show they cared about *their* recovery process and *their* integration back into the community, not just being dumped off at the hospital. It would also be a great media story to show that the mental health community cared about Robert, their mental health deputy. He knew the lieutenant's little wheels were turning.

"Well, Adam, you're probably right. It wouldn't hurt anything. You're going to watch her?"

"Yes, sir," he said.

"You guarantee she's not going to lose it during the service?"

"*No...*" he answered sarcastically.

"Yeah, I guess that would be a little too much to ask wouldn't it?" he laughed.

"If she freaks, which I don't think she will, I'll get her out of there," Adam assured him.

"I'm going to leave it up to you, Adam. If you think you can pull it off, it's okay with me."

Adam remembered his last sentence, before they hung up. "I'm going to leave it up to you." That, of course meant that if everything went as planned and the media got wind of the "Emotionally Disturbed Person," or more likely, "the Mental Health Client" that was at the funeral, the lieutenant would be right up front, face in the camera, spouting out all kinds of mental health community cooperation plans and programs the unit is currently involved in, or going to be in, or looking at being involved in.

On the other hand, if Myrtle did decide to take cover from the laser beams or charge the mass of paratroopers assaulting the funeral, Adam would be the one answering the questions, and the media wouldn't be the ones asking. Internal Affairs would.

Adam looked at his watch then got out of the car. He walked over to the door and looked in. A purple haired girl in her early twenties came to the front door with a wad of keys, and after a few tries, she finally found the correct one and opened the door. She didn't look at him or even say "good morning." She just turned back around and headed behind one of the display counters.

Adam let himself in and asked her, "Where are your hats?"

The girl was trying to unlock one of the cabinets with the keys and pointed to the corner of the store.

The store was stuffed, rack-to-rack with any kind of garb you can imagine. This was one of the largest costume shops in town, and the owners couldn't fit another piece of clothing in it. Adam thought about going to the mall or to a specialty store, but decided this would most likely have what he was looking for. He worked his way around suits of armor, ladies in waiting, Bugs Bunny, a gorilla, and a dozen other characters, heroes and villains, before he arrived at the hats. And hats they had. He searched through racks and racks of pointed, round, flat, tall, and everything in between until he saw it, perching on top of one of the stands. A tall, black fur, Russian style, winter hat. It was perfect. Adam pulled it down and checked the price tag, RENT: $10 / PURCHASE: $35. He would have to buy it; he knew she would never give it back once she got her hands on it. He walked back up to the front to discuss the purchasing arrangements with the shop's customer service specialist, and she was as helpful as before.

"Thirty-seven forty-five," she sighed.

Adam handed her forty-two dollars and forty-five cents. The girl looked at it and put the money on the counter. She separated it, the two twenties, two ones, and change. She shook her head and with a puzzled look on her face, typed forty dollars into the register. The drawer came open and she counted out the two dollars and fifty-five cents displayed on the screen. She handed the money to Adam, picked up the two twenties, closed them in the drawer and walked to the back of the store. The rest of Adam's change was still sitting on the counter.

"Could I get a receipt?" Adam asked, just to be annoying.

A voice came from the back, "We're out of paper."

Adam smiled. This did not bother him as it did many times in the past because he realized, as long as the world had creatures such as these, he would be higher on the human, evolutionary food-chain. They made him feel better about his position in life. He scooped up his money and went back to his car.

Adam sat in the driver's seat and worked feverishly on his project. This type of work, this type of modification could not be done in haste. It must be deliberate and with specific purpose. All components in place, and all parts secure. When he finished, he admired his work. Satisfied, he headed to Myrtle's. It was fifteen minutes before eleven.

As he pulled into her complex, he noticed the beautiful day; there wasn't a cloud in the sky, and the temperature had warmed to the mid-fifties. *A perfect day for a funeral*, he thought, and parked in front of her door. As he got out, Myrtle came out to meet him. She was dressed in a long black, multi-layered dress. It had high padded shoulders and long cuffed sleeves with silver clasps. It reminded Adam of a cross between an oriental and mid-eastern cut. It was quite exquisite, and he assumed her husband had brought it back with him from one of his trips overseas. She locked the deadbolt and came over to the passenger's door where he met her. He noticed her colander and foil helmet matched the dress's cuff clasps.

"Nice contrast you got goin' on," Adam complemented, as he opened the passenger door. "Mid-eastern Asian with a touch of kitchen cuisine?"

"Don't start with me," she said. Then added, "You're going to let me sit in the front this time?"

"Hard to believe, isn't it?"

Carefully, she got in.

Adam shut the door and walked back around. As he sat down, he noticed she was truly in rare form. She sat, back straight, nails, eyes, make-up, all perfect. She even straightened the two foil receiving antennae protruding from the sides of the colander. They had been bent at odd angles for the whole time he had known her, but now stood like two silver soldiers at attention.

"Your car stinks," she said.

"Hello? What do you think I do for a living?"

"I don't care what you do for a living; your car still stinks. If you're going to pick up a lady," she looked over at him, "for any reason, you should make sure your car doesn't stink."

He actually planned to spray some deodorizer this morning, but forgot. "Sorry. There is some air freshener spray in the glove compartment."

She reached in and got the can. She prayed two squirts toward the back seat, a couple toward the ceiling, and then one at Adam. She put it back and once again, sat still, staring straight ahead.

"Your dress is really pretty," he said, trying to soften the atmosphere and get her mind open to suggestion. He didn't know how she would react to his idea.

"Thank you," she said, holding her chin up.

"I picked up something you might like," he said.

"Is that so?"

"Yeah, uhm, since we're going to a funeral—"

She looked over at him and raised an eyebrow.

He continued, "I thought you might want another hat. Something that matches your dress." He reached around into the back seat.

Her face softened when he held it up. "It's beautiful Adam, but not today. If they are going to do anything, it will be today."

"No, I don't think you understand; it's not just a fur hat," he said as he turned it over showing her the inside.

A smile grew on her face. It spread slowly, wider and wider. "You did that?"

Adam nodded.

"You're the crazy bastard, not me!" she laughed, and grabbed the hat from him. She looked down into the hat, lined completely from crown to rim with silver aluminum foil. She pulled at the edges. "How'd you get it to stick in there?"

"Double sided carpet tape," he smiled.

"The edges are so smooth."

"I just folded them over," he added.

Immediately, she pulled the colander off and put it in her lap. She studied it and Adam thought she might be having some kind of nostalgic moment, but suddenly she pulled off one of the antennas and tucked it into the foil rim inside her new hat. She put the hat on her head and adjusted the rear view mirror to see herself. She straightened it, then grabbed the skinny tube of foil hanging out from the edge and molded it upward so once more, it could receive the long awaited message.

"It's perfect," she said to the mirror.

Adam smiled. He installed the foil on the inside of the hat, concealed completely by the fur with the intent that no one else would notice it. He guessed one antenna was a small price to pay for ridding her of the colander helmet.

"Thank you."

He smiled, and they rode to the funeral together.

After the family had their private service, the honor guard brought Robert to the awaiting procession. The trip to the grave site took about one hour, and the graveside service, another. Hundreds of police officers in as many different uniforms lined the site in row after row to pay their respects. Adam and Myrtle joined the group of mental health officers near the coffin. They all shook hands and gave Myrtle brief hugs. Lieutenant Martin secretly pointed out the antenna to Adam and smiled. The area was so crowded that Adam could barely see the immediate family. He saw Marla a couple of times, but couldn't tell if she was looking at him. She wore large black glasses and kept her head down most of the time.

After the eulogy of a chief of police that never knew him, and a chaplain that had never met him, the honor guard commander called the ceremony to attention. All three times, as the seven shotguns fired in a twenty-one gun salute, Adam flinched. They were slight movements, and well guarded, but they were there, and Myrtle was the only one who seemed to notice. She reached over and held his hand.

As the last shot echoed, an emergency tone screeched over a patrol car's loudspeaker, startling the entire crowd. Immediately, a dispatcher's voice broke the silence, "Unit 1274, checking status—" the call broadcasted across every stone in the cemetery.

There was a long silence, and everyone in the crowd felt his heart being torn.

Again, the call was blasted through the crowd, "Unit 1274, checking status—"

This time, out of the corner of his eye, Adam could see the rhythmic shoulder movements from the strongest uniforms and hear their quick inhalations, but all of them stood stoically. None of them looked at each other; an officer's grief is his own.

For the last time ever, dispatch called out to Robert, "Unit 1274, checking status—"

The family and close friends were now all in tears, and the ceremony came to a close.

"To all officers, Unit 1274, is out of service."

Adam and Myrtle started walking back as the ranks of officers slowly dispersed. He wanted to get out of there, but they were delayed by the recognition of some people he hadn't seen in a while, and a few handshakes. Eventually, they made it back to his car and sat a long time in silence, waiting for the traffic to clear.

"Have you ever been to a military funeral?" she asked.

"Yeah. Have you?"

"Of course I have," she said.

"Whose?"

"That's a stupid question; who do you think?" she said.

Adam looked over at her. "I thought you said he lived in France with his boyfriend."

She pulled off the fur hat and straightened her hair in Adam's mirror. "Sometimes he does," she answered, calmly. "Sometimes it's better that way."

Back at her apartment, Adam walked her to the door and she turned to give him a hug. The fur hat in one hand, the colander in the other. "Thank you, Adam. I know you took a chance on me."

He smiled. "You had me guessing."

"I suppose I'll talk to you later," she said, unlocking her door.

"You know where to find me," he said and walked back to his car. Like always she stood and watched as he drove away, waiting until she could no longer see him before closing her door.

That was the end of their first and only date.

At 2:25 pm Adam decided to check on duty. He had only one more shift to survive before his weekend. He already had plans; unplug the phone, turn off the pager and sleep.

"Unit 1273," he called to dispatch.

"Unit 1273, go ahead."

"1273, hold me in service, en route to the mental health office."

"Unit 1273, 10-4, I have one call holding," dispatch advised.

There was a long pause, then he finally answered them, "Go ahead with it."

Dispatch gave him the information and he jotted down the address on his notepad. He told them he would be en route and pulled into the afternoon traffic. He rolled down his window and felt the crisp air hit his face. He inhaled and felt it deep in his lungs. For a few moments he forgot all the things he dealt with this week and just drove, knowing he only had a few more hours separating him from his weekend.

After all, what more could happen in just a few hours?

ABOUT THE AUTHOR

In the past twenty years, Greg Lawson has served the interests of the United States as an Army Infantry Parachutist, Navy Operations Specialist, and Air Force Combat Arms Instructor on five continents and four oceans. Between stints in the military, Greg has worked as a Deputy Sheriff in Central Texas. His assignments have included Patrol Deputy, Drill Instructor, SWAT Team Member, and Mental Health Investigator. Trained as a Hostage Negotiator and Suicide Mediator he was relayed upon numerous times to resolve violent confrontations with emotionally disturbed persons.

In 2000, Greg was inducted into the Phi Theta Kappa Society, International Scholastic Order for academic achievement and is a member of the Writers' League of Texas.